Over Her Dead Body

Bradley Bigato

Over Her Dead Body
By Bradley Bigato

1st Edition

ISBN-13: 978-1466367623
ISBN-10: 1466367628

This book is dedicated to Jamie Motts for her words of encouragement, to Ellen Watkins for her inspiration, and to my wife Rachel for both.

Preface

"Writing is a form of personal freedom. It frees us from the mass identity we see in the making all around us. In the end, writers will write not to be outlaw heroes of some underculture but mainly to save themselves, to survive as individuals." This quote from novelist and playwright Don Delillo sums up in part why it is that I write.

Since I was a child, there have always been stories coming to me at all hours of the day. In class, I always thought of myself as a "space cadet". Despite my efforts not to, I would always find myself in the middle of some story that my mind had just randomly conjured. Today I'm still a bit of a "space cadet" but I now see myself as some sort of magnet for unwritten stories.

In college, I had always found pride in the fact that many of my English teachers would use my work for examples for the rest of the class. Today, nearly fifteen years later, I am just now beginning to understand what Don Delillo meant. There is a freedom in writing. The freedom to express ideas, to become anyone or anything. And to "...save themselves, to survive as individuals." as Delillo puts it.

Now I find myself finally putting pen to paper so to speak. I hope that I still have that talent for writing that my teachers would beam about years before. More than anything, I hope that I've been able to captivate and entertain.

Should you desire to comment on my novel, inform me of any mistakes, or be added to my mailing list, please send me a message to my email address: bradleylutes@yahoo.com with the title of my novel in the subject area. Thanks for reading.

Other Great Novels From Bradley Bigato:

Finding Mommy
King's Rook

Chapter 1

Amber and Maria pulled up in front of the large two story house. The house, a Victorian mansion built in the early 1900's sat back off of Sterling Drive on the outskirts of Angel Falls, NY. The driveway led from the street through two brick pillars connected to brick walls that surrounded the property. There was no gate between the pillars so Amber and Maria led the 2008 black Toyota Camry down the winding driveway until they pulled up abruptly in front of the house belonging to Dr. Benjamin Wimonowski. The house looked new despite the vines that stretched from the ground to the top of the building. To the left of the door was a single window on the lower and upper floors. To the right, there were two windows on each level overlooking the drive. It appeared that the blinds separated for a moment on the window to the left of the front door.

Amber looked at Maria. Maria put the car in park and exhaled loudly through her lips. "So how are we gonna do this?" Maria asked.

"I don't know. I guess we just go up and knock on the door."

"Don't you think one of us should stay in the car in case there's trouble?" Maria sounded like her nerves were getting the best of her.

"Why would there be trouble? It's just a doctor's house for Pete's sake." Amber brushed back a strand of brown hair from her face.

"I know, I know. It's just...something about this place gives me the creeps." Maria played a serious stare at Amber. They both let the stare hold while reading each other carefully. People always assumed that twins can read each other's thoughts but Maria and Amber needed to see into each other's eyes to know what each other were thinking. As they stared, Maria's serious and semi scared expression buckled into a smile and they both broke out in laughter. "I'm being paranoid aren't I?" Maria said as she wiped away the tears that came from laughing too hard.

"Probably, but then again...it wouldn't hurt if one of us just went up." Amber said

"So we gonna flip for it? Or rock, paper, scissors?'

"Let's flip for it," Amber said as she took out a quarter from her pocket. "I call heads."

"Hey, I wanted heads," Maria chimed in as the coin went airborn. Amber caught the coin and flipped it over on her arm. Tails. "I mean tails, I wanted tails." Maria backtracked.

"Alright fine. I'll go," Amber said as she opened her door. She began to get out and then leaned back in before shutting the door and said "chicken." Maria began a retort but the door closed quickly.

"Be careful." Maria said quietly to a now empty car. A shiver ran through her and she reached out to turn up the heat.

Dr. Wimonowski was inside sitting at the kitchen table. He was about to sink his teeth into a succulent piece of barbecued ribs when he heard a car pull up outside. He went to the window and peered out through the blinds. *Who the hell is this?* He didn't entertain friends or guests, nor did he have family that dropped in to visit. He would get the occasional politician or salesman, but they didn't come around too often. Sometimes children would get close enough to see the house, probably wanting to sell cookies, magazines, or fruit, but they always got spooked in the end and ran back out the entrance.

Dr. Wimonowski watched the car for a moment. It looked like a couple of girls inside arguing about something. *I suppose they're spooked too*, he thought. *Probably arguing about who's going to come up to the door to sell me something. Hmmm.* The passenger door opened and a girl got out. A minute later the doorbell rang.

Amber stood outside waiting. It was just the beginning of October so it wasn't exactly freezing, but it wasn't exactly warm either. She began to bounce a little, as her nerves and patience began to get the best of her. She reached out and was about to push the doorbell again when she heard a deadbolt unlock and the door swung open. "Dr. Wimonowski?" she asked.

"I'm Dr. Wimonowski. What can I do for you?" The doctor seemed nice, but Amber could tell he didn't like visitors. He had grey hair on both sides, separated by a long bald spot in the middle. He pushed his spectacles up that had slid down onto his nose and repeated "what can I do for you Mrs...?"

"Oh, I'm sorry. My name is Amber. Amber Farmer."

Dr. Wimonowski didn't recognize the name. He looked her over carefully. Brown curly hair that went just past the shoulders. Brown eyes. Beautiful face. She wore blue jeans and a button red flannel shirt that was unbuttoned at the top to expose a lighter red t-shirt underneath. She was gorgeous, but he didn't know her. "What can I do for you Mrs. Farmer?"

"Um Miss Farmer," she corrected. "Back in 1990," she began, "you had something special dropped off on your doorstep...didn't you?" His reaction was immediate. His face went pale like he had seen a ghost. His lips began to tremble and his eyes filled up with fear...and tears. He looked like he was about to collapse. "Dr. Wimonowski? Are you ok?" she asked worriedly and braced herself to catch him should he fall out the door.

"I think you better come in." he said. And stepped aside and shut the door behind her.

Maria watched everything from the driver side of the car. She couldn't make out what was being said but she could see the expressions on the doctor's face. First he looked annoyed, then curious, and then he looked frightened like he might run away or pass out. Maria's bad feeling began to disappear and she could have kicked herself for not going in. *Chicken!* Maria heard Amber's taunt echo in her mind and snickered. *I guess I am a big chicken* she thought. *And all for nothing. What a dork!* Maria just sat there and laughed at herself. She wondered what was being said inside.

Almost an hour had passed and Maria was starting to get bored...and a little nervous maybe. It's not like she expected this to take fifteen minutes...or even thirty for that matter. But one hour seemed like five out here in the car in front of this creepy mansion/house thingy. *God! Here I go again being creeped out over nothing. And why? Over some creepy vines that went up the side of the building? They're just vines!* Maria shook her head not understanding why she felt so on edge. The hair on the back of her neck stood up and all her senses where on high alert. *But why?*

A few minutes later the front door opened and Amber stepped out. She turned, gave the doctor a hug and then started for the car. The doctor stared at Maria for a moment, gave a brief smile and then stepped inside and closed the door. Maria pushed the window button for the passenger side. Amber was almost to the car when she began to brag "see, I told you nothing was..." Amber stopped short her sentence when seeing Marias eyes grow big. A large, heavyset man had come around the corner of the house and behind Amber so fast Maria wasn't able to get a sound of warning out of her mouth. Amber, seeing the startled expression, turned to look but a big gloved hand shoved a cloth over her mouth and the man opened the back door to the Toyota and shoved Amber and himself into the back seat. He shut the door and shouted "drive!" at Maria. Maria sat stunned with a look of shock on her face. She tried to move but she was frozen like a deer in headlights. The man still had a cloth over Amber's mouth to keep her from screaming. Amber was thrashing around both trying to get away and trying to breathe at the same time. The man reached into his black leather coat with his right hand and produced a gun. "I said drive! Now!" and put the gun to Amber's head. Maria's witts came back to her and she put the car in drive.

"What do you want?" Maria was now crying. "You can have the car. You can have our money...just please...let us go."

"Shut the fuck up and drive or so help me I will shoot her!"

Maria steered the car through the brick pillars. She wiped her sleeve across her face. She pulled up to the road and stopped. "Which way?"

"Turn right. And if you try anything, I'll kill her. You got that?"

Maria nodded her understanding.

"You got that?" the man yelled so loud this time Maria about hit her head on the ceiling.

"I got it," Maria bawled through tears. "Just...don't hurt us."

The man relaxed his hand that was around Amber's mouth. "You scream or hit, I shoot. Understand?" Amber nodded agreement, mouth still muffled. "Good. Now put your hands behind your back. Amber did as she was told and felt something go around her wrists and then heard a zip sound as the zip tie was pulled tight. "Good. Now open your mouth." Amber hesitated. "I swear to Christ I'll knock your fucking teeth out. Open your Goddamn mouth!" Amber did as she was asked and felt the cloth go into her mouth almost choking her. The man pulled silver duct tape out his pocket and wrapped it around her head and mouth three times. Amber was relieved that she could breathe out of her nose. A week ago she had a cold and her nose was so stuffed up this little event would have killed her in thirty seconds. The man shoved her down onto the floor and then sat back and pulled out his cell phone. “Turn right here,” he directed Maria.

Maria glanced in the mirror and back at the road. The man was dialing a number on the cell phone. *She offered her car. She offered money. What did he want?* Maria had found that there were only a few things that drive men. She shuddered at the realization that if the man didn't want money, they only had one other thing he could want. Maria felt her leg begin to tremble on the gas pedal. It was all she could do not to pee herself.

“I got em. Now what?” The man barked into his cell phone. “Where? You sure it's empty? Ok. Then what?” The man met Maria's gaze in the mirror and she quickly looked away. “Fine. Gotit.” The man clicked shut his cell phone and pocketed it back in his jacket. “Turn left at the next street,” he told her. Maria's stomach turned as the realization dawned on her that not only had their fate just been decided, but there was more than one kidnapper. She began to cry again.

The man continued giving out directions for the next five minutes before instructing her to pull into a parking garage that appeared to be empty. She drove half way up the garage when he told her to park.

“Now put your hands behind your back.” The man ordered. Maria did as she was commanded and felt something go around her wrist and the same zip sound she had heard when the man had bound her sister. The man reached into his outer jacket pocket and produced another cloth and the duct tape. He then took her through the same awkward steps as he had done to Amber. Maria about threw up when the cloth struck her gag reflexes. She had to completely relax her body to shut it down so that she did not vomit and drown herself in the process.

The man stepped out of the car and opened Maria's door. He took the keys and pocketed them and then hit the trunk button. Maria's eyes grew large as she looked from the trunk button and then back at the large man. The man grabbed Maria's brown hair and pulled her out of the car. Maria winced in pain but followed his lead still trying not to throw up. The man pulled her around to the back of the car by her hair. He raised the trunk and pushed her in, picking up her legs and shoving her in all the way.

Amber was listening and watched as he walked by the window with her sister. When she heard the trunk button she knew there was a possibility that they were going to be put in there. *But why?* None of this made any sense. Amber nearly came to the same conclusion that her sister did, that they were about to be the victims of rape when it occurred to her that it was highly unlikely considering where they were abducted. Not only was it somebody else's property, the whole thing was nearly sealed in by a brick wall. This wasn't some dangerous or high traffic area where predators hung about. No, this was personal somehow. *Could the doctor have been involved?* It didn't seem likely. He was a very nice man from what she could tell. *Oh God, why is this happening to us?*

The man opened her door and grabbed her by the wrists and jerked her forward. He picked Amber straight up and dropped her...hard onto her sister in the trunk. Then everything went dark as the trunk slammed down on top of them. At first, both of the girls lay still as they tried to recover, Amber from being dropped, and Maria from having a hundred and twenty pounds dropped on her. They heard a loud slam as the driver's door shut and the car started.

Amber wiggled around in the trunk, trying to get off her sister and trying to get more comfortable. Maria wasn't moving at all and Amber was beginning to worry that she may have been knocked unconscious when the man dropped her so hard. Amber tried to make a sound, but the muffle was barely audible and it nearly choked her. She went quiet but was still struggling to get off her sister. To Amber's relief, Maria started wiggling underneath her.

They both wiggled around until they were able to get side by side on their backs. Their knees were bent awkwardly as the trunk wasn't big enough for them to lay flat. They could see the red lights of the car but it didn't illuminate them enough to see anything else.

Amber lie there looking up into the dark. *How did this happen to me?* She thought. Everything was going so well. Up until last year she never even knew she had a sister. Maria had figured it out somehow and had come and found her. When Maria's parents had been killed in a car accident, Maria had been told by her surviving aunt and uncle that she had been adopted and that she had a twin sister. Maria, feeling desolate and lonely after the loss of her parents, set out to find out who she really was and wanted more than anything to meet their biological birth parents.

Amber, who had moved out of her parents home four years prior at age 17, was living in an apartment with her roommate Samantha and going to school full time while working nights as a waitress at Jared's Restaurant. Amber had moved out of her parent's house early because they were fighting all the time. She had become more like their personal Cinderella and they didn't hold back telling her what a shitty daughter she had turned out to be and how it was no wonder her birth parents didn't want her. Samantha was also in a rough home and the two of them decided to get out and salvage what was left of their souls. Amber completed high school, got a job and was earning good grades in college. She was working at the diner one night when her sister had come in and sat down in her section. When Amber approached her table to ask about a drink, Amber just stood there and stared, mouth ajar. "Oh my God," she had said. "You look...you look...you look..."

"Like you?" Maria had finished for her.

"Ya." Amber's eyes had grown big.

"Well chickie, there is a good reason for that. What time do you get off work?"

"Thirty minutes."

"We'll talk then and I'll explain everything. Now what's good in this joint?"

After work Maria and Amber had sat and talked over pie and coffee. She just couldn't believe what she was hearing. Her parents had told her she was adopted, but didn't say anything about having a twin sister. She'd read before in the newspapers how every once in a while someone would run into a twin that they never knew they had, but the thought that it could happen to her....was just so weird. Maria moved into town and they began to spend a lot of time together. She found out that they both liked much of the same things. The same tv shows, the same food, and the same clothes. Maria had told Amber that she wanted to go find their birth parents. Amber didn't want anything to do with it. "They gave us up," she had said. "Why would you want to find parents that don't want us?"

"I don't know. I guess I just don't want to feel so alone in the world." Maria had said.

"Alone? You got me now. You're not alone."

"No. We've got each other," she corrected. "But, still, I have unanswered questions and I'm curious....please?"

Amber had fought her for a month about finding their birth parents. It just didn't make sense. Amber had planned to be rude and give them an earful if she ever found them.

It doesn't look like that's going to happen now. She thought. Amber looked around trying to see something...anything. But it was just too dark. She inched close to Maria and found that she was laying the same way she was. Amber turned over on her side and began pushing her head hard into her sister's shoulder and mumbling "turn over" through the gag.

Maria couldn't understand a word Amber was saying. Amber kept pushing her head against her shoulder and now was burrowing trying to get under her butt. As Amber pushed and burrowed, it occurred to Maria that she was trying to get her to turn on her side. Maria turned on her side toward the back of the car. She could feel Amber's face brush up against her hands. She was surprised she could feel at all. The plastic ties were bound so tight she thought her fingers must be blue by now and probably ready to fall off. The car hit a bump and both girls mumbled a gasp as they went slightly airborne and then back down again. Maria began wiggling her fingers. The more she wiggled, the more she felt blood rush back into them which only caused even more pain.

As Amber tried to push her face against Maria's hands, Maria could tell Amber was trying to do something, but what? How could she do anything with her hands bound like this?

Maria moved her fingers some more. She could feel the duct tape that was wound tightly around her sister's mouth. As she poked at the tape with her fingers, she found she could just about push a finger into an opening above where the tape went across Amber's mouth. What good would that do? Maria thought. Even if I get my finger in there, the tape is wrapped several times and way too tight to pull off. Maria stopped for a moment, but then Amber tried yelling something through her gag that came out like a muffle. Maria thought if she could get her fingers on that cloth, just maybe she could pull it out and hear her better.

Maria pushed hard into the top of the tape with her middle and index fingers. She felt her fingers go in and began to wiggle them from side to side as she pushed. She felt like she was tearing at Amber's lips and gums. Maria felt the cloth and pushed to get her fingers on it. When Maria pushed her fingers, she accidentally pushed the cloth further back into Amber's throat. Amber began suffocating at once and began kicking her legs in a panic to get air. She didn't dare roll away from Maria's fingers lest she take away the only things that can now undo what had been done.

Maria could tell something was wrong when her sister began to thrash around. Maria guessed that she had shoved the rag back further in her throat and that her sister was choking. Maria made another attempt to grab the rag but the binds on her wrist buckled down and wouldn't let her grasp it.

Amber was about to pass out. If she could see, she was sure her eyes would have gone out of focus but she could feel it in her head. She began convulsing as her body made a last effort for air. *Oh my God! I can't believe I'm going to die like this.* She thought. She didn't even have control now. Her body took over convulsing violently as it tried to take a breath.

Maria felt the convulsions. Tears began pouring out of her eyes as she knew her sister was dying and there was nothing she could do to stop it. Maria tried and tried but she was just digging her fingers into the roof of her mouth and grasping at air. Just as she made a grab for the rag, Amber convulsed and thrust her head further onto Maria's fingers, ramming the cloth further into her throat. Maria's fingers grasped hard through the stinging pain and found substance. She squeezed her fingers together as hard as she could, screaming pain into her own gag as she jerked hard and pulled the rag free of Amber's mouth and free of the duct tape.

Amber's reaction was immediate. She gasped and sucked hard as if being held under water for too long and then surfacing just in time. Her cloudy head started to clear and she breathed in and out deeply several times. The car took a hard turn that sent both girls rolling. They both rolled back onto their backs and rested. Maria could hear Amber's labored breathing as she struggled to catch her breath. Maria had pressed and stretched the tape enough that the hole that remained toward the top of the duct tape was just enough to allow the air to move freely in and out.

"Thank you," Amber managed through the duct tape. It wasn't clear, but it was audible. Maria just stared straight up into the darkness, trying to regain her strength and energy.

"Maria, if you can hear me, kick me with your foot." There was a pause, then a kick. *Good*. Amber thought. *She can hear*. "I'm going to turn sideways toward you. You are going to turn away from me." Amber sucked in another hard breath. "Reach into my pocket and grab my house keys. I'm going to turn the other way and I want you to saw at the plastic ties. Use the long sharp key." Amber thought her motorcycle key would work the best. It was long and had lots of shallow teeth that might just cut the plastic...or fray it. The car hit a bump and the girls bounced again. "If you understand what I said, kick my leg again." There was another kick. *Thank God*. Amber thought. "Okay, good luck."

Maria turned sideways again towards the trunk. Amber turned toward her and scooted up close into a spooning position. She felt Maria's hands reaching and feeling, trying to find her pocket. She hadn't turned far enough so her hands were too low. "Higher," Amber said.

Maria turned downward a little more which brought her hands higher. This position made it significantly more difficult for her to breathe. She tried to relax, to slow her body's need for oxygen. When she felt her breathing slow, she began to feel for her pocket. She found it right away and slid her hand in. Navigating Amber's pocket seemed a little easier than trying to grasp the gag cloth but it was no less painful. Maria felt Amber scoot up a little which allowed her to go deeper. She felt the keys and quickly grasped them. She began to shout in triumph into her gag.

"You got em?" Amber asked. There was a muffled "Mhmm" sound. "Alright. I'm going to slide down and turn the other way. Remember, use the long key." There was another confirmation muffle and Amber slid downward effectively pulling Maria's hand and keys out of her pocket. Amber turned the other way and scootched back into her sister. The car was still moving and making turns. Amber was beginning to feel claustrophobic. She took another breath and waited patiently for the keys to begin their work.

Maria fumbled with the keys trying to feel each one until she was sure she had the long one. The pain in her hands was severe but she was growing accustomed to it. When she felt like she had secured the long one, she felt for the plastic zip tie around her sister's hands and began moving the key back and forth across it. She couldn't move very fast but she put as much pressure and speed into it as she could. Every push and pull sent agonizing burning sensations and stabbing pain into her hands. It only seemed like seconds and Maria stopped as the burning pain became too severe. She squeezed her eyes shut and took another deep breath. *Come on Maria. You can do this*. After she felt the blood return and the pain subside, she began sawing again.

Amber felt her sister stop and wondered if she was ok. She could only imagine how her hands must be feeling. She was beginning to get the feeling that they didn't have much time. She gritted her teeth at the thought of what horror might await them. Amber pressed her fingers together and pulled tighter at the wrists hoping the pressure would make the plastic easier to cut. She felt Maria stop two more times and then finally, a snapping sensation and her hands were free.

Amber immediately reached up and tried to pry the duct tape all the way away from her mouth so she could speak. She knew she wasn't going to be able to find the ends and unwind them in the dark so she just stretched it down below her chin. "Thank God!" she said as she moved closer to Maria. "Turn toward me," She said. Maria dropped the keys and turned over quickly. Amber felt for her face and then wedged her fingers in the upper portion of the tape and pulled and twisted backwards, stretching the tape until it was below Maria's chin. She reached in and grabbed the gag cloth and pulled it free. Maria also took a deep breath and coughed a few times.

"Thank you. Oh dear God thank you." Maria said still gasping.

"Ok, now turn back over so I can get your hands free." Amber commanded. Maria did as she was told. Amber felt around the floor for the keys and found them laying half under Maria. She pulled them out and felt through them for the long one. "Ok. I'm going to start. Pry outward against the ties as I cut them ok?"

"Got it." Maria said and began to pull outward with her hands. Because Amber's hands were free, she was able to move fast and steady and within a minute she felt a snap and Maria's wrists pulled free. "Oh my God. Oh my God," she said quickly, "I'm free! Now what?"

"Now we find our way out of here." Amber chimed back.

"Ya, but how are we going to do that?" She wondered.

"I think these newer cars have safety latches on the inside. We should be able to pull it and jump out." Amber said

"Um, aren't we going a little fast for jumping out of a car?" Both girls went silent as they tried to judge the speed. It was over fifty for sure. They must be on a highway or a country road.

"Ya your right. We're definitely going too fast," Amber agreed, "but if we pop the trunk maybe someone will see us and come for help."

"Or he may jump out and kill us before we can even get out."

"Maybe," Amber said, "but I have a feeling if we stay here much longer we're going to die anyway." Before Maria had time to respond, they felt the car slowing down and coming to a stop. The girls could hear their own breathing. "Maybe it's just a stop sign." Amber hoped. Then the motor was shut off and a car door opened. "Oh no. Oh God. We're too late."

Amber began whispering hurriedly to Maria. "Quick, put your duct tape over your mouth and your hands behind your back." Maria did as did Amber. She pulled it back down a little. "Let me in front. When he picks me up, I'll stab him with my keys. You kick him hard and we will make a run for it. Got it?"

"Got it." Maria muffled through the duct tape and began to slide over Amber so she was toward the back. Her stomach filled up with butterflies and she felt like she would vomit. *Don't puke now girl. Not with this thing on your mouth*. She wondered how her sister could be so brave and so calm. Maria felt like she wanted to scream.

Amber had the keys in her hands with the long one between two fingers. She heard keys and then scratching against the car. The trunk popped open. Amber could see that it was dark out but a full moon lit the sky enough so she could make out the man and his face easily. The man sneered as he stared at the girls who looked all sweaty and ragged. "Don't worry ladies. It'll all be over soon," he said as he reached in to pick up Amber. Amber moved fast. When the man's head was close to her, she quickly pulled the keys around and stabbed him straight in the eye. His hand went to his eyes as he stumbled backwards cussing and groping at his face.

"Now!" Amber said and both girls jumped out of the vehicle and attacked some more. Maria landed a hard kick to the man's groin while Amber kicked hard at his left knee. "Let's go!" Amber shouted at Maria and they darted towards the woods closest to them. A quick glance showed that they were surrounded by woods with nobody there to scream to. The girls were running through a short grassy patch and were only five feet from the woods when a loud bang echoed out. Amber looked back over her shoulder as she reached the woods. The man was still cupping one eye but had a gun out and pointed toward them. Maria had fallen down a few feet behind her.

Amber ran back and kneeled down and grabbed Maria by the shoulders helping her up. "Are you ok?" she asked her.

"Ya, I think so." Maria said as she got up and moved with her sister into the woods. Three more shots were fired at them as they went, but two hit the ground next to them and one blew away a patch of tree to their left. The man began screaming at them. "You fucking bitch! I'm going to kill you!" But the girls kept on going into the woods.

"Amber..." Maria said in a gasp as she began to slow down.

"Come on hun, we gotta keep going. He'll catch up with us." Amber said.

"Amber, I'm cold. My chest feels funny...can't breathe." Maria slowed down to a halt and fell to her knees. She braced her hand on the ground and then she lay down face up to look at her sister. Amber glanced toward the edge of the woods. They were only about twenty feet in. The man would be here shortly. She was sure of it.

"Maria, we have to go. You have to keep moving." Amber tried to pull her to her feet when she noticed in the moonlight that the front of Maria's shirt was glistening and a dark color had spread across it. "Maria, what's wrong? What is this? I don't..." but then it dawned on her that the first gunshot didn't hit the ground or a tree. There was a thup sound that Amber had never heard before. "Oh my God! You've been shot. No...no...no...this *can't* be happening. You can't be hurt!" Amber pulled Maria's head up into her lap and began rocking her. "Please be ok, please. We can make it to a hospital. They can fix it..." Amber was sobbing now, hugging and rocking her sister. Crackling sounds came from the front of the woods and thud. The man was coming and had tripped. He began cussing again.

"Amber...," Maria said through a hoarse voice.

"Ya babe. I'm here." Amber said.

"Go." Maria coughed and blood sprayed out of her mouth. She ran her sleeve across her mouth to dry it off. "Go on without me. He'll kill you."

“I’m not leaving you.” Amber declared through her tears. “He’ll have to kill us both.”

“No,” Maria said. “You can get away. I can’t. There’s no need for you to die too.”

“No. You’re not going to die!” Amber shouted through sobs.

“Do you love me?”

“Of course I do…but…”

“Then don’t let me die in vain. Find the police. Find our parents and tell them about me.” There was a long pause. “Please…”

“Ok. I will.” Amber said as she hugged her sister tight. “I love you so much!” A gunshot rung out and a piece of bark exploded nearby.

“Go.”

“But…” Another gunshot and a thud as dirt exploded near Amber’s foot.

“Go now!” Amber hugged her sister one last time and laid her gently down. Bullets were coming faster now. “Bye sis…” Amber took one last look and darted off into the woods. Amber ran and ran until she was out of breath. She stopped and listened. The only sound she heard was the wind blowing through the trees. It was comforting somehow...until...bang! One shot rang out off in the distance from where she came. She felt her sister's life fade away. Amber went down on the ground sobbing. She began hitting the ground again and again. "Why?" she cried. "Whyyyyyyyyy!" She yelled out into the woods. A gust of wind brushed by her and in it she could hear her sister's voice. "Run!" it whispered as it blew on past. Amber got back up and bolted into the woods.

Chapter 2

Dr. Wimonowski was getting scrubbed up and preparing for surgery. He'd already done four tonsillectomies that morning and it was only ten o'clock. His last surgery of the day was at two so if everything went smoothly, he should be on his way home by three. John Derrington, the surgeon on E.R. duty right now had given him a recipe for steak rub and he was itching to go home and try it. "This is the best seasoning I've ever put on a steak," he had said. "Rub it in, sear it on both sides and cook it to medium. It will melt in your mouth." Dr. Wimonowski was salivating just thinking about it. A short nurse with curly blonde hair poked her head into the scrub room. She was new and Dr. Wimonowski had only spoken to her a couple of times. She looked to be about mid-twenties and had a very pleasant demeanor.

"Dr. Wimonowski," she said, "there are a couple of detectives at the nurses' station that want to speak with you."

"What? What about?" Dr. Wimonowski looked perplexed.

"I don't know. They wouldn't say." The nurse responded matter of factly.

"Well, I'm scrubbing for surgery. Tell them it will be about thirty to forty-five minutes."

"Ok. Will do." And with that the nurse backed out of the room.

Why the hell would detectives want to speak with me? He wondered. Dr. Wimonowski just shook his head and went back to scrubbing.

After the surgery, Dr. Wimonowski came out to the nurses' station. The petite blonde nurse was nowhere to be seen. Dr. Wimonowski looked around and spotted a brown haired man with a mustache leaning up against the south wall. He wore an older looking grey suit and a trimmed brown mustache. The man shifted and when his jacket separated, he noticed a badge attached neatly to or over his belt. Dr. Wimonowski approached the man. "Can I help you?" He asked.

"Are you...," the man fumbled in his pocket for a notebook which he produced and scrolled over it. "Dr. uh Wimon....wimon..."

"Wimonowski." The doctor spared him the embarrassment. "Yes, that's me. What can I do for you uh...Detective...?"

"Detective James. And yes that's my last name."

"Ok, Detective James, what can I do for you?"

The detective looked at the doctor and then around the room. “Is there a place where we can speak in private?” The detective asked.

“The uh…cafeteria will be about empty. I was heading there for some coffee. Will that suit you?”

“Yes that would do nicely.” The detective said. “My partner had to step out and was supposed to meet me back here. I’m going to make a phone call real quick and I’ll meet you in the cafeteria.” The doctor nodded and headed for the cafeteria.

The doctor had gotten his coffee, two creamers and some sugar and had sat down in a quiet spot toward the back. There were two other people nursing drinks as well. Both women and both had solemn downturned faces as if they had the weight of the world on their shoulders. Dr. Wimonowski had seen this all the time in the hospital. It usually meant they were waiting on the outcome of an important surgery. It was saddening to see. The detective approached the table with a cup of his own. He took note of the wrappers on the table. “So you’re a cream and sugar guy huh?” The detective said.

“Huh?” a pause as the doctor followed his stare. “Oh…uh ya. I have to have my cream and sugar. You?”

“Na, I like it black and strong. All that other gunk makes it too much like candy.” The detective took a seat opposite of the doctor. The detective’s brown hair was parted down the middle.

His blue eyes pierced him like he was staring straight into his soul. "I'm sure you're wondering what this is all about so I'll just get to it." The doctor nodded his head with a concerned expression. The detective reached into his jacket and produced a photograph which he smacked on the table in front of him. He watched the doctor's expression for a moment which seemed to register fear or surprise. "Do you know this girl?" the detective asked. The doctor squirmed in his seat looking suddenly uncomfortable.

"Well, yes. I've only met her once. I guess twice maybe. What's this all about?" The doctor took a defensive tone like he'd been accused of something.

"Well, which is it Doc? Have you met her once or twice?"

"Er, well the thing is..." the doctor stuck his finger in his shirt behind his tie and stretched it outward in a circling motion as if the tie was now constricting him. "I met the girl when she was a baby, see."

"Go on." The detective took a sip of coffee.

"Well, a little more than twenty years ago, two babies...twins...were left on my porch." The detective scribbled into a notebook.

"What year was that?" The detective asked.

“I can’t say for sure,” said the doctor “1990 maybe. It was in the news.” The detective scribbled some more and then gave a look that indicated for the doctor to continue. “Anyway, we called the authorities...”

“We?”

“Er..my wife and I.”

“And you’re wife’s name is?”

“Ex wife”

“And your ex wife’s name is?”

“Jane.” The doctor was looking more nervous and began fidgeting.

“So you and Jane called the authorities? Then what?”

“They sent out child protective services who took them in and after the parents were never located, they went up for adoption. It is my understanding that they were both placed in homes.” The doctor looked relieved to have the attention focused on the two girls and not on his wife. He took a sip of coffee. “What’s this all about Detective?”

“You said you met them twice. Tell me about the second time.”

"Well, a couple of days ago two girls came to my door claiming to be the girls that were dropped off twenty one years ago."

"What day was this?"

"Today's Thursday, so Tuesday I guess."

"What time Tuesday?"

"Well, I was just sitting down to dinner so probably about five pm." The doctor took another sip from his cup.

"Were you expecting them?" The detective asked.

"No, they just showed up."

"Who else was with you in the house?"

"Nobody. I live alone."

"Was there anybody outside your home? Lawn care people, landscapers, etc?" The detective asked.

"No, I do most of that stuff myself."

"What do you mean most?"

The doctor thought for a moment. "Well, if I get too busy or I'm not feeling well, I call Nathan's Lawn Care. But I really haven't had to call them for most of the year. Are you going to tell me what this is all about detective?" The doctor was getting aggravated. He glanced down at his watch.

"Sorry doc. This shouldn't take too much longer. Tell me about what happened. What did the girls want? Don't leave out any details."

The doctor took a long sigh and leaned back. "Well, I only got to meet one of them. Amber, I believe her name was. Her sister was with her but stayed in the car. After Amber knocked, she told me something special had been dropped off at my doorstep twenty one years ago and I concluded that it must be her. So I invited her in."

"What did you talk about?"

"Well, she and her sister were trying to locate their birth parents. She wanted to know if I had any ideas or if there was a note with them when they were dropped off."

"And was there?"

"Nope. Nothing. Neither we, or the authorities were ever able to determine where the babies came from."

"Why you?" The detective asked.

"Excuse me?" The doctor looked perplexed.

"You're not an Obgyn are you?"

"No. I'm a surgeon. Ear, nose, and throat primarily."

"So, why would someone choose you as a place to drop off babies? I would suspect they must have known you."

"I just assumed someone thought we had money because of my profession and the large house. They probably thought it would be a good home for their babies."

"I see. And why didn't you keep them?"

"I don't know. I guess my wife and I weren't ready to have children yet."

The detective scribbled some more into his notebook and sat back. He took a long swig of his coffee. "When the girls left your house on Tuesday, did you see anything odd, suspicious, or out of the ordinary?"

The doctor thought for a moment. He looked up as if he were playing back the night in his mind. "No, not that I recall. Did something happen?"

"What kind of car were they driving?"

The doctor reflected again. "I don't know what kind. Small, black. Toyota maybe." The doctor took another sip of coffee.

The detective put his own cup down and leaned back. Now it was time to watch for a reaction. If there was one thing Detective James was good at, it was reading people. He'd asked enough questions to get a base line and read his reactions. So far he didn't believe the doctor had been deceptive about what he had seen or heard. He was nervous and appeared to be hiding something...but what? The detective leaned forward and pierced him with his cold blue eyes.

"Dr. Wimonowski, Amber came in Wednesday morning and reported that she and her sister had been kidnapped. She claims that her sister was shot and killed while she managed to escape."

The doctor's hands began to tremble, shaking the coffee cup. He placed it down on the table. "That's...that's...terrible. Who would...Killed you say? What...what...why?" The doctor's eyes were beginning to water up.

"That's what we are trying to figure out doctor. Amber claims they were kidnapped from your property."

The doctor had a look of shock on his face. "That's impossible. I saw her out the door myself. They were both fine when they left."

"And you saw them both drive away in their black car?"

"Yes. Er, well..." The doctor looked up trying to remember. "I guess I just walked her out the door. But she was only parked twenty feet away. She couldn't have...I mean...my place is surrounded by a brick wall. It just doesn't make sense."

"Did Amber feel threatened or scared of anything or anyone?"

"No. not that I recall. She was a real sweet girl with a kind demeanor. Who would want to hurt her?"

"What about you? Have you had any threats or have any enemies that might have thought the girls were your relation?"

The doctor looked stunned by this. He thought for a moment fidgeting with his cup. He took his glasses off, pulled out a cloth and cleaned them; then replaced them above his nose. "Detective, I don't have enemies." The doctor adjusted his tie. "I can't think of anyone who might want to harm me or anyone that I know."

The detective just stared at him for a moment. The doctor held his gaze but felt like he was going to vomit. It was like the guy was looking right through him. Could he tell that he was lying? He didn't think so. But that stare sure gave him the creeps.

"Well, I'll let you get back to your work doctor. I know you are busy. If you think of anything else..." The detective reached into his inside jacket pocket and produced a card. "Please call me right away."

"Will do." The doctor said taking the card. "What about the other girl?"

"Amber? What about her?"

"Is she ok? I mean…she's not in any danger is she?"

"Physically, she's fine. Whether she is still in danger or not, we won't know until we determine who attacked them and why."

"She was such a nice girl. I sure hope she will be ok. The other girl…?"

"Maria." The detective said.

"Maria. Was she robbed, violated?" the doctor asked.

"We can't say. We haven't been able to find the body." The detective was still piercing the doctor with his eyes suspiciously and giving him the creeps.

"Well, if there is anything more I can do, please let me know."

"You just give it some more thought doctor. You may remember something that might help us."

"I sure will. And if I do, I'll call you right away." With that the doctor headed out the door and the detective headed for a refill.

Chapter 3

Spring time in upstate New York. A sparrow sat perched quietly in a tall pine that overlooked a 20 acre field. The morning breeze floated across the treetops and made a swishing sound as the trees swayed gently. The sparrow was watching the house across the highway. A small one story cottage was nestled in on a ten acre wooded lot. The house was white with a large bay window in the front. And ten feet out from the bay window was a bird feeder that had been empty for two seasons now. The birdbath next to it though, had been a regular source of water for a week or two after a good rain. The sparrow launched itself out of the tree and darted down and came to perch on a barbed wire fence at the edge of the field. There were a couple other sparrows and a squirrel drinking from it now. Once the sparrow had felt it was safe, it glided across and joined its companions at the birdbath.

Michael and April pulled into the drive in their green Ford Explorer. There was a sporty looking silver car in the drive and Dawn, their real estate agent stood outside of it waving to them. April hit Michael on the arm, “Look hun, we’ve got squirrels and birds already!” April, an outdoor enthusiast loved gardening and nature. If it were up to her, she would have made the whole state a nature preserve with their house in the middle.

"Well, it is the country dear, there are bound to be some natives out here." Michael looked at April and smiled.

"Smart ass." She said hitting him in the arm again. Her dark curly hair fell forward and she brushed it back and looked at him out of her big brown eyes. Michael had dark and curly, short hair and a strong chiseled face. When he smiled back at her, dimples formed on his cheeks that just warmed April's heart every time she saw them.

The real estate agent waited patiently by her car. Michael and April got out and met up with her. Dawn was an older lady in her fifties with gray curly hair and fierce green eyes. Those eyes lit up as the couple approached. "And how are the two of you this morning?"

"We are ready to do some house shopping!" April said with a smile.

"And I'm here to keep her happy and the budget balanced." Michael said with a smile. April gave him a look that said *watch it buster!*

"Well, let's take a look shall we?" Dawn said while shoving her clipboard under her arm and heading for the door. Dawn stopped on the walkway leading up to the front door. She pointed at some tiny bushes behind some landscape timbers. "Oooh aren't these adorable? I think these are called Wisconsin

Juniper bushes. They don't get very big but they do bush out a little more. Are either of you into gardening?"

"She is. Me...not so much!" Michael said. April was looking over the bushes and reached out and touched one.

"While we're here, I'll also point out that this siding is vinyl and less than three years old. The color is called feathered brown. The windows are also new and were put in at the same time the siding was done. What a beautiful color. Doesn't it give it almost a log cabin kind of look?"

April nodded and Michael was looking the structure over carefully. "Is this a crawl space?" he asked.

Dawn pulled out her clipboard and flipped through a page or two. "It sure is." She said. "That should make it easy for you should you ever need to work on plumbing or anything." Michael nodded agreement and rubbed at his stubble.

"What about the roof?"April asked looking up. They were too close to the house to get a good view. She backed up a bit, stumbled over a brick used in the landscaping and fell backward onto the grass.

Dawn gasped and put her hand to her mouth as Michael stretched out his arm to help her up. "Are you ok?" Dawn asked.

April took Michael's hand and pulled herself up to a sitting position. For a moment Dawn thought April was going to break out into tears, but she suddenly broke out in laughter. "Of course I would have to be wearing a skirt on top of it all," she said while still laughing. Michael, still holding her hand, put his other hand on her arm and hoisted her to her feet. April brushed off the back of her skirt with her hands. "Do I have any dirt on me honey?" She asked.

"Nope, you got it all." Michael said. "Did you get a good look at the roof from down there?"

"Ha ha very funny..." April gave him a look.

Dawn flipped through a couple of pages and traced down with her finger. "It says here that the roof is about five years old." Dawn looked up. "Wow, new siding, new windows, new roof, you just about have yourselves a new house. You ready to check out the inside?" They both nodded and followed Dawn as she unlocked the door and went inside.

The inside of the house smelled of fresh paint and new carpet. There was a living room directly to their right and straight in front of them was a dining room with a big open sliding glass door. It overlooked a small but cute walk-out deck and a beautiful back yard.

April immediately headed to the back door. "Gosh this is nice hun. Look at the back yard!" April was excited and her voice was getting high pitched. "Just look at all the birds and squirrels!"

"Honey there's like three birds and one squirrel." Michael corrected. He had told her not to act excited around the realtor so they could negotiate a better deal. *Too late for that*. He thought.

"Ya but they're really cute and they're soo close! Look at the woods out there." April made an arc motion with her hand indicating the woods surrounding the property. "I'll bet deer come through there all the time!"

Nice...Michael thought. *She's going to do all the work for the realtor*. Michael smiled and nodded his head. He was happy to see her so excited anyway.

"Are you a deer hunter Mr. Bander?" The realtor asked.

Great...two against one. "I do a little hunting from time to time." Michael answered. *Now she's going to tell me there are deer everywhere out here*.

"Well you are in luck. I have it on good authority that there are deer everywhere out here." Dawn was watching them. She wasn't sure he was on board, but the woman had sold written all over her face. "Would you guys like to see the other rooms?"

April smiled and grabbed Michael's arm and put hers through the crook of his elbow so they would be arm in arm. And then she dragged him around the house that way.

It was a cute little house. The realtor took them from room to room and throwing in the 'Wow look at that's!' And the 'did you see this?' And the 'Oh isn't this adorables' and so on. Michael put up the best fight he could to try and negotiate a better price. He was sold on the house just like April, only he knew to control himself when negotiating a deal that could cut five thousand or more off the price. If the realtor knows you're sold, they won't push for a better price. The more money it sells for, the more they all get.

After showing the place thoroughly, the realtor finally grew silent. "So, what do you guys think?" She asked.

There it was. The test close. April looked up at Michael with her eyes beaming and a big smile stretched out across her face.

"Well what do you think honey?" She asked.

Michael looked at her and then at the realtor. The realtor was smiling too. "It's a nice little house, I admit. But I think the price is way too high. I think we should look around a bit more." Michael threw out phase two of his negotiating. Phase one, don't look excited even if you are. Phase two, act like the price is too high and like you're not interested.

The realtor was experienced and savvy. She knew they were going to buy this house. And she knew he knew. But she followed through with her phase two of closing the sale. phase one, point out all the good things and leave out most of the bad. (She always tried to point out at least a couple of bad things that were minor to get the clients arguing against the bad and for the house. They would say “Oh I can fix that” or “that’s no big deal” and then she could gauge how interested they were. If they argued in favor of the house, she knew they liked it. If they just agreed, she knew to move on to a different house.) These two were sold on this one. But phase two, give them some urgency, was about to begin. “I understand. Prices always seem high when times are tough. I have some other houses I would be glad to show you but we better get moving along because there’s two other couples coming to look at this place before noon.”

The smile disappeared off April's face right away. She turned her big brown eyes and sad little expression up to Michael. “They’re coming to look at our house.” She said.

Oh crap. Michael thought. *So much for negotiating a better price*. Michael looked at the realtor who quickly looked away like she had found something else worth checking out. He knew she must be exploding on the inside. Easy sale. “Can we have a moment alone?” He asked her.

“Sure, take your time.” Dawn said and stepped into the next room but didn’t stray too far out of hearing distance. If there were objections, she wanted to know what they were so she could tackle them head-on.

April watched the realtor leave and then looked up smiling at Michael. Michael just looked into her eyes and his heart melted at the happiness he saw there. April threw her arms around him and hugged him tight. After a moment she pulled back a little and looked into his brown eyes. “What do you think hun?” she said.

“You’re sure this is what you want? We haven’t really looked at that many places. This place is cozy, but it’s not *that* great. We could do better is all I’m saying.”

“I like it here. I can’t really explain it, but I feel like a piece of me belongs here. I kind of feel drawn to it. Is that weird?” April was holding his hands in hers and looking up at him.

“No. I mean yes it is weird, but I’ve been having a sensation of something. It’s almost like I’ve been here before. I guess something draws me to the place too. It appears that we are both weird.” He said with a laugh.

“Are you making fun of me?” She said.

“Would I do that?”

April punched him lightly in the chest. “You better stop it.” She said playfully. “So what are we going to do?”

"Well, if you are set on this place, and I can see that you are, then we should put an offer in. We'll shoot for ten thousand below the asking price and hope they counter offer with five below. Would that suit you?"

"I don't want it if you don't. I want us both to be happy. We can look at some more places..." April's face had a sad look.

Michael's heart was warmed by what she said. He could see that she really wanted this house and he was moved by the fact she would give it up for him. "You know, I would be happy anywhere with you. As long as I have a place to put my recliner, a garage to work in, and a backyard to barbecue in, I'm in heaven. Besides, as you pointed out, there are woods to hunt in, and plenty of gardening space and wildlife. The price already isn't bad. I say we go for it."

April's face lit up and she hugged him again and then started jumping up and down. In the next room a smile spread across the realtor's lips. Three down and the month's just beginning.

Chapter 4

It had only taken about three months to close on the property and get moved in. April's sister and Michael's parents all showed up to help move the boxes into and out of the moving truck. There was a barbecue and it became a fun event. Two weeks after that, the boxes were unpacked and everything seemed to have a place. April had made the house into a home. Michael had put up shelves, hung pictures, and made a mancave out in the garage. April had painted, decorated, and added the personal touch that only a woman can, to give the home a cozy cottage feel. April had put bird food out and had regular attendance from blue jays, cardinals, and squirrels. Michael had walked the woods and found signs of deer tracks. They were both settling in very happily. Until the fourth Tuesday night.

Sheriff James Watley, was out for a late drive on the back roads. He was feeling restless and cooped up. He wanted some country air. There was a bridge out this way that had been getting vandalized most likely by some rowdy teenagers and he was hoping to catch them in action so he could get them started on getting the graffiti cleaned off. There were words stenciled in like Asshole and Fuck. That was typical of bridges out in the country, but they got him involved when one of them wrote: for a good time call Mary B. and then added a phone number. I'm sure they thought this was a funny joke, but Mary Beaton's mother did not and made sure the sheriff knew it when she called in to complain. "Don't you guys ever stop any crime?" She had said, "get off your lazy asses and patrol something for God's sake. Maybe... I don't know, you might actually prevent some crime? My daughter's getting calls from perverts. If you don't do something, then I will!" And with that, Sherriff Watley figured he better get it cleaned up. He'd picked up a can of black spray paint to blot out the name and number, but would prefer to catch the perpetrators in action so they didn't continue doing it.

Up ahead in the road, Sheriff Watley could see a reflection of metal almost like a vehicle in the middle of the road. There were no lights on. *It's probably some tractor.* The sheriff thought as he slowed down and approached it slowly. It was a truck, stopped in the road with no lights on and the driver side door open. The sheriff reached over and grabbed his flashlight and directed it toward the cabin of the vehicle. Nobody home. At that, the sheriff pulled up ahead and did a three point turn and came around behind the truck so he could call in the plates.

"Base."

"Go ahead." Came the sweet voice of Leah Ashley. Leah was a heavy set gal with long brown hair and pretty brown eyes. It was always nice to hear her voice come across the radio because she was always in a good mood.

"Got a Ford pickup abandoned on Cherry Blossom Road by the old Danken house." Charles Danken had passed away about a year ago. Jenice Danken had held onto the house for a while, but was unable to keep up with all the work on her own. She had finally succumbed to family requests for her to move into a retirement home. Last Watley had heard she had moved into Wondering Garden's Retirement Home in town and was doing well. He had also heard the Danken house was sold not too long ago, but wasn't sure who had moved in.

"James, you gonna call the plates or keep me in suspense the whole night." Leah said across the radio.

"Ya, ya...don't get your drawers in a bunch." The sheriff peered ahead at the plates.

"You can't bunch whatcha ain't wearin sweetie." Leah retorted. James made a face.

"Too much information Leah. You ready?" He asked.

"Go ahead Darlin."

"5, 4, Echo, Delta, 7, 6, Frank." The sheriff called out the plates into the radio.

"The truck is registered to one Michael Bander. 3274 Cherry Blossom Road. Yep, the old Danken house." Leah said.

"Bander..." Watley said. "Is that Larry's kid?"

"I believe so. I think I heard he had a boy named Michael."

"Huh."

"Is the truck off the road?"

"No. It's right plumb in the middle of the lane. With the door open." The sheriff looked down at his watch. 11:58, almost midnight.

"That's just weird. Well, watch your six cowboy."

"Will do. Out."

The sheriff got out of his car, put his hat on and grabbed his flashlight. He left his lights on so nobody would hit the car from behind. He walked around the blue Ford pickup looking it over carefully. There was nothing to indicate an accident. *Probably got out to take a leak and hid when he seen me coming.* The sheriff thought. Would make sense if he'd been drinking. He wouldn't have wanted a DWI charge. The sheriff pointed his flashlight down the road past his car. The Danken house was no more than fifty yards south of here. These woods are probably part of the property. Who would get out and take a leak fifty yards from their home? It just didn't make any sense. Sheriff Watley moved his flashlight over the woods looking for somebody. Nothing. *Maybe he saw an animal and went to investigate.* Hell it wasn't a mile up the road a few weeks back that the sheriff had come across farmer Dirby rounding up some cattle that had gotten loose late at night. There must be some logical explanation. The sheriff reflected that law enforcement such as himself often jump right into worse case scenarios. It often blew things out of proportion, but it kept him alive for the times when it was the worse case scenario. With that in mind, he walked toward the woods slowly with his left hand holding the flashlight and his right hand unsnapping his gun and resting his hand snugly on the grip.

What was it about woods in the night? Sheriff Watley was contemplating the question as he felt a small breeze and the hair on the back of his neck stood up. He had the heeby jeebies. As an avid hunter, he had spent many mornings and many nights in the woods and it never ceased to amaze him how you never quite get used to how it makes you feel. All your senses are on alert. You can feel the presence of the world as if the whole forest itself were alive. You didn't just feel like a predator, but like prey as well. That's how he felt now anyway. Vulnerable. Sneaking up on some unknown situation at midnight in the middle of the damn woods. *Should have stayed in town*. He thought as he forged deeper into the woods.

A brush of wind whipped across Sheriff Watley's neck sending a cascade of goosebumps from his neck on down to his arms as he ventured a little further into the woods. His Maglite was bright and he used it to look around. The problem with looking for trouble in the dark was that you have no peripheral vision. A person could see more in the daytime with one eye than you could at night with two eyes and a flashlight. But he had been through this before. Nine out of ten times you find a car or truck running on the road, the person just got out to take a piss or crap. Or puke. Or all three. So, he really expected to find this guy just doing his business and that he just couldn't hold it. Some officers wrote citations for public indecency. He just couldn't understand that. Who the hell hasn't had to stop their car on a long trip occasionally to either get out and take a piss or let your kid out to go? What kind of idiot moron officer could really write a citation for that? An asshole kind that's what. And there were plenty of them out there. The worst of it is now these poor folk just trying not to piss themselves are considered by law to be sexual predators and have to inform neighbors, schools, and law inforcement every time they move. They become humiliated, alienated, and victims of hate crimes all for pissing on the side of the road. Good grief. What's wrong with the world anyway?

He was about to give up on this side of the road and search the other side when he heard something up ahead. It sounded like leaves crinkling and maybe a soft thudding like something hitting the earth. He pointed his Maglite up ahead. He could just barely make out something. He crept forward carefully keeping his right hand on the butt of his gun. "Hello, who's out there? This is the Sheriff." He spoke loud and confident despite his tingly guts. He could definitely make out something up ahead. It almost looked like bare feet. It looked as though somebody was bent over on their knees with their feet tucked under them. *Looks like another puking case after all.* He thought. *Probably another drunk*. He moved a little closer.

"Hello? This is the Sheriff. Identify yourself." As he got closer, he could see that there was definitely somebody on their knees but it almost looked as though they were digging in the dirt. Their body would make reaching motions forward and then dragging motions back and dirt was being flung backward. They were definitely digging. The sheriff moved closer still. He was nearly up behind the guy now and moved to his right about ten feet out to get a better look. As he moved around the side, he could see the guy didn't have any pants on. He was a dark haired man maybe in his thirties with a white t-shirt and grey briefs on. He was pawing frantically at the ground. Sheriff Watley drew his gun.

When an officer pulls his gun, either his life or someone else's is usually in danger. Maybe it was the dark. Maybe it was the wind. Or maybe it was the half naked guy clawing at the ground in the middle of the woods at midnight, but Sheriff Watley wasn't convinced that he was safe. He just kind of stood there and watched for a moment. His legs were positioned with his front leg slightly bent and his back leg straightened. He was positioned for stability and braced to dart in any direction if the situation called for it.

The man on the ground acted unaware that anyone was in his presence. He continued on pawing at the ground and flinging dirt. He was mumbling something. It was almost a sob really. Sheriff Watley couldn't be sure but it sounded like "Mayuh" and then he would dig even harder. The man seemed relatively clean cut. He had dark curly hair and dark but short stubble on his face. He just kept digging absentmindedly as if the sheriff wasn't even there. "Excuse me." The sheriff said sternly. There was no reaction.

"Sir I need you to stop what you are doing and stand up slowly." Still no reaction. The man continued to dig at the ground. Shit. He thought. This guy is either drunk or has completely gone nuts. Either way, that still made him dangerous. The sheriff tried again. "Sir. I need you to stop digging and stand up slowly." Still no reaction. The sheriff moved in closer and pushed the guy over by pushing his foot against his shoulder. It wasn't a kick, just a push. The guy fell over still making digging motions while lying on his side. He mumbled something again that sounded like "Mayuh" and righted himself and went back to digging. He didn't even take one glance at Sheriff Watley and the sheriff had a pretty good suspicion that the man was unaware of his presence. "Sir!" The sheriff said louder this time. No reaction. The sheriff pointed his gun in the air and fired. The shot that rang out was deafening. The man stopped digging.

The man looked straight up and then toward the sheriff. The light appeared to blind him and he tried to shield the light with his hand. "What the...where am I? Who are you?" The man said and looked down to see that his hands were deep in soil.

"Sir, you need to stand up slowly and keep your hands where I can see them." The sheriff said sternly.

"I don't understand. How did I get here? Where am I and who the hell are you?" The man began to stand up while keeping his hands visible. "And can you not shine that damn thing in my face please?"

The sheriff lowered the light a little so it wasn't blinding the man, but allowed enough to still see his face. "I'm Sheriff Watley and you are clearly intoxicated. You're truck is parked on the road and running. I found you here without your clothes clawing at the dirt. Can you tell me how you got here sir?"

The man looked around a little trying to evaluate his surroundings. He didn't recognize them. It was pitch black and hard to see. "I don't know how I got here. Where am I?" he said again.

"What's your name sir?" The sheriff said shortly.

"Michael. Michael Bander." A gust of wind pushed past and Michael shivered in it. He couldn't understand how he had gotten in the woods with his clothes off.

"And what is your address Michael?" The sheriff asked.

Michael looked around again and then back toward the light. He couldn't even see the guy except to make out a silhouette. "I live on Cherry Blossom Road." He said.

"Where at on Cherry Blossom?" The sheriff continued gathering the information.

"I live at 3274 Cherry Blossom Road. Now where am I and how did I get here. It's cold and I need some clothes." Michael was becoming agitated.

"You're in the woods about fifty yards from your house. As I was saying, your truck is parked on the road with the door open. Let's get back to my car and I'm sure we can sort this all out. Just start walking that direction and keep your hands above your head where I can see them. Understand?"

"Ya, I got it. I didn't do anything wrong though. I really don't know how I got here." Michael sounded a little whiny. He was hurt by the idea that somebody was treating him like a criminal. *Like he would really harm anybody*. Who was this guy?

"I'm sure there is a logical explanation. We'll get to the bottom of it. Let's just get moving shall we?" The sheriff pointed his light in the direction and Michael began to walk. *You're drunk and you blacked out. That's the logical explanation we'll get to once I've given you a breathalyzer*. The sheriff thought. Michael kept walking wincing and making oww sounds as he stepped on twigs and hard rocks. He was moving slowly because of his bare feet. *What a dumbass. How drunk do you have to be to end up out here naked and barefoot?* The sheriff thought as he followed behind. He kept his flashlight just up ahead of the guy but made sure the light touched him enough to keep an eye out for any sudden movements.

"I haven't been drinking if that's what you're thinking." Michael hollered back over his shoulder. "The last thing I remember is lying down to sleep next to my wife."

"I'm sure you're right. I still have to check...you understand I'm sure." The sheriff repeated. He sure hoped the guy was drunk because if he wasn't then he was liable to find the wife murdered or something crazy. He just had a feeling. Guys just don't go digging in the woods at midnight with no clothes on unless they are either drunk, high, or had a mental breakdown. He was still betting on drunk though.

Michael stumbled through the woods. Every step was like needles in his feet. A couple of times he stubbed his toe on a rock and almost went sprawling into the darkness. *How the hell did I get here?* He wondered. *If I was him I would arrest me*. The thought didn't lighten his mood. *What would April think?* Did she know he was missing? *Is she ok?* What if someone had broken in and hit him over the head and drug him out there? *That wouldn't explain the digging though*. Michael tripped over a branch and just caught himself before falling.

"Keep your hands up in the air please."

"I'm not going to hurt anyone," Michael said, "and I'm not drunk!" He was sure he wasn't on the good side of the sheriff and who could blame him. It just didn't make any sense. *God I hope April is ok...and I hope she knows what the hell is going on.*

Michael stepped out into the clearing with the sheriff right behind him. He could see the car behind his truck. It looked like his truck anyway. He had no idea how it got there though. He had no memory of driving or being driven. This was weird. Something wasn't right.

"You need to step toward the back of my car and around to the driver side." The sheriff said as he walked. He still had a flashlight in one hand and his gun in the other. He wasn't taking any chances.

Michael walked up to the sheriff's car and rounded the back side. He was really cold and the pavement was burning his feet as he stepped onto it.

"Put both hands behind your back and lean forward onto the trunk please." The sheriff said.

Michael turned around with his hands still in the air. "Am I under arrest Officer?"

"Until I can determine whether or not you are intoxicated and why you are in the woods at night without your clothes...yep, I would say it's safe to say that you are under arrest. I'll read you your Miranda rights later. Right now just do as I asked."

Michael put his hands behind his back and leaned forward onto the trunk. He had never been arrested before. This might be kind of funny if he actually had any idea about how he got here. But as it were, he was cold, in pain, confused, and now humiliated. How much worse could it get? He could only think of one way...*Please be ok April*. "I need to call my wife." Michael said as the sheriff put the cuffs on his hands. The metal ground into Michael's wrists and he gritted his teeth as they bit into his skin.

"I'm sure you do." The sheriff turned, pulled Michael back and turned him around. "As soon as we're done here I'll drive you up there and we can check on her together and she can follow us down to the station."

"Down to the station? On what charge?"

"I guess that depends on what this breathalyzer has to tell me." The sheriff said. "Now open your mouth." The sheriff produced a package from his pocket and began to tear off the plastic.

"I told you Officer, I haven't been drinking. I just need to call my wife and make sure she's ok."

"Why wouldn't she be?" The sheriff hesitated with the test.

"Well, I don't exactly remember getting here. What if I was hit over the head and dragged out here?" Michael retorted. He felt harassed.

"Well, that wouldn't exactly give you cause to go acting all stupid digging in the dirt now would it?" The sheriff asked.

Michael couldn't disagree with him and just shut up and opened his mouth. The officer put a small plastic device in and said "now I need you to inhale as deep as you can and blow out as long as you can until all the air is out of your lungs. You need to blow hard. If you don't do it right, we can go on down to the station right now and I'll tell them you refused the test. Got it?"

Michael nodded and inhaled a deep breath and blew as hard as he could. He felt light headed and thought for a moment he was going to faint. *Shit I'm so freaking cold*. He thought. He started shivering a little and his teeth began to chatter.

Sheriff Watley shined the flashlight onto the breathalyzer. He couldn't believe it. It was a good blow and nothing. Not one percent of alcohol. That worried him. He began to worry about the wife. *This is not going to be good at all*. He thought. "Get in the car." He said as he opened the door and pushed down on Michael's head and into the back seat. He slammed the door behind him and got into the front.

Michael was glad to be off the concrete and away from the cold wind. It was still cold in the car though and he was getting increasingly worried about April.

Sheriff Watley got on the radio and reported what had happened. "You mean naked digging in the dirt?" Leah said across the radio.

"Not naked. He had his underwear and a t-shirt on." The sheriff said shaking his head.

"Does he do landscaping? I've got a patch that's overgrown that's just begging for a man to come crawl around in his drawers and trim up for me. He can dig around all he wants..." Leah said across the radio again.

"He's not goin anywhere near your patch Leah. He'd have to be drunk and I just tested him. I guess your outta luck tonight." The sheriff looked in the rearview mirror at the guy in the back. "I'm going to run him up to his house and check on the wife. Make sure she's ok. Shouldn't take longer than fifteen. Twenty at most. We got some room down there for this guy?" the sheriff asked.

"Well, all we got tonight are a couple guys in a bar fight and Lewis again." Leah said.

The sheriff nodded his head. Lewis was the town drunk. He never hurt anybody, but would always pass out in gas stations and public places so he could get a warm place to sleep and some food. "Alright. I'll let you know. Out."

"K. Out." Leah said.

Sheriff Watley put the car in drive and started for the old Danken house. He pulled up in the driveway behind a green Ford Explorer that he assumed was the wife's. There were no lights on in the house but as the headlights flashed across the door, he could see that it had been left open. “You stay put. I’ll be back in a moment. What’s your wife’s name?”

“April.” Michael said

The sheriff opened his door and closed it behind him. He took the flashlight with him but left his gun holstered. He did unlatch it though. He didn’t expect trouble but he had to admit that it wasn’t beyond the realm of possibilities that the guy could have been knocked cold and drug into the woods. The screen door was shut and the sheriff shone the flashlight through the screen to the interior of the house. He looked around. There was a couch and a recliner. Nothing seemed to be out of the ordinary. He rapped on the screen door loudly three times. “Anybody there?” He hollered in through the screen and rapped again.

He was about to knock again when he heard a noise and a voice holler from around the corner. “Who is it? Michael? Is that you?”

“No ma'am, this is the Sheriff. I have your husband with me. I need you to come to the door please.

There was a pause and then a woman approached the door cautiously and turned the porch light on. The sheriff could see her clearly reflected in the porch light. She was beautiful with curly dark hair and brown eyes. She had a bit of a bed head as her hair was tuffled in places and sticking up. It was obvious she had just been asleep. She rubbed her eyes and looked out the screen door. “What can I do for you Officer? Is something wrong?” She had no idea why a sheriff would be knocking on her door at all much less this time at night.

“Are you April Bander?” The sheriff asked.

“Yes. I’m April Bander. What’s this all about? Is something wrong? Why is Michael with you?” Her expression went from sleepy to concerned.

“And your husband is Michael Bander is that correct?” The sheriff continued.

“Yes, Michael’s my husband.”

“When was the last time you saw your husband?” The sheriff asked.

“Well, we just went to bed a few hours ago. He fell asleep before I did. But you just woke me up and he’s not in bed. I assume he couldn’t sleep and went out to the garage until you said he was with you. Did he call you for some reason? Has something happened?” She was beginning to panic.

“Is your husband taking any medications right now or is he on drugs of any kind?” The sheriff asked.

“Drugs? Are you kidding me? Michael? I don’t think so. He’s not on any medications right now. Why are you asking me this? Where is Michael? I want to talk to him. You're scaring me." April had tears welling up in her eyes.

"Ma'am, I found your husband's truck parked in the road, running, about fifty yards from here." The sheriff pointed in the direction he had come. "There was no one inside and so I went into the woods to investigate. I found your husband barefoot, in his t-shirt, and underwear on his knees digging in the dirt."

"What?" April looked shocked. "What was he doing digging in the dirt?"

"Well, I was hoping you could tell me." The sheriff said.

"I have no idea. He hasn't done anything like this before. What did he tell you?"

"He said he didn't remember how he got there. He acted like he was in a trance or something. I had to fire my gun just to get him to stop digging."

"You fired your gun? Is he ok?" A tear fell from her right eye.

"Yes. He's fine. I just fired it in the air because he wouldn't stop digging."

"Is it possible that he was asleep? I have a sister who used to sleep walk and she made it out to the car a couple of times." April sniffed and wiped the tear off her cheek with her fingers.

"Well, I tested him for alcohol and there was none."

"No, there wouldn't be. We didn't have anything to drink last night." April said.

"I guess it's a possibility. I've never heard of anyone sleepdriving before, but I do get occasional calls about sleepwalkers. It's pretty spooky stuff. It would explain a lot though. The bare feet, the lack of clothes, and why I had to fire my gun to get his attention." The sheriff shook his head and looked back toward his car. "You say he's never done anything like this before? Never had a problem with sleepwalking?" The sheriff asked as he turned back to look at her.

April shook her head. "No. I'm always up before he is and he's always been a really sound sleeper. I can't explain it."

"Well..." The sheriff looked back toward his car. He seemed to be contemplating. "I really don't have much to hold him on. I guess I'll release him back to you. You need to keep an eye on him though. Maybe get him to a doctor or something." The sheriff said.

April nodded. "I will. I'll set an appointment right away. Maybe they could do a sleep study or something."

"Something." The sheriff agreed. "I'll go get him and be right back." The sheriff said as he marched off toward his car.

April saw the sheriff open the back door and pull Michael out. The sheriff turned him around against the car and took his cuffs off. April gasped seeing him in handcuffs and put her hand over her mouth. The scene looked barbaric and she felt like she was on an episode of “Cops”. Michael saw April and started walking toward her. He walked up to her and threw his arms around her. “Look at you, you’re covered in dirt.” She said

“I was so worried about you. I thought something had happened.” Michael said.

“Something had happened? To me? You were the one out digging in the woods in your undies Michael Mcreary Bander!” She said.

“I don’t know how I got there. I just woke up and I was there. This is embarrassing.” He said.

The sheriff had walked up behind him. “I’ll let you folks be. If you have any other troubles, just give us a call.” He said looking directly at April. "And don't forget to get your truck out of the road before someone gets hurt running into it."

April nodded. “Thanks Sheriff.” She said as he headed back toward his car. “Let’s get you inside and cleaned up. You really don’t remember anything?” She said to Michael.

“No. Nothing”

It was a long night. April walked up and retrieved the truck, helped get Michael cleaned up, and then fixed them a snack of caramel apple slices and hot cocoa. Michael recalled to her all the things that had happened. April sat there and shook her head in disbelief. "I just can't believe he pulled a gun on you. Much less fired it." She said shaking her head.

"I know. I thought the guy was going to shoot me for sure." Michael said.

"And he put you in handcuffs. Imagine. My husband in handcuffs!" At this April couldn't help but begin laughing. She laughed until tears ran down her cheeks. "What will the ladies at work say?" She laughed some more. "What would your mother say?"

"Seriously, you're really going to tell everybody about this aren't you?" He said in disbelief.

"Are you kidding me? And pass up the best water cooler story of the decade? You bet." She said.

Michael just raised his hands and dropped them into his lap, a sign of defeat. "Ok, but just remember, it will be your turn for something humiliating one of these times and I'm going to remember this." He said to her. Then he moved in closer to her and grabbed her hand and lifted her up so she was face to face with him and he moved in to kiss her and just as she moved for the kiss he retracted. “Isn’t there anything I can do to silence these beautiful lips of yours?” He asked.

April pulled her head back and looked at him. “Are you trying to bribe the storyteller?” She said.

Michael nodded. “Maybe...”

“It’s going to take a lot more than a kiss to seal these lips!” She said with a grin.

“Really. Do tell.” Michael hoisted her up into his arms and carried her into the bedroom. After a long night of passion, lust, and bribery, they decided they would call in sick the next day and sleep in.

“No more sleepwalking in the woods?” She whispered to him as she drifted off to sleep.

“No more.” He said quietly as he drifted off to sleep with a promise rolling off his lips that was no sooner spoken than broken.

Chapter 5

The following day, April and Michael spent relaxing at home. There was an awkwardness in the air as both of them tried to take in the previous night's experience and find some purpose or meaning in it.

Michael spent most of the afternoon pacing in the kitchen with a cup of coffee. He would just stand and stare out the back door. There was so much to take in; the squirrels, the birds, the trees, and every other living thing that created a community in their backyard. But Michael didn't see any of it. He stared in the right direction but he looked past it all into an area in his mind where he replayed the gunshots, the handcuffs, the feeling of the soil under his toes. Why was he out there? How did he get there? He had never had any troubles with sleepwalking before. Why now? Was there some logical explanation that he just couldn't see? He stood there and wondered. He reflected to his childhood and couldn't recall having had any instances of sleepwalking. Could this be a sign of some medical condition that is about to make itself known? He took a sip of his coffee and shook his head to himself. *Handcuffs. Me in handcuffs. What's next?*

April was also deep in thought. Instead of pacing, she found solice in research. What is sleepwalking? Is it dangerous? Could it be cured? These were the kinds of questions she was plugging away into a search engine on the internet and reading page after page. Some of the sites claimed to be written by doctors while other sites were built by individuals who've had to deal with personal sleepwalking or that of a loved one. She read stories about people who managed to drive from one place to another while asleep. People who've opened their doors at two o'clock in the morning to a neighbor, friend, or relative who had shown up dead asleep with strange requests or statements.

Some sites claimed there were treatments and medicines for the treatment of sleepwalking. April leaned back on the couch and stretched. Her laptop was on her lap and nearly fell off. She glanced up at Michael. He was at the back door again looking out with that far away look. Did he need medicine? It only happened once, but what if he had gotten hurt? What would have happened if the sheriff hadn't found him? Hypothermia? Truck accident? Who knows... She didn't want to see him on medicine but she didn't want anything to happen to him either. It was clear that he was just as worried as she was. She put her laptop aside and went to him.

"What are you thinking?" She asked as she wrapped her arms around his neck from behind.

"What makes you think that I'm thinking?" he turned around and slid his hands around her waist.

"Just a hunch." She said while she looked deep into his brown eyes. She always felt herself getting lost in those eyes. Sometimes she would look into them and they seemed bottomless, like she could fall in and continue falling forever. Sometimes the feeling would overcome her and her knees would get weak until she felt like she would topple over. As she looked now, she had the same feeling and she tightened her grip a little more and found herself determined to hang on. How could he be so calm? She could sense that he was concerned because of the pacing and the staring out of the back door. It's what he always does when he's worried or in deep thought over something. But, he always seemed so calm. Inside her was a tsunami of waves being thrown about. Her emotions and thoughts went sliding all over the place from one wave of emotion to another. She felt like she was on a boat in a massive storm and the waves would come in pounding against the ship, tossing it in different directions. Then, just when she thought her ship was about to sink, she would look into Michael's eyes and find calm water; an undisturbed lake. In her mind she could see herself sitting on a dock in her orange sundress and dipping her feet in the calm water. And her ship would begin to settle. The waves would get smaller and smaller until her boat was anchored next to the dock on the still water while she lost herself in his eyes. She looked away now for fear she wouldn't return and just put her head against his chest and cried.

The day winded down without anything exciting. Michael and April went for a walk down the road. Michael pointed to about where he had come out of the woods. They spent more time researching sleepwalking and decided that if it happened again that he would see a doctor and maybe have a sleep study done where they watch you while you sleep. They sat on the couch for most of the evening just sitting quietly and holding one another. They weren't sad or depressed, it was just that they didn't get many opportunities to just sit during the week and be with one another. It always seemed like during the weekends they were so busy running errands and managing the honey do list that they hadn't had an actual break to rest in ages. It was nice. It felt nice. They shared a sizzling hot steak, broccoli, and a potato for dinner. Then they settled in to watch their evening show. Monday night. "Lie to me" was on. It was a show about a deception expert. Dr. Cal Lightman was the lead character who would help solve crimes for the FBI or the private sector. They enjoyed a glass of red wine and began their nightly routine of preparing for bed. They were all settled in and April was about to turn off the light when she turned back and looked at Michael. Michael smiled because he knew what she was worried about and what the look was for.

"I'm not going to have to chain you to the bed am I?" She said.

"I'll be good," he said. "Scout's honor." He held up two fingers which was the symbol for a good scout.

She smiled and said "you better mister...or you will be court marshaled!" She kissed him and turned out the light. They both lay there in deep thought looking up into the darkness until finally succumbing to sleep.

Chapter 6

Sheriff Watley was back on duty again. It was a fairly slow night. There was a domestic disturbance at the Reighly house...that was nothing new. At least once a week he would have to report to the house and help settle the argument. He had gotten accustomed to the flying dishes and the yelling. Now he would just walk straight in and start ducking right away. Eventually he would get the two of them sitting down at the table and talking. It usually took about an hour but they would wear down and the voices would go from yelling to a soft retort until finally they couldn't remember what they were fighting about in the first place.

He had given out three tickets after that. Two speeders and a right tail light out. A group of kids were in the car with the tail light out and he could smell marijuana on them. The driver didn't appear stoned, but rather a shy kid toting around his friends. Sheriff Watley confiscated paraphernalia and a small bag of weed and sent them on their way with a warning. He wondered if these could be the same kids that spray painted the bridge. He didn't find any spray paint on them though. As things winded down and the streets became empty, the sheriff figured he had some time to go finish the job on the bridge that he didn't get to finish the night before. He still couldn't get that whole situation out of his head. It just didn't seem right somehow. He made a left and turned onto Cherry Blossom and headed the same direction he had the night before. He didn't figure he'd run into any trouble tonight. As he wound his way down the road, it didn't take long for him to realize that he had figured wrong.

Angel Falls, NY was officially named back in 1803. The town began not unlike many others, by a few small families living close enough to one another that some entrepreneur decided to set up a shop in between homes and make a small profit by trading and selling goods. In the case of Angel Falls, it was a young man by the name of Judiah Branshire that set up a small blacksmith shop and bartered merchandise in exchange for various commodities. One family may be in need of horseshoes for instance and would come to Judiah and trade the horseshoes for corn. Another family might need corn and trade for hogs. Eventually enough passerbys took notice and settled nearby so as to always have things available to them that they would need. It didn't take long for other entrepreneurs to join in alongside Judiah and soon there was a liquor store, a hotel, and a bank. It had always been said that Angel Falls got its name from the small waterfalls that flowed down the Raquette River downtown. There are others who claim the name came about after a bad case of smallpox wiped out a generation of children. They called the children their angels and because they had "fallen", they named the town accordingly.

Sheriff Watley had lived here all his life. His father was a sheriff and although he had always had dreams of going off to college and making family history by being the first to earn a college degree, he couldn't settle in on anything and after picking up a job at the station part time, he eventually was consumed and grew into the role. He loved the job anyway. He could understand why his dad had done it. It was a damn good feeling to be able to help so many people. He had built a reputation just like his father of being tough but compassionate. Angel Falls was his playground. He knew a lot of folks and they all seemed like family to him. The crime was about what you would expect in any small town. Most of the calls were for domestic disputes, bar fights, or petty theft. Sometimes there would be a big drug bust, but usually things were pretty quiet.

Sheriff Watley was driving down the road, thinking about the graffiti on the bridge. Kids. He thought. Will they ever change? Better to be patching up some graffiti than cleaning up after a drive by. Sometimes you just have to be thankful for the small crime. The sheriff stopped suddenly. In the road up ahead was the same truck from the night before with the door open. "You've got to be kidding me." He said under his breath. He just sat there staring for a moment trying to understand. Is somebody fucking with me? A guy wouldn't just sleepwalk to the same spot in the woods twice in a row...would he? He shook his head and pulled off to the side and placed the car in park. He picked up the CB and called it in.

"Base," he said.

"This is base, watcha got James? Over." The sound of Leah's voice filled the car.

"You on duty tonight Leah? I thought it was your night off. Over." Sheriff Watley said.

"It wouldn't be a night off If I couldn't harass you now would it? Sara's kid's got a touch of the flu so I'm fillin in for her tonight. Watcha got sweetie? Over."

"Well, I'm out here on Cherry Blossom again. Over."

"That graffiti thing? I thought you took care of that last night. Did them boys get it prettied back up already? Over."

The sheriff looked down and then back up shaking his head. "I got a little distracted last night remember? Over."

"Oh yeah, the sleepwalker right? How'd that go anyway? Over."

"Well, let's just say I'm getting distracted again. Over."

"You've got to be kidding me. Is that old boy out there again? Over."

"Well, his truck is here in the road again. So, I'm going to assume it's him. Unless his wife has decided to give it a shot. I'm going to check it out. I should check in in about ten. Over."

"K. Be careful James. This is getting kind of creepy. Over." Leah's voice echoed in the car.

Tell me about it. The sheriff thought as he put on his hat and stepped out of the car.

Chapter 7

The night air was cool and moist. There was a slight wind blowing gently across the sheriff's pant legs as he began his trek across the ditch and into the woods. He wasn't entirely sure the guy would be in the same spot, but he figured he would check there first. He held his Maglite with his left hand and unsnapped his holster with his right. He kept his hand near his weapon as he made his way through the woods. Even though Angel Falls wasn't a big crime town, his father had always taught him to error on the side of caution because even the most innocent situations can turn on you in an instant. One thing he had learned from watching the news in the bigger cities is that often you only get one chance to make a mistake and keeping your guard down is always a mistake. This guy must really have a medical problem. This was going to seem like dejavu. What is his wife going to say this time? She didn't seem very happy last time. Hell, the sheriff thought, if my wife caught me out sleepwalking a couple of times, she'd handcuff me to the bed. The sheriff thought he might just suggest that to her this time. He could just hear himself now; ma'am, I think it would be wise to invest in some handcuffs for your husband at night. Of course his luck, she would do it and then there'd be a fire and he'd die because he couldn't escape. And who would she blame? The sheriff who was only trying to help. But truth be told, the guy was going to be in more danger driving while asleep or getting hypothermia and dying alone in the woods. The sheriff kept walking and soon he could hear the sound of flinging dirt like the night before. He tightened his hand down near his gun and moved toward the sound.

The sheriff could make out the form again as he lit up the man with his flashlight. Once again the guy was out in a white t-shirt and tan briefs. He was on his knees again clawing at the dirt and muttering something under his breath as he flung the dirt to either side. The sheriff stood watching in dismay. The guy was digging frantically. What was he saying? It sounded like Myah. Mayeeah? No that wasn't it either. Some more dirt was thrown back hard and landed on the leaves. The sheriff looked around the woods with his light. The man continued to dig and mumble something. His speed picked up and with it his voice. "Maria." That's what he said. Maria. The sheriff made a coughing sound to try and get his attention. The man continued digging like he wasn't aware of the sheriff's presence. The sheriff looked around again and then back at the man. This was going to be awkward. Not only was he going to have to explain to the guy's wife that he was out digging in the woods in his underwear again, but he was chanting another girl's name as well. This should be interesting. *I guess the girl's number on the bridge will have to stay public for a while longer*. He thought. He was just about to holler at the guy when he noticed that the guy had actually dug down quite a ways into the dirt. He had clawed nearly a circle about two feet out and about a foot deep. He was trying to go deeper but a root or something kept catching on his hand and flapping around. Every time he would reach out and attempt to claw at the dirt, his right hand would come back clawing at the root and dirt would only go flying on his left side. The sheriff moved in closer and lit up the hole with his flashlight. The root that was stopping him from going any deeper was thick and bounced around every time the man tried to claw at it. The Sheriff leaned down low for a better look and suddenly fell over backwards in shock. He quickly picked himself up and drew his gun at the same time. He blinked his eyes in disbelief and traced the root back one more time with his eyes to make sure. His eyes confirmed what he thought he saw. Right next to the guy's legs, attached to the root which was not a root but was a human arm attached to a small hand. "Oh my God! Oh my God! What the fuck!" The sheriff said to himself. He stood back, the gun still drawn on the man digging. A breeze brushed up against him and he heard the man say "Maria" again. He swore he could hear it in the wind. The sheriff pointed the gun at the man and said "Mr. Bander." No response. "Mr. Bander, I need you to stand up and put your hands on top of your head." Still no response. The sheriff fired the gun in the air and then pointed it back at Michael. The man stopped digging like he had the previous night and sat still for a moment. He began to look around trying to gather his bearings when he looked toward the sheriff and was blinded by the light. He put his right hand up in front of his face to try and keep from being blinded.

"Sheriff?" He said

“Mr. Bander, I need you to put your hands on your head and stand up real slow.” The sheriff said in his stern voice, trying hard not to let the panic going on in his body to come through into his voice and show any sign of weakness.

“Oh man...” Michael looked around. “Not again! You’re not going to put me in handcuffs again are you Sheriff?” Michael put his hands up and tried standing up. In the process, he stepped on the arm and he fell backward into the dirt. “What the...what the heck was that?” He held up his hand in front of his face trying to keep the light out of his eyes. He tried standing up again.

“Sir, I need you to stand up and keep your hands where I can see them.” The sheriff repeated. He kept the light in the man’s face to keep him blinded. It’s much more difficult to attack when you can’t see what you are attacking.

Michael stood up and put his hands on his head. “I’m sorry Officer. I must have come out in my sleep again. I...I don’t understand what’s going on. My wife has scheduled an appointment at the doctor’s office for a sleep study next week. You’re not going to put me in cuffs again are you?” Michael asked.

“Turn around and face that tree.” The sheriff said and jerked the flashlight toward a tree and back.

"Seriously. I'll go with you, this really isn't necessary." Michael pleaded but turned toward the tree anyway.

The sheriff needed his handcuffs but both hands were full. His left held the flashlight and his right held his gun. He tucked the flashlight under his arm. The sheriff quickly pulled the handcuffs off his belt and grabbed the flashlight again. The sheriff stood there for a moment. He wasn't going to be able to cuff him; the guy was too big and could turn around and get the advantage. Instead he tossed the cuffs next to Michael's feet. "Pick up the cuffs and put them on behind your back." The sheriff said.

Michael looked down at the cuffs and then over his shoulder at the light. "Seriously? We really have to do this? It's just sleepwalking man. I'm not going to attack you."

"Put the handcuffs on!" The sheriff said sternly.

Michael took a long breath and bent and picked up the cuffs and put them on behind his back. The sheriff stepped toward Michael and put the flashlight under his arm again, long enough to clamp the cuffs down extra tight.

"Goddamn it! That hurts! What the hell are you doing?" Michael yelled. His skin was being pinched in the cuffs.

The sheriff grabbed the flashlight from between his knees and took a step back. He ignored Michael's shout of pain and grabbed the CB on his shirt collar. "Base." He spoke into the CB.

"Base. Over."

"I've got a 187. Send backup to Cherry Blossom. I repeat I've got a 187. Suspect in custody. Send back up right away. Over."

There was a moment of silence. 187 was code for murder and wasn't used very often in Angel Falls. Leah came back on audibly shook up. "Confirmed. Back up on the way. Over."

Michael turned around toward the sheriff. "What's a..."

"Turn back around sir!" The sheriff yelled.

Michael just stood there mouth open. "I don't under..."

"Sir, turn around now or I *will* shoot!" The sheriff said again.

Michael couldn't believe what he was hearing. He turned back toward the tree and mumbled under his breath. "God. You'd shoot me for sleepwalking? What the hell?"

"I think we're a little bit beyond sleepwalking." The sheriff said.

"I don't understand. What does that mean? And why'd you call for backup?"

"Who's the girl?" The sheriff asked sternly.

"What girl?" Michael asked still facing the tree.

"Well that sure as fuck looks like a girl's hand to me unless you know something I don't asshole."

"Wha.." Michael turned his head and followed the flashlight beam toward the ground. He didn't see it at first. There were scrape marks in the dirt where he'd been digging. He could feel the dirt packed under his nails. He had made a small crater in the dirt but no more than about a foot deep. He followed the shape of the hole upward until he saw it. Right there at the far left a hand hung out from the dirt. It was dirty but the skin looked soft and the protruding nails with orange fingernail polish indicated that it was indeed likely a girl. A dead girl. A dead girl that *he* dug up. The implications hit him and his face grew pale. He turned and vomited.

"Get back against the tree." The sheriff shouted. Michael was leaning over and vomiting. He stayed where he was at until he had finished and leaned back against the tree resting his head on it.

Michael mumbled something under his breath about this being a dream. He rapped his head against the tree a few times hoping it would jar him awake but no luck.

They stood there quietly for what seemed like an eternity. Michael, with his head against the tree mumbling to himself and the Sheriff with his gun and light pointed at Michael.

"So who is the girl?" The sheriff asked again while scanning for his backup. He wished they would hurry up and get here. There was no response. "We're going to find out one way or another so you may as well tell us. Who is she? Girlfriend? Hooker? What?" Still no response. "You know a lesser cop would just shoot you now and save the trouble of having to feed you in prison. Who the fuck is she?"

"I don't know." Michael said. "I don't even know how I got here."

"Right. You just happened to sleepwalk to a random place in the woods next to *your* house where there just happens to be a dead girl?" Flashing lights appeared through the woods as cars began to arrive. The sheriff flashed his light in the direction signaling their location and then put it back on Michael. "Well, I guess we'll find out one way or another. I hope they fry your ass."

More cars pulled up and soon there were lights and voices all around. Michael was tired, shaky and confused. Cold. He could barely stand up. He felt embarrassed to be out here in the woods in his briefs, surrounded by strangers, and next to a dead girl. He began to feel like he was going to throw up again.

A bald officer approached the sheriff, flashlight trained down on the girls arm. "Jesus Christ. What have we got here James?" The bald officer was Frank Calhoun. He was about 6'2", two hundred fifty pounds of muscle. And an asshole. The sheriff wasn't fond of him but he was happy for the backup.

"Did they wake you up Frank?" The sheriff asked.

"Not quite. The old lady was about to give me a piece of ass when I got the call. Can't say I'm very happy about it. This the perp?" Frank turned his light on Michael who was still leaning against the tree in nothing but a t-shirt and briefs.

"Found'em out here last night digging. He claimed to be asleep. You know. Sleepwalking. Not sure I believe that now. He won't say who the girl is." The sheriff said.

"That right asshole?" Frank spit some chew on the ground to the left of Michael. Michael didn't say anything. "Oh, I'll bet I can get him to talk. Give me about five minutes alone with this asshole. He'll tell us everything we need to know."

"Frank. Don't go fucking this up. He's nailed to the wall dead to rights. You go leav'n bruises on him and he'll say he was beat into confessing and walk. So just let him be. I'm sure Detective James will get it out of him. He always does." More people arrived with lights and soon there were voices all over. Everyone seemed to be either looking at the body or at Michael. Soon they began taping off the crime scene.

Frank approached the sheriff again. "Hey James, Gary and I are going to escort him to the station. We'd like to ask him a few questions on the way. Figured you'd want to stay here and see this through." Gary was standing next to him. He was thin, ugly, and had only been on the force a couple of years. He didn't say anything. He just stood there staring at Michael and chewing his gum.

"Ya, I'll want to try and I.D. the vic and get some info to the detective. Then I've got to go talk to the wife. Like I said, don't fuck this up. We can't have bruises showing up on him. Take him straight to the station. Got it?"

Frank spit again. "Ya, ya, I got it. He won't have a mark on'em. You got my word." Frank said.

"Then get him out of here before you fuck up my crime scene with all your goddam spitting." The sheriff said.

The two officers trodded off toward Michael, muttering something about the sheriff being an asshole. The sheriff ignored it and turned back toward the body. Some of the CSI team had already begun their work. There was a young CSI wearing glasses and slightly balding taking pictures and working around the crime scene in a counterclockwise direction. Two others were canvassing the area with flashlights. They were at arm's length moving side by side in the same direction working the area like a grid.

"What have we got here James?" A rough voice came from behind the sheriff. Detective James appeared on his right and looked down toward the girl. "What do we know?"

The sheriff looked toward the detective and then back toward the girl. “Well…about midnight last night I came across the perp’s truck sitting vacant in the road. His name’s Michael Bander. Frank and Gary just took off with him. Did you see him?”

“Ya, I seen him,” the detective said. “he in his skivy’s and t-shirt in the middle of the woods?”

“Yep. He was last night too. Claimed to be sleepwalking. Don’t know if I believe him, but I had to fire my gun to get his attention. He seemed genuinely confused.”

“Where’s he live?”

The sheriff glanced back toward the road. A car was leaving and a couple more flashlights were coming in their direction. *Probably the coroner and lead CSI*. He thought. “He lives about fifty yards to the west.” The sheriff pointed in the direction to his right.

“Did he say anything? Did he mention who the girl is?”

“No he didn’t say anything other than he didn’t know how he got here. Threw up over there when he found out there was a body here.”

“That’s not the reaction I would expect from the guy who put her there. He does match the description though.”

"Description? You got a case?" The sheriff asked.

"Well, it's about seven months back, but maybe this is her. Had a girl come in saying that her and her sister were abducted. She got away but her sister was killed. She didn't know exactly where, but she said it was out in the country with no houses nearby. She claimed to have run through a lot of woods. The girl disappeared before we could find the place." The sheriff nodded and the detective continued, "I remember the description she gave us of the perp was tall with dark hair. I know it describes half of Angel Falls, but this guy's not looking too good both matching the description *and* being at the crime scene."

"You think this is her? You're not missing any others?" The sheriff said. He realized it was a pretty stupid question once he said it. This was Angel Falls after all and people just don't get murdered here every day. But then again he hadn't heard of this missing girl either. "I mean from a while back?" Another stupid question and the sheriff realized it the moment he said it. The victim's arm wasn't in full decomp which mean that the girl had been buried in the last six to twelve months. "No, she's gotta be recent huh?" The sheriff said correcting himself before the detective did it for him.

"Well, the girl who was reported missing, or murdered rather, was said to have been wearing orange fingernail polish." The detective nodded toward the girl's hand. The whole area was lit up by lights and the CSI had already begun working the soil around the body. They used gloved hands to carefully pull away at the soil while another scooped the soil into large evidence bags to be taken back to the lab and searched for trace. "I'm just bettin this is our girl." The detective said.

"Maria," the sheriff said.

"That's right. The girl who's missing name's Maria. So you have heard of the case."

"No," the sheriff said, "The Bander guy was muttering something while he was digging. I remember...he was saying 'Maria' over and over."

The detective took out a notebook and jotted something into it. "If this guy's not our killer, he sure is in a whole lot of trouble. He got any family?" The detective asked.

"Wife. Spoke with her last night. She seemed pretty nice. She said he'd never sleepwalked before last night. They haven't lived here that long."

"How long?" The detective asked looking up from his notebook.

"I don't know. Couple of months maybe? I can't say for sure."

"You going up to talk to the wife?" The detective asked.

“Ya, someone’s got to break the news that her husband’s in a whole lot of shit. I’m sure she’ll be thrilled knowing the man she falls asleep next to, gets up and comes out into the woods to dig up a murder victim and is most likely the killer.”

“Find out how long they’ve lived there will ya? And see if she knows of anybody named Maria. I’ll call in a warrant so we can search the place.”

“Alright. I’m on it. Good luck Detective, it’s going to be a long night.” The sheriff took off in the direction of his car.

Chapter 8

Michael was riding quietly in the back of a squad car. The two officers who had taken him were discussing quarterbacks in the front. Michael's wrists were burning and his skin was bruised. The officers had made sure to inflict maximum pain by yanking upward on the cuffs as they pushed him through the woods and toward the squad car. They forced him to trip several times and made sure to pull him up hard by the cuffs. He felt like his wrists were broken and he had scratches all over his legs. The officers talking up front grew to a whisper and the one on the passenger's side leaned over and whispered something to his partner while making glances toward Michael. Michael was already feeling sick to his stomach, confused, and scared. The look the officer was giving him, the look that said he was planning something sadistic, made Michael's stomach churn and he felt like he was going to vomit again.

Michael's suspicions were confirmed when the squad car went off course from the station and veered through dark streets on the bad side of town. The car came to a stop and parked in front of an old run down ranch style house that was overgrown with weeds and vines. It was clearly vacant.

The officer in the passenger seat turned back looking through the metal grate at Michael. "What do you think Frank, we gonna get this guy to talk?" The officer sneered and then looked over at his partner.

"Oh he'll talk alright," Frank turned around and looked back toward Michael, "They might be tough at first, but they all talk by the time I'm done with'em." Frank gave an evil smile back at Michael. Michael just glared at them. He wasn't sure what he was in for, but he was starting to doubt he would ever see April again.

"Anything you want to tell us before we get started?" Frank said to Michael.

"I told you I don't know anything." Michael said calmly but sternly.

"Well I'm convinced. Aren't you Gary?" Frank said sarcastically.

"Oh I'm convinced alright. Convinced this guy's full of shit. You think you're going to convince us that you strayed into the woods by accident and just accidently began digging where a dead girl was buried? I think he thinks we're idiots Frank."

"Well Gary, let's educate this son of a bitch shall we?"

Gary revived his sneer "Let's do it," he said and they both turned and got out of the squad car.

When they opened the door, Michael tried to lean the other direction so they couldn't grab him, but it was in vain as they grabbed him by the feet and yanked him out hitting his head on the bottom of the door frame and then the ground.

Michael began thrusting around like a fish out of water. Gary drew his arm back and was about to strike Michael in the face when Frank grabbed his arm. “Whoa, easy there buddy. I told the sheriff that we wouldn’t put any marks on him and I intend to stand by my word.” Gary began to let his arm drop. “So hit’em in the stomach.” Gary grinned and drew his arm back and laid out a full force punch into Michael’s gut. The wind was knocked out of him so forcefully that he nearly passed out for lack of air. Michael was still gasping when Frank reached behind him and dragged him up to his feet by the cuffs. Michael was in so much pain from the blow that he couldn’t feel the cuffs cutting into his skin. “That ought to tame you down some. Now fucking walk or he’ll do it again.” Michael was still doubled over but managed to keep his feet moving as they led him toward the door. Gary tried for the doorknob.

“It’s locked.” He said to Frank.

“See that rock over there?” Frank nodded to the left. Gary pointed to a small grey rock. “No, the red one to the right of it.” Gary pointed to the one to the right. “Ya, that one. There’s a key underneath. Put it back when you’re done.” Gary turned the rock over and found the key. He unlocked the door and put the key back. Michael was shoved through the door and into a room on the left. Gary flipped on his Maglite and flashed it around the room. Frank was holding Michael up by the cuffs with one hand. He pointed with the other. “See that door over there?” Gary turned the light in the direction that Frank was pointing. There was a brown door, dirty with black spray paint on it. The words 'death to malboc' was written on it in terrible handwriting and there were some symbols scribbled below it. "That's the basement. Let's take him down there."

Michael's mind was beginning to clear as he was being led down the wooden stairs into the basement. They couldn't mark him up and they had to get him to the station before too much time had gone by or there were going to be questions. How bad could they possibly hurt him? April's gotta be worried sick. He'd need to call her as soon as he arrived at the station. If he really gets a phone call that is. He was starting to think that was all just in the movies. He didn't see a phone call in his immediate future.

"Here, hold the prisoner." Gary grabbed Michael's cuffs where Frank had held them. "Let me see your light." Gary handed Frank the Maglite. There was a dividing concrete wall that ran down the middle of the basement dividing it in two. There was a doorway cut into the wall but Frank didn't go into it. He leaned down next to the wall. There was a car battery resting on top of a couple of two by four's. Frank grasped a couple of metal clamps and connected them to the battery. The room was lit up by two lamps. One lamp was in the far corner and the other was directly in the middle. The basement wasn't very big, in fact it didn't seem to be more than fifteen feet to the back of the wall. There was a wooden bench underneath the light in the middle. It was stained red in various places

Michael assumed it to be blood and his heart sank when he began to realize that this was going to be worse than a few punches to the gut.

“So how are we going to get him to talk without making any marks?” Gary said looking over at Frank. Frank smiled.

“Ever hear of waterboarding?” Frank said.

Michael’s eyes went wide and began to jerk back and forth trying to break free of Gary’s grip. Frank quickly rushed over and landed a solid blow to Michael’s gut and grabbed him by the throat and jerked him up into the air and onto the table. Michael was trying to push off the table by his feet while frank was holding him down by his throat. The cuffs bore into Michael’s hands even further underneath him.

“Grab his feet and hold’em to the table.” Frank said to Gary. Gary had trouble catching Michael’s feet as they flopped about. Finally he was able to grasp one and then the other and hold them down to the table. Michael was still trying to wiggle but Frank had his neck pinned so hard to the table that he was losing circulation. His vision was going blurry and he felt like he was about to pass out. “That a boy.” Frank said. “You just calm down now.” Frank kept his left hand over Michael’s throat and reached to the right of the table. Hanging on a nail on the side was a nylon ratchet strap. He put one of the ends in his mouth and uncoiled it. He laid the strap over Michael’s throat and let each end dangle over the sides. Frank let go of Michael’s head and disappeared under the bench to grab the other end of the strap. Michael tried to lift his head up but had got jerked back down when he felt the strap tighten on his throat. He heard the clicking of a ratchet and felt the strap go tight against his throat threatening to cut off his breathing and circulation if it went any tighter. Frank stopped tightening the strap and came back up to check his work. He tested the tightness with his finger to verify that Michael could still breathe. Once he was satisfied, he grabbed another strap and strapped his feet to the table just below his knees. This strap he pulled much tighter. Gary watched Frank work with a grinning sneer on his face. He would chuckle or laugh when Michael would grunt or make any sounds of pain. Frank stepped back and observed his work.

Michael tried to move but couldn't. He was helpless. He began to worry he might not survive. He and April had only been married for such a short time. They never even had a chance to take a honeymoon or a vacation. He wanted to swim in the ocean. She wanted to show him the Bahamas. Michael often wondered if they would have children. They had never really discussed it. What would they have looked like? Would they have had a boy or a girl? Would he have taught him how to fish, hunt, or work on a truck? Would she have looked like an angel in a prom gown? Images flashed in Michael's mind of a family that he had never had, and dread came over him as he realized that he probably never would now. Even if he survived, how would he convince anybody of his own innocence? He wasn't even sure himself.

"Look at'em Frank. He looks scared don't he?" Gary said.

"He looks guilty to me." Frank said. "What about it boy? You guilty? You ready to talk yet?" Michael just laid there looking straight up at the ceiling. The metal lamp was swinging back and forth on its cord. There wasn't much of a ceiling. The basement was never intended to be a finished one. Michael could see floor joists and hardwood floors. He let himself get lost in the swinging lamp. "You look at me when I talk to you! You hear me boy?" Frank grabbed Michael's hair and pulled his head up slightly and slammed it hard against the back of the table. Michael continued to look up, lost in the lamp. Frank snorted and spit in Michael's face. Michael felt the spit burning his eyes and a glob ran down his cheek. His eyes were welling up with tears. He didn't want to give them the pleasure, but despite his fighting it, a tear fell down the right side of his cheek.

"Aww now ain't that cute Frank? You gone and made him cry." Gary said.

"I'll bet he didn't cry for that girl before he killed her. What about it asshole? Did you cry for her? Did you make *her* cry?" Frank yelled at Michael. Michael looked straight ahead at the lamp emotionless. "So you're not ready to talk yet eh? Welp, we can fix that right quick let me tell you." Frank grabbed an old towel lying on a wooden chair nearby. "Gary, see that gallon of water over there in the corner? Ya, that one. Bring it over here."

Gary grabbed the water and brought it to Frank. “Now here is how we solve crimes where I come from. Pay attention newbie. We’ll have this bird singin in no time.” Frank said as he threw the towel across Michael’s mouth. Michael’s eyes went wide and he tried moving his head from side to side in panic. He had heard about waterboarding and knew what was coming. His body flexed hard against the straps but he couldn't move. Each time he tried to move his head, he felt the straps cutting into his neck.

Frank unscrewed the cap to the water jug. He looked at Michael and smiled at the panic in his eyes. “Calm down, calm down now.” Frank said quietly. “We gave you the opportunity to tell us what happened and you refused. Is that our fault?” Frank said quietly.

“I don’t know what happened. I’m telling you the truth. I didn’t kill anybody. I was s-s-sleepwalking.” Michael said from under the towel.

“Well, that’s a cute story and all buddy, but it just don’t add up. You see, you couldn’t have been there unless you done it or was with the person who did. So, you just need to quit the bullshit and tell us what you know. Savey?” Michael looked at Frank expressionless. He couldn’t believe this was happening. That this guy, this “cop”, was going to torture him.

“Alright Gary, you keep the towel pulled tight over his mouth. Got it?” Frank asked.

"Good God Frank. This damn thing stinks. What the hell you got all over it?" Gary asked as he pulled the towel tight over Michael's mouth.

"Oh I may have wiped my ass with it a time or two." Frank said.

Michael felt as if he was going to vomit. He didn't want to open his mouth to breathe. He knew very shortly he was going to though. He focused on the lamp again. Gary had hit it with his head and it was swinging again causing all the shadows of the room to move. He began to drift to a happier place. For a moment he was back at home with April and they were sitting on the couch. He had his arm around her and she had her head buried into his chest. They were watching something on TV though he couldn't tell what. He could smell the apple blossom scent in her hair from her favorite shampoo. He could feel the softness of her shirt and the skin underneath it. He could almost...Michael was pulled away with a rush of water across his face. The towel soaked it up instantly and clung to his face like peanut butter on a knife. Water streaked down the sides and even went into his eyes which became immediately blurry. He was still calm but as the need for air built within him, he could feel panic rising from within. He strained against the straps trying to move his body, trying to move his head, to get out from underneath the towel. His lungs began to burn and he could feel the fire within his head as his body cried out for air. But no air came. Michael continued to hold his breath and Frank continued to pour the water ever so slowly across his mouth and nose. Michael felt the world begin to spin. The light above was swinging slower now but became blurry. There were two lights now swinging slightly overhead back and forth. All at once Michael's need for air overtook him and his body tensed as he sucked in for air. The towel that now gripped his face tightly pulled slightly inward sending small sprays of water and feces into his mouth. But he couldn't pull enough air through the towel. His eyes began to bulge and became bloodshot. Michael's head began to thrust and the towel across his mouth made little indents as Michael continued to try to pull air through the towel. But Frank kept pouring the water across it and the towel was so saturated with water that the air just couldn't come through. Michael was suffocating. He may as well have plastic wrapped across his face. He felt himself fading out of existence. His body began to relax as his eyes rolled back in his head. The lamps were not swinging anymore. In fact the lamps ceased to exist. The room went black and Michael found April sitting on the beach beside the ocean. He went to her. She looked up at him and smiled. Michael offered her his hand and she took it. He pulled her up close to him and they embraced in a sweet passionate kiss. Michael and April turned toward the ocean and watched the waves come in. It was so peaceful. He put his hand around her lower back and together they walked toward the water. As they approached the water, the sand grew wet and the next wave came up and the cool water surrounded their feet and ankles. Then bright light appeared overhead and Michael was brought back to reality with a foul burning in his nose. He looked up to see that the lamp was moving once again and Frank was holding something under his nose. An ammonia capsule.

"Look. See, nothing to worry about newbie. It brings'em back every time. Well, not every time. Sometimes they drown and you have to do it manually."

"Fuck that. You kill this S.O.B. he stays dead. I'm not sticking my mouth anywhere near his with all that shit on his face. It's probably on my fucking hands!" Gary looked at his hands and wiped them on his pants.

"Ah don't worry about that. If he dies we can always say he escaped custody. That happens from time to time you know." Frank said. Gary didn't seem to hear him. He was still studying his hands and wiping them aggressively against his pants.

Michael was still gasping but was relieved to have so much air to breathe. He could feel his life force coming back into his body. He was jittery but felt his strength returning. His cheeks were wet with water and tears. His breathing was raspy and labored. He coughed and water sprayed the air.

Gary wiped sweat from his forehead and looked over at Frank. "You think he's ready to talk?"

Frank reached to his side and pulled a cell phone out of a pouch. He flipped it open, checked the time and flipped it closed. "He better be. We're running out of time and I'm starting to get pissed." Frank grabbed Michael's hair and pulled his head up a little and slammed it against the table again. "So...man who likes to murder little girls, you ready to talk?"

Michael looked him in the eyes. "I told you. I don't know anything. I don't. I swear." Michael turned his head back toward the lamp.

Frank and Gary exchanged a look. "I guess we've got time for another round or two." Frank said. "Gary, toss that towel back on his face."

A look of disgust crossed Gary's face as he eyed the shit stained towel on the floor. He looked back up at Frank. Frank nodded. "Do it." He said.

Gary leaned down and pinched the towel by the tips of two fingers and held it away from him like it was a poisonous snake. He threw it over Michael's face.

"Pull it tight on the ends. Make sure it's across his nose and mouth." Frank ordered.

Gary's eyes gave another look of disgust and looked at Frank as if to say 'are you fucking kidding me?' But he did as he was told. He took the corners of the towel and spread them out across Michael's face so only his eyes were showing. Michael began to look panicky.

Frank picked up the water jug. “Alright, hold it tight. Here goes round two.” Frank held the water up over the towel. Michael began thrusting and jerking again but was getting nowhere. The water came and the towel began to stick to his face.

Mumbling came from under the towel and Frank stopped for a minute. "What’s that asshole? You got something to say now?”

“Ohaylhellyou,” came a muffled yell again.

“Gary pull that back a sec.” Frank said. Gary pulled the towel aside. “Say again.”

Michael coughed and sprayed some more water. “I said I’ll fucking tell you.”

“You’re damn right you will. Now who the fuck was she?”

Michael looked over at Frank and then back at the lamp. “Her name is Angela Jacobs. She’s a girl I worked with.”

“Wohoo...I knew it.” Gary said slapping Frank on the back. “You fucking killed that girl didn’t you asshole?”

“Yes. I killed her.”

Frank flipped out his phone and checked it again. “Times about up. See newbie, works every time. I’ve helped solve quite a few cases the perp would have gotten off if I hadn’t intervened. Now undue that strap and stand this asshole up." Frank reached under and loosened the strap on Michael's neck. Gary loosened the one on his legs.

Michael's hands and arms had gone completely numb underneath him. He felt pain and a burning sensation, but could no longer feel his individual fingers. He wasn't sure he could move them.

Frank grabbed his feet and slipped them off the table until Michael was nearly standing up. As soon as Michael's feet hit the ground Frank let loose with a powerful punch to the stomach. Michael bent over and vomited. He was trying to gasp for breath when Frank spun him around and slammed his head on the table pinning him down. Michael's t-shirt was soaked with water. His briefs were urine soaked. He couldn't remember at what point he'd pissed himself. Frank held his head down with force. "So you like to murder little girls do ya? I'm bettin you raped her too am I right? Am I right asshole?" Frank pushed down hard on his head. "Gary, what do you think? You think we got us a rapist here?"

"Don't know why else he'd do it. Must be." Gary said.

"Here. Hold his fucking head down." Gary came over and pushed down on Michael's head and neck with both hands. "You know what they do to rapists in prison? Well I'm going to show you. I'll be the first one to pop that fucking cherry of yours." Frank grabbed Michael's briefs by the sides and yanked them to the floor. Gary looked back at Frank with his mouth half open looking appalled. Then his mouth closed into a sneer and he pushed harder on Michael's head and neck.

Chapter 9

April lay in bed asleep, oblivious to the fact that her husband had left her bed several hours ago. She remained oblivious to all the flashing lights passing in front of the house. And now she lay there semi oblivious to the knocking that came at the door. There were three hard knocks, a pause, and then another three hard knocks. She was at an amusement park feeding food to the fish. She had just put another quarter in the machine and turned the handle. A heaping pile of pellets rolled out into her hand. Michael was next to her. He held out his hands and made a scoop with them. April poured half of the pellets into his hands. She looked up and he was smiling at her. They both laughed and turned and sprinkled the food into the water a little at a time. It seemed like hundreds of big carp skimmed the surface sucking the pellets in with their little carp mouths. They looked like little vacuum cleaners and they made funny little noises each time they sucked a pellet into their mouth. After they emptied their hands, April turned toward Michael and their eyes connected. Michael smiled at her and reached up and tucked a stray hair back from her face. He pulled her close and she embraced him. It was beautiful out; there were kids and families all around running excitedly. Then Michael pulled back a little. April felt something tugging at her pant leg. She looked down and found a beautiful little girl smiling up at her. She had beautiful brown curly hair, warm brown eyes that glistened as she smiled, and a beautiful face of an angel. The little girl was smiling. She was holding an ice cream cone in her right hand. She held it out and offered it to April. April smiled and took the cone. She gave it a single lick and said "yummy" to the little girl and handed back the cone. The little girl smiled and then something like a look of concern crossed her face. April and Michael both bent down. "What's wrong sweetie?" April asked the little girl. A tear had begun to fall down her left cheek and Michael scooped it up with his finger.

"Why are you crying?" He asked.

The little girl looked up at both of them. "Please. Please help me."

"Help you what honey?" April asked.

"I can't find her. Can you help me find her?" The little girl said.

"Who are you looking for sweetie? Are you lost?" asked Michael.

"I can't find my sister. She's lost." A big gust of wind blew past kicking up dirt and debris into April and Michael's face. April shielded her eyes with her hand. It grew darker as clouds filled the sky and blotted out the sun.

"Where's your mommy honey? Is your mommy with you?" April asked.

The little girl turned her head so that she was staring straight into April's eyes. Her ice cream slid sideways and fell from her cone to the ground. Her eyes reflected concern, fear, and welled up with tears. "You're my mommy silly" the little girl said and threw her arms around April. April hugged the girl and smiled at Michael who was smiling back at her. The sky grew darker and April looked around to see people running and screaming. She looked back at Michael and he had blood running down his chin. His clothes were gone and he was wearing nothing but his briefs and a t-shirt. Then a loud knocking sound came from nowhere and April sat straight up in her bed gasping for air. She took a deep breath and listened to the silence. The knocking returned. It had followed her out of her dream, or interrupted it.

You're my mommy silly. The voice came back to her in her head as she slid out of bed and grabbed her robe off the closet door. She looked at the bed and made a note that Michael wasn't there again. She hoped he was in the other room and not out digging...but if that were the case he would have answered the door. She shook her head as she tied the robe around her waist and headed for the door. The door was slightly ajar. "Who is it?" She hollered through the crack in the door. *Where the hell is Michael?* She felt a cold chill run up her spine. She didn't like strangers knocking on her door in the night.

"It's Angel County Sheriff ma'am."

"Again?" She said as she opened the door and peered at the man in uniform standing outside. It was the same sheriff as the night before. He didn't look very happy. "He did it again didn't he?" She asked.

"Yes ma'am. I'm afraid he did." The sheriff replied.

"You're not going to arrest him are you? I mean...he hasn't had a chance to see a doctor yet. It's not his fault." April pleaded.

"I'm afraid it's a little more complicated than that. May I come in so we can speak?"

April's look suddenly changed to one of extreme concern. "I...I guess. I don't know what there is to talk about though. He really just needs to see a doctor." She opened the screen door and let the sheriff step through. The sheriff followed her in and she signaled him to be seated on the couch at the end. She took the recliner right next to it, folded her robe tight around her legs and placed her hands in her lap. "We looked it up online today. It turns out it is a common problem. Different sites said that there is medication for it but we probably won't be able to get him to a doctor for a week." She hesitated watching the sheriff's concerned face. "I suppose I could tie him to the bed or something. Lock him in a room?"

"Ma'am, we found your husband out digging in the same spot again tonight." The sheriff looked around for a moment like he wanted to find something better to talk about. Some sort of small talk like 'oh that's a nice vase you have over there, where did you get it?' or 'hey that's a pretty picture, where was it taken', but finally he heaved a big sigh and turned back toward April.

"And? You brought him home again right? Is he out in the car?" April looked toward the window. She could see the headlights beaming through the curtains. "Did you cuff him again?" She asked sternly.

"Mrs. Bander, there was a body found."

"Wha..?" April clasped her hand over her mouth and stifled her own scream. She bolted straight up out of the chair. "Is Michael ok? Where's Michael? Where's Michael? Tell me he's ok. Oh God tell me he's ok..." Tears were starting from the corner of her eyes. She made her way toward the door.

The sheriff stood up. "Mrs. Bander, your husband isn't in the car. Please sit down."

April's eyes went wide and she covered her mouth again. "Oh my God! Is he...is he..?"

"Ma'am, your husband is fine. He's in custody at the station. Now please sit down so I can ask you a few questions."

April stood there for a moment lingering, thinking, running the scenarios. She couldn't find one that fit so she looked back at the sheriff and finally returned to her seat in the recliner.

"Mrs. Bander, your husband was found digging again; only this time he unearthed human remains." April's eyes grew big but she remained silent. "The body appeared to be female."

"Oh my God! What happened to her?" She said quietly.

The sheriff could see that it hadn't registered with her yet that her husband must have known that she was buried there and that he was not only a suspect, but also most likely the killer.

"We don't know yet, there will be an autopsy though. The detective thinks it might be a girl who went missing a few months back. Does the name Maria mean anything to you?"

April thought for a moment. "No...er...well, I have an Aunt Maria. But I don't think she's gone missing. I'm sure I would have heard about it."

"Has your husband ever mentioned anyone named Maria? Maybe someone he'd met at work?" The sheriff asked.

"No, not really. He's never mentioned anyone. He might have a student named Maria or something. I don't know."

"So he's a teacher?"

"Mhmm."

"What does he teach?" The sheriff had pulled out a little notebook and was scribbling in it.

"He's a Biology teacher."

"At the high school?"

"Yes. Why are you asking things about my...oh my God! You think Michael had something to do with this? Are you nuts? Are you fucking crazy?" The sheriff looked up from his notebook a little shocked. He had been wondering when it would register. "Michael Bander a Killer? You guys are waaaaay off!" April wasn't yelling but she was pissed and speaking very sternly.

"Calm down Mrs. Bander. Put yourself in our shoes. We find a man out in the middle of the woods in the dead of the night with nothing on but a t-shirt and underwear digging up a body."

April's pissed look melted away into a look of concern and worry as the depth of the situation began to wrap itself around her.

"Now Mrs. Bander, could you find a body buried in the woods without a flashlight in the middle of the night?"

April turned her head. Tears were running down her cheeks. She wiped them away with the cuff of her robe.

"You couldn't possibly walk right to the spot unless..." The sheriff was hesitant to complete the sentence.

April turned and looked the sheriff in the eye. "Unless he knew she was there." She completed the sentence for him.

"Now you understand why he is a suspect."

"I want to see my husband."

"I only have a couple more questions for you and then you will be free to call around and get yourself a good lawyer. I'm sure he can arrange for a visitation, but I wouldn't hold your breath on getting to see him anytime soon. I'm sure he'll be formally charged with murder tomorrow and I'm not guessing that the judge would allow him to post bail." The sheriff broke the news as softly and politely as he could. He believed it to be better to just be straight with her than to sugar coat it.

April clasped her hands over her face and began to cry.

Chapter 10

Michael had never been a violent man. He had been in only three fights. Ever. In fact, he considered himself to be humble, fair, respectful of others, and always treated others the way he would want to be treated. But that didn't mean he was unlearned in the ways of combat. In fact, his father had forced him to learn to fight at about the age of ten. Michael was on his way home from school. He lived just a little over a mile away. Too close for the busses, but too far on a rainy day. But that day, the sun was shining. It was hot. Very hot. Michael's backpack weighed more than he did and the straps were cutting into his shoulders with each bounce. Michael had just crossed a street and had cut through a church parking lot. There was a shortcut this way that knocked about five minutes off his walk home. There was a grassy hill in the back of the church. Michael made his way down it. He was staring at the ground as he walked, lost in space. Well, it wasn't space that occupied it. It was Sarah. She had passed him a note today at the end of math class. He took a minute to read it before walking home and was replaying it in his mind. She had asked him to the Saity Hawkins dance. He liked the girl, but just wasn't much of a dancer. If he went, she would be expecting him to dance with her.

Michael was trying to picture him dancing with a girl when a rock bounced off his cheek. He immediately doubled over, cupping his cheek. Blood began to drip through his fingers. Two boys stood laughing at the bottom of the hill. Mike Cofner and Jacob Brask. They were both laughing and pointing.

Michael looked at the boys and then at his hand with blood all over it. He had never seen so much blood. He decided the shortcut wasn't such a good idea today and turned and headed back up the hill.

"Where ya goin sissy?" Jacob hollered from behind. Michael heard foot thuds as both boys ran up the hill behind him. He was almost at the top when a hand grasped his heavy backpack and pulled him backward. The bag weighing more than himself, took the side of gravity and propelled him backward to the ground. Over and over, Michael rolled to the bottom of the hill. Both boys were on him immediately, kicking and punching. Michael barely knew them. He hadn't done anything to these guys. He had seen them from time to time beat on other kids though.

Michael curled into a ball and suffered about two minutes of kicks and punches. Then one of them saw another young boy that must have deserved a beating because they abandoned Michael and left him for death. Well, he felt like death anyway. More likely sore ribs, black eye, cuts, and a bruised ego. Michael managed to pick himself up and drag himself home. When he walked in the door, he did not get the pitiful reaction he had expected. His father, John, had been in the Special Forces. He was upset, but more at himself than Michael, for not having taught his son how to defend himself.

John was kneeling before Michael with a cloth wiping away the blood. He went to the sink, rinsed it out and kneeled down before him again. He dabbed gently at Michael's busted lip and dotted up the blood. "We start tomorrow." He said. "After school. You understand?" Michael nodded at his dad. His mouth was too sore to be asking a bunch of questions, but he was fairly certain his dad intended to teach him how to fight. And teach he did. Until the end of school and the rest of the summer, Michael's dad taught him how to defend himself in all the ways he knew how.

"Michael," his dad had said to him one day. "I've never taught you these things because I didn't want you to become a bully. You have to understand, the more you fight, the more fights will come to you. The best way to win a fight is to avoid it. The moment you have to strike another human being, you've already lost. A little piece of you dissapears each time." He tapped Michael on his heart to emphasize. "Can you understand that?"

"Yes dad. Don't fight unless there is no other choice." Michael said. Michael's dad nodded, happy that his son understood. He embraced him. "I love you son. I've only taught you these things because one day it might save your life, or someone else's. I hope you never have to use what I've taught you."

Michael had, on two other occasions needed to use the skills that his father had taught him. There was never a fight really. Michael's defense was good and swift, and he was able to make his point before he ever had to strike anybody. He had taken what his father had told him to heart. He had avoided fighting on almost every occasion. But now, here he found himself in a dark basement with two men, not unlike the two boys who had beaten him so many years ago. He was wet, cold, and sore. He was trembling. One man held his head to the table and the other was dropping his pants, hell bent on raping him. Michael's mind had been cloudy from the waterboarding. It was quickly clearing as he assessed the situation. He wasn't likely to die here. He figured the two officers had a name, and now were about to get what they were really after in the first place. He would then be dragged back to the station and charged with murder. He was sure of it. And if he himself was on the jury, would he not convict any man who had been digging up a body in the woods at midnight? His dad's words echoed in his mind: "The best way to win a fight is to avoid it." Was there any way to avoid it? Certainty of rape, certainty of a life sentence or worse. He had to go. He needed to understand what was going on. Who was the girl? How had he found her? How did she die? He would not go down this way. He would not live out the rest of his life as a murderer. The decision was made. There was a clank on the floor as Frank's belt hit the concrete. Michael felt two hands grab him from behind.

Chapter 11

Detective James was still at the crime scene. The body had been unearthed. It was Maria. It had to be. Her description and clothing matched the information her sister had given about her. She had been shot twice. Once in the abdomen and the other in the head. The coroner ruled the shot to the head as the likely cause of death, but said she would likely have died anyway because of the injury to her abdomen coupled by the fact the nearest decent ER was over forty miles away. The girl never had a chance.

Detective James scribbled down some thoughts in his notebook while waiting for the last of the soil samples to be bagged. The girl had been hefted onto a large tarp. It was important to capture any loose trace that might fall off her clothes on the way to the lab. Two CSI personnel grabbed the tarp at each end and carried the girl off toward the vehicles. Detective James looked in the direction that the sheriff had gone and wondered how he was doing with the wife. Shitty part of the job. He thought. He looked down at the two remaining CSI's who were shoveling the last of the dirt into ziploc bags that were about two feet wide and two feet long. "That's the last of it Detective." The younger one said. He had red curly hair and freckles. He looked smart. Probably was. Most of the CSI team here were over qualified for this little town. Many of them were brilliant. The best CSI's were filling in the little towns because the big cities had gone broke and weren't able to afford them. It crushed their dreams of working a big city, but there were always small cities that would swipe them up for half the pay they would have gotten in the big city. The other CSI was a woman. She was a few years older. She had brown hair pulled back into a pony tail. There was dirt smeared on her face and nose. Detective James looked from one to the other. "I appreciate you guys getting out here so quick. I've got one more thing I need you to do when you're done though."

"What's that?" The red haired CSI asked wiping his sleeve across his forehead.

"I've got someone bringing out four metal detectors. I'd like both of you and two officers to sweep the crime scene with them. The weeds are high which makes finding anything by sight alone tough. We didn't come up with any shell casings and there should be two or more. Start at the road and do a twenty five yard grid and extend it past the hole by twenty five yards. Any questions?" The CSI's looked at each other and nodded their heads. "Good. I'm heading in to question the perp. I'll check in with you guys later." They nodded and Detective James headed toward the road. The sheriff was right about one thing; It *is* going to be a long night.

Chapter 12

The human brain is an amazing thing. Like a computer, it can do the most complex calculations in a fraction of a second. A person can get lost in a thought or daydream and what may seem to go on for hours in their head, may have all taken place in only five seconds of reality. When Michael felt two hands grab hold of him from behind, there was instant clarity and his mind began calculating and assessing the situation. Like a grandmaster chess player calculating his next move, Michael ran through many scenarios in his head attempting to predict several moves ahead and their outcomes.

It all came down to a gun. There were two of them. Gary's was around his waist and Frank's was lying on the floor, around his ankles with his pants. If his hands weren't handcuffed behind his back, he would have a fighting chance. But with hands clasped tightly behind him, his brain was having a difficult time pinning down a winning scenario. If he went for either gun, the other officer was likely to pull his own before Michael could get one in his hands and aimed properly behind his back.

There was no winning scenario. Michael knew it after running half a dozen options through his mind in a second. Each attempt to escape ended with him getting shot. There was one scenario in which the outcome was uncertain. He would blast his foot backward into Frank's knee hopefully breaking it. He would then kick Frank straight back into the upper chest which would disorientate him and knock the wind out of him depending on whether or not he was wearing a bullet proof vest. As Frank was falling backward, Michael predicted that Gary would release his hold in shock and possibly go for his weapon. Michael would then head butt the officer in the face, spin around so his back was to him and grab the gun from his holster. It was all just speculation. If one thing went wrong, Michael would die. Death didn't seem like such a bad option when faced with being raped and life imprisonment.

"Aw look at that Gary. He's as gentle as a pussy cat. He'll fit right in with them big boys in prison now won't he?" Frank said to Gary.

Gary laughed. "He'll be somebody's bitch alright."

"He'll be my bitch first. This is for the girl you killed asshole."

Frank was about to make his move and Michael wasn't going to wait to be violated before acting. He thrust his foot backward into Frank's knee as hard as he could. He heard it break. He thrust kicked Frank. Hard. In the chest. Frank flew back against the wall clutching his chest trying to breathe. As Michael predicted, Gary released his hold and turned toward Frank, eyes wild in disbelief. Michael stood up and smashed his forehead right into Gary's nose. Blood came pouring out and Gary cried out in pain.

"Oh my nose! My fucking nose! You broke it. You Fuck!" Michael spun and was pushing him back toward the wall, feeling and trying to find his belt and get his hand on Gary's gun. Michael's hands were so tightly bound and swollen he couldn't hardly move them much less grasp anything. He was watching Frank who was starting to breathe easier. Michael saw that Frank was beginning to lower himself in order to reach for his gun. Michael moved fast. He let off of Gary and ran straight over to Frank and threw a roundhouse kick hard at his face. Frank's head exploded back into the wall and Frank slid down to the floor unconscious. A shot rang out that sent concrete spattering by Michael's face. Concrete exploded from the wall stinging his face and the bullet ricocheted around the room. Michael ducked down and moved closer to the table he had been strapped to.

"Fuck!" The young officer shouted out. "You fucking shot me! I'm hit."

Michael hesitated. He hadn't shot him. The ricocheting bullet must have got him. *That dumb cop thinks I have Frank's gun*. Michael thought for a moment; *how can I use this?* Then it hit him. "Gary, I've got Frank's gun aimed right at you." Gary was still swearing though much quieter. It sounded more like pouting. "You've got until the count of three to drop your weapon and kick it under the table."

"But..but.."

"One..."

"How do I know you won't just shoot me anyway?" Gary was near tears.

"Two...keep holding that gun Gary and you'll find out for sure."

"But I.. "

"Three!" Gary's gun hit the floor and he kicked it under the table. Michael was still just out of his sight. Michael smiled and shook his head. He looked back toward Frank. He was still out.

"Please don't kill me."

"You want to live Gary?" Michael asked.

"Ye..yes." *Weird how he doesn't sound so tough now.* Michael thought.

"Then listen to me very closely and do exactly what I say and I'll let you live. Throw the keys to your cuffs under the table."

Gary did as he was instructed. The keys hit the concrete under the table. Michael looked at them. He wanted to grab them desperately and get out of the handcuffs. But to do that, he would have to flip upside down on his back which would make him vulnerable and give Gary too much time to build up courage and come up with a plan.

"Good. We're almost done now and then I'll be on my way. You still want to live?"

"Yes." The response was quiet. "I...I'm shot."

"Yes, I know. I'll call an ambulance before I leave you have my word. Where are you shot at?"

"My arm."

"Ok, do exactly as I tell you and you'll live through this." There was no response. "Take your shirt and vest off and throw it on the floor by the table." Michael said.

"My...my shirt?"

"Do it now Gary or I'll fucking shoot!" Michael yelled. He looked back toward Frank. Frank's head moved a little. He was going to come to. A shirt fell to the floor in front of the table.

"I don't have a vest on."

"Then you're an idiot. Cuff yourself behind your back. If they're not cuffed as tight as mine were I'm going to break all your fingers. You got that Gary?"

"I got it." There was the sound of chains and then the unmistakable sound of cuffs being closed. One. Then another. Michael looked back toward Frank. His eyes were open and staring right at him. Michael Froze. Frank would be able to see

Michael clearly. He'd know that he doesn't have a gun. He'd know that he was still vulnerable.

Michael remained frozen for a second. He could hear his heart beating loudly in his ears. Is this where he would die? Naked in a dirty basement of a vacant house where nobody would find him for months? Visions of April passed through his mind. She was dressed in black and crying. It was his funeral. He could see his parents, her parents, friends... Then he saw something else. Frank wasn't looking at him...he was looking through him. He was still out of it. Probably had blurry vision. Frank closed his eyes.

Michael reached under the table with his foot and slid the keys toward him and dropped to the ground on his butt. He was still watching Frank. Frank's eyes had opened again. Michael could tell he was trying to regain his focus. Frank began to stir.

Michael's hands had clasped the keys. The blood had begun to flow and there was just enough feeling in them to tell when they had grasped something solid.

"Ca...can I go now?" Gary's voice echoed from behind the table.

"Gary, you put your face up against that wall and keep it there. You'll get out of here soon enough." Michael said. Frank seemed to stir even more now with the sound of the voices. He was beginning to focus his eyes on Michael. Frank's eyes suddenly went wide and he sat up with a jolt. He looked at Michael and then looked down at his pants. His gun was not visible but would be under them, in the holster attached to his belt. Frank sat up and leaned forward. He started feeling through his pants, trying to find his gun.

Michael began to panic. His hands were shaking and he was having a hard time getting the key into the keyhole. Frank had located the lump where his gun appeared to be and was flipping over his pants. Michael felt the key go in. He turned the key and the lock clicked and let loose. His hands were free. Frank had his holster in his hands and looked up at the sound of the cuffs clicking. But it was too late. Michael was pointing Gary's gun directly at him.

"Don't even think about it." Michael said. Frank paused and then let the holster drop back onto his pants.

"Wha...what's going on over there? Frank? Frank?" Gary's voice was shaky.

"We're fucked you idiot. That's what's going on." Frank's voice was weak. He still hadn't recovered from the kick to the head. Michael stood up but kept the gun trained on Frank.

"Stand up!" Michael ordered Frank.

"I can't you fucking asshole. You broke my goddamn knee."

"Then I guess you better use the other one and stand the fuck up!" Michael was angry. He was tired. And he was dirty. And he needed to let April know he was ok.

Frank just sat there and shook his head as if to say 'Nope. Go fuck yourself.'"

"I'm in my fucking rights to kill you right now and I'll do it. I'm leaving this place in five minutes whether you are alive or dead. So if you want to live to rape some other poor innocent fucker, then I suggest you do what I say and do it now!" Michael's voice had worked its way into rage.

Frank looked Michael directly in the eyes and found no sign of weakness. There was nothing there to suggest that Michael wouldn't shoot him if he didn't do what was instructed. Frank struggled but managed to get himself up and stood on one leg. He kept his right leg slightly elevated off the floor.

"Take your shirt off." Michael ordered. Frank just stared at him. "You didn't seem to have a problem undressing *me,* now did you?"

"Well we're not little girl rapists either now are we?" Frank retorted but started unbuttoning his shirt.

"Well, we know *you're* a rapist now don't we?" Michael retorted. Frank threw his shirt on the floor by Michael's feet. He was still wearing a vest and a t-shirt.

"Vest and t-shirt too." Michael said while still pointing the gun at him.

Frank hefted the vest over his head and dropped it onto the floor. He grabbed his t-shirt from the bottom and almost fell over trying to get it over his head while balancing on his left foot. Frank pulled it over his head and dropped it onto the floor. He looked pale. *Probably from pain from the broken knee.* Michael thought. There were blood smears on his face and it glistened in the lamplight. Frank was now naked and vulnerable. Michael looked over at Gary who was watching the commotion silently. "Put your face against the wall and turn the other direction!" Michael yelled but kept the gun pointed at Frank. He noted that Gary still had on a t-shirt. He wanted them both to feel as cold and violated as he had felt.

Michael looked back at Frank. "Get over to the table and lean over it." Michael signaled with the gun.

"What are you going to do, pop my cherry? See Gary, I told you this asshole's a rapist." Frank started hopping on his left foot toward the table. Gary stood quietly. Frank started to fall because his pants were still wrapped around his ankles. He caught himself on the table and pulled himself up and over so most of his weight was supported by the table. His left foot was still on the ground and his right foot was slightly off the ground.

Michael bent down by Frank's right foot and grasped his shoe and pulled and twisted to get it off. Frank howled out in pain from the pressure on his broken knee.

"Owww..you asshole!" Frank yelled. His shoe popped off and gave some relief from not having the weight of his shoe bearing on his knee.

"Lift your other foot." Michael commanded.

Frank put all his weight on his belly across the table and lifted his other foot. Michael twisted the shoe off and his pants and tighty whities fell off in a pile. Michael grabbed the keys off the floor and undid the other cuff still attached to his left wrist.

"Put your hands behind your back." Michael commanded. He expected Frank to mouth off with more insults and degradations but none came. Frank put his hands behind his back. Michael cuffed him and tightened them until Frank cried out in pain. Michael smiled at this and then grabbed his legs and hoisted him up, naked, onto the table face down.

Michael approached Gary from behind and placed the gun against the back of his neck. "You still want to live?" Michael asked.

Gary nodded. "Yes." He said quietly.

"Then do exactly as I tell you. Kick your shoes off."

"Wha…what?"

"I didn't stutter, kick you damn shoes off or so help me…"

"No…no…I got it. I'm taking them off." Gary scraped one foot against the other until both shoes were off.

"Good, now walk over to the table." Michael said.

Gary's eyes widened at seeing his partner handcuffed and naked on the table. He walked up and stopped at the table's edge in the middle.

"Good. Now lean over." Michael pushed Gary's back forcing him to fall over onto his partner. Gary landed face first onto Frank's bare ass. He quickly tried to pull himself up but felt a hand on the back of his neck. "I think you can stay right where you're at. Don't you dare move!" Michael said. Gary stopped pushing and kept his face planted face down in Frank's ass crack.

"Not so fun when your face is in his shit is it?" Michael said as he reached around Gary and undid his belt and pants. Gary didn't respond. Michael dropped Gary's pants and boxers. With the exception of Gary's t-shirt, and their socks, both officers were naked and vulnerable. Michael stood and looked around. He spotted two more jugs of water by the far wall. He went and grabbed one and brought it to the table. He unscrewed the cap and started at Frank's head and worked his way down to his feet, going right over Gary's head, drenching them in water. He threw down the jug and grabbed the other one. Gary had turned his head sideways in order to breathe.

"What, you think you need to breathe? That's more than you let me do. You guys are the ones that should be behind bars, not me." Michael went around to the other side of the table, unscrewed the cap and poured it over Gary's shirt until he was soaked. "Stand up!" Michael shouted at Gary. He grabbed Gary by the cuffs and pulled him backward hard. Gary winced and cried out in pain. "Doesn't feel so good does it?" Gary was standing up now and Michael poured the rest of the water over the front of his shirt. Gary shivered. Michael pushed him toward the front of the table and made him lean forward again. This time, he was leaning over the back of Frank's neck. Michael picked up his legs and hoisted him the rest of the way on top of his partner so he was lying on top of him. Michael reached down and grabbed the strap they had used on his neck and threw it over Gary's shoulders. The strap fell to the floor and Michael reached down and grabbed it and fed it through the ratchet and pulled until it was tight. He ratcheted it until it was tight enough where they couldn't move but not so much that they couldn't breathe. Frank and Gary had their heads turned toward the wall away from Michael. Michael picked up the other strap and threw it across the back of Gary's legs above the knees. Michael grabbed the other end and began to ratchet it tight. "This might sting a little bit." Michael warned as the strap came taught. He cranked it tight and Frank screamed out in pain with the pressure on his broken knee.

"Owww…oh you fucking asshole. You fucking prick asshole. You are going to pay! I am going to fucking kill you! You hear me? Fucking kill you asshole!" Frank yelled. Michael just ratcheted the strap that much harder.

Both officers were grunting and trying to move. Michael had a feeling if Frank kept wiggling long enough, karma was going to get him in the ass…literally. Michael grabbed Gary's pants and slipped into them. It was a tight fit, but it would keep him warm. He felt better right away. He picked up Gary's shirt and put it on, buttoning it up. And here April thought it was funny that he was in cuffs…if she could see him now…the thought reminded Michael that he needed to call her. Gary had a cell phone attached to his belt. Michael grabbed the cell phone and tinkered around with the buttons until he found the one he was looking for. Michael went to the end of the table and pulled off Gary's socks. They were damp from the water but not completely soaked. "I'm going to ask you guys some questions" Michael began. "And how honestly you answer them will determine how long I decide to wait before calling you some help."

"Fuck you." Frank managed to get out underneath the weight of Gary.

"Ok, never mind. I'll see you boys later." Michael acted as though he was going to leave.

"No…no…ask." Gary said. "I'll be honest. I swear."

"Shut the fuck up you idiot." Frank said.

"I ain't gonna die here man. I'm fucking shot. Don't you get it? He leaves and doesn't call for help...we die!" Gary said. Frank didn't respond. Michael turned around and headed toward the table. He was tinkering with the cell phone again.

"Whose idea was it to bring me here?" Michael began. There was a pause.

"It was my fucking idea. You happy?" Frank said.

"What's the address?" Michael asked. There was only silence. Frank didn't speak and Michael figured Gary didn't actually know. "I can't call you an ambulance if I don't know the address."

"514 Lincoln Street." Frank mumbled.

"Ok. Good. Now why did you bring me here?" Michael asked. He moved the phone to his left and ran his right hand through his hair shaking out water and debris.

"Are you fucking stupid? We brought you here to find out who the girl is. Who *you* fucking killed." Frank said.

"And you thought torturing me and waterboarding me would get you that information?"

"Well, it worked didn't it? We found out you killed Angela Jacobs. Between that and what you've done to us, you're going to fry asshole. You resisted arrest, escaped custody, kidnapped and tortured two police officers, and shot one."

"First, you kidnapped me. Second, I haven't tortured anyone, and third, I didn't shoot anyone, he was hit by his own ricochet."

"That may be true. But do you think they're going to believe you, a felon on the run for murder, or the word of two law abiding police officers who got hurt trying to keep a murderer off the streets?"

"Last I knew, law abiding police officers don't torture people into confession. And they sure as hell don't rape them."

"Ya, well good luck trying to prove it." Frank said.

Michael hit a button and put the cell phone back in the holder on his belt. He'd have to wait until he was outside to call April. Michael grabbed Frank's pants and emptied the pockets. There was change, a zippo lighter with a confederate flag on the front, a receipt, keys, and a pack of smokes. Michael pocketed the lighter, the keys, and the change. He then pulled Frank's wallet out of the back pocket. Michael quickly thumbed through it. There was eighty three dollars in it which he took out along with a debit card. He dropped Frank's belongings on the floor and stood up and took out Gary's wallet. Gary had forty six bucks. Michael added in the eighty three and the debit card. A hundred and twenty nine bucks wasn't going to get him very far. He stood up and approached the two officers who were throwing their arsenal of cusswords into the air. Most directed at Michael.

"I'm out of here boys. Here is the deal." Michael held up a cell phone and snapped a picture of the two officers lying naked on top of each other. I'm heading straight to the ATM with your cards. I'm going to withdraw 300 from each account. That's the least you can do for me after torturing me. Consider it a victim's severance."

"Fuck you. You don't know our pin numbers." Frank still had enough energy to be a wise ass.

"And after I have entered the pin numbers that you are about to give me," Michael continued "I will call an ambulance for you. But...if the pin numbers aren't correct, no ambulance, and this picture I just took will be on the front of tomorrow's paper.

There was more swearing but both men gave up pin numbers. Michael knew he couldn't return home. He figured if both the numbers were correct, and the officers weren't sitting on empty accounts, he would have close to eight hundred dollars. That would buy him a little time to figure out what the hell was going on. Before he left, Michael picked up Frank's phone, dialed a number and hit the speaker button. He moved to where the officers were facing and as he tested the straps to make sure they were taught, he quickly slid the phone underneath the strap but out of site. His own cell phone would be turned on silent and charging next to his bed. By calling his cell phone and letting it go to voicemail and leaving this phone on speaker, he thought he might get to listen to an interesting conversation someday. He wasn't sure how long it would record though if it did at all. Michael picked up the Maglite and the two guns. He knocked both bulbs out of the lamps leaving the basement pitch black. Both officers immediately began yelling at him, but their voices faded as Michael climbed the steps out of the basement. Naked and cold, strapped to one another in a dark basement in a bad neighborhood. Karma. Michael smiled and stepped out of the house.

The first thing on Michael's agenda was to call April. She would be worried sick about him. There were probably cops crawling all over the place asking questions. Michael hopped in the police car and fumbled through the keys until he found one that worked. He started the car and took out Gary's phone. He dialed the number to the house phone and waited for April to answer.

Chapter 13

The sheriff had given April a few minutes before continuing on with his questioning. She had begun crying uncontrollably. He knew she wouldn't be able to answer any questions confidently in this state. He offered to get her a tissue but she waved him off and used the sleeve of her robe to dry her face. Her eyes were beginning to puff up and swell. It took a little bit, but the graveness of the situation had sunk in. Her soon to be failed marriage, her failed first home, the center of a scandal. She would always be known as the girl who was married to the murderer. She would have to leave her home town...and her family just to get away from it all. She could live with all that. What was destroying her right now at this very moment was Michael. She loved him so desperately. She couldn't believe that the sweet man she loved would ever harm another human being. She missed him so much and he'd only been gone for a few hours. She needed him. She needed him right now to help her through all of this. He was her rock. She felt like she was betraying him somehow, sitting here talking to the sheriff. But, if she believed in his innocence, couldn't she somehow convince the sheriff? But she was torn between how she felt, what she knew of Michael, and the evidence. How did he know where a girl was buried? And right on their property? Is that why he wanted her to look at this house to begin with? Is that why he went along with her so easily when she said she wanted it? Was he simply trying to make sure that the girl's body was never found? Were there other bodies? Why would he risk exposing himself by digging her up? Was he really sleepwalking? Did his guilty conscience drive him there? Did he want to be caught? She just didn't understand. She dried her cheeks off with her robe again and looked up at the sheriff.

"I'm sorry ma'am, I know this is tough. I just have a couple more questions." The sheriff said. April nodded and looked down lost in thought. "How long have you lived here?" The sheriff continued.

April looked up. She was quiet for a moment and then "About four weeks." She said quietly.

"Did the two of you buy the house at that point or had you owned if for a while?"

"No. We had just bought it."

The sheriff remembered the detective saying the girl had been shot about seven months ago. That meant she was buried here before they bought the house. "Was it Michael that led you to buy *this* house?" The sheriff continued. He knew the question was going to sting. The answer could further implicate her husband.

She looked up eyes wide, mouth slightly ajar. She wasn't sure how best to answer the question. "Well…I…um…the thing is…" Her home phone rang. She looked up at the clock on the wall. Two-thirty in the morning. Who would be calling at two thirty in the morning?

The sheriff gave her an inquisitive look. “Go ahead.” He said. “You can answer it.”

April looked at the sheriff and then back at the clock puzzled. She got up and crossed the room to the cordless phone that was standing upright, nestled in its holder. She looked at the callar id. She didn’t recognize the number. “Hello?” She said.

“Don’t say a word.” It was Michael’s voice. Her heart did a flop in her chest. She about lost her breath.

“Mi...”

“Not a sound.” He said sternly as he cut her off. She stopped, glancing at the sheriff who seemed to have her full attention.

“If you have company, say ‘yes mom’”

She glanced at the sheriff again. “Yes, mom.”

“Now say everything is fine.” She did. She was facing the wall. She wanted to go into the other room but didn’t want to arouse any more suspicion than she already had.

“All I can tell you right now mom, is *Michael...*,” She paused, “sure has a lot of explaining to do when I see him.”

There was a pause on the other end of the line. April began to feel nauseous. There were butterflies in her stomach and she could feel prickles running up her neck.

"I just..." Michael paused. "I just want you to know that I love you. I don't know what is going on, I swear. But I didn't do this. You've got to believe me." There was a pause. April didn't say anything. "Remember where we had our first picnic?"

"Yes." April said quietly.

"Two o'clock. Tomorrow. Meet me there. Make sure they don't follow you." There was another pause. He was in police custody. How was he going to meet her? Her mouth was half ajar, confused. She glanced at the sheriff and she could tell her reaction was causing some concern. He stood up and stretched his back. He was trying to hear the conversation.

"Just say I'll call you tomorrow mom." Michael said as if understanding.

"I'll call you tomorrow mom." She said, a tear running down her cheek.

"I love you." Michael said quietly.

"I love you too." She said. She heard a click. He was gone. She set the phone back on the charger and turned around and shrieked. The sheriff was standing right there not even inches from her.

"Who was it?" He asked.

April stammered for a second. She wasn't sure whether or not he had heard Michael's voice on the earpiece. "That was my mom" she said as she reached up with her sleeve and dried the remaining tears on her cheek.

The sheriff looked at the clock and then back at April. "At two thirty in the morning?" He asked accusingly.

April's heart about stopped. She felt like she was going to vomit. He didn't believe her. Should she tell him? Was she going to be an accomplice? Wasn't this obstruction of justice? *You've got to believe me. You're my mommy silly*. The voices ran through her head. "She listens to the scanner. I told her what happened yesterday. She's worried about me. That's all." She lied.

The sheriff nodded. "Well, I think I'm done here for the night. You call me if you think of anything you need to tell us."

April nodded and showed him to the door. After he left, she closed the door, leaned against the back and slid down to the floor crying uncontrollably.

Chapter 14

Michael put the phone away and took a deep breath. He fought back the urge to cry. He could tell April was an emotional trainwreck. All the things she must be thinking right now...Would she think he murdered the girl? Surely she knew him better than that. He was sure of it. They were so close. They were so in tune with one another that they always knew what the other was thinking without even saying a word. But now...now everything was becoming blurry. It was all happening so fast. *What would I think if it was her who had dug someone up in the woods? Wouldn't there be a cloud of doubt? Wouldn't my faith have been rattled? Would she ever be able to kiss me or hold my hand again without at least wondering if I am a murderer? How could this have happened? Why me?* Michael thought and leaned forward and rested his head on the steering wheel. *I've got to fix this. I've got to find out what happened.* There had to be a logical explanation for everything and he knew if he couldn't find it...his life...and everything he loved about it would be over. Forever. Michael looked up at the road. *You can do this.* A voice inside his head lifted his spirits. Do it for April. Do it for me. Michael wiped a tear from his cheek. He didn't know how he knew, but he knew. The voice in his head, the voice calling out to him, wasn't April's, it was *hers*. Do it for me... "Maria," He said out loud and put the car in drive.

Angel Falls was a pretty small town and it only took Michael five minutes to get to the ATM at the Angel Falls

National Bank on Center Street. Normally, Michael would have been worried about being seen by another police officer, but he knew they were at least two short, and the rest were probably tied up with more important things. Michael smiled at the thought. *Tied up...Normally...* If he couldn't laugh at that, he couldn't keep his head through all of this. *There was no normality about this and two of Angel Fall's finest are tied up alright.*

Michael pulled through the ATM and took out Gary's wallet. He pulled out each card and put the cards in one at a time, entering the pin numbers that they had given him. Both pin numbers were correct and Michael was soon stuffing six hundred extra dollars into his wallet. Well, it was his now anyway. He glanced at the balance on the ATM receipts. Gary had only about $800 dollars left after the $300 had been taken out. That's about what he'd expect out of a "newbie" as Frank had called him. But Frank on the other hand, had over $26,000 in his account. That was a little more than he would have expected on a police officer's salary. *Not my business*. Michael thought as he put the cards and receipts to the side. *I've got my own problems. Crooked cops are their problem.* Michael thought as he put the car in drive and pulled up by the bank doors. Michael put the car in park and got out. He reached back in and grabbed the Maglite just in case. He had no place to go. They would check the hotels, friends, and family. He was exhausted. Both mentally and physically. He doubted his mind would let him sleep after all that had happened but he had to try. He needed a fresh mind tomorrow. He was going to need to think clearly. April was going to need him to think clearly. He had to try and get some sleep. But where? He ran possible locations through his mind. There was an abandoned brick building on the other side of the river but he couldn't take the bridge and it was too deep to wade across. He had to meet April on this side of the river tomorrow so he needed to be somewhere nearby. He knew after he made his phone call he was about to make, the police would be driving around looking for him. But where would they look? And where is a safe place to rest? Michael considered hiding out in the back of a random vehicle, but if the owners left for work at seven or earlier, it wouldn't give him much sleep. And if they spotted him sleeping in the back and called the police, it would all be over. He thought about hiding out under bridges, but he figured it would be one of the first places a police officer would check. That's where *he* would check. Michael looked around. All he could see were houses, cars, garages, and businesses. Garages...Michael thought about it for a moment. Not all, but some garages have lofts or rafters where men store their extra lumber. If he could find one unlocked, he could sneak in and lay in the rafters out of sight. But if they park in their garage...it was risky but he was running out of time. Michael flipped through the keys and found the trunk key. He opened the trunk of the squad car. There were various pieces of police gear all stowed in cases or nets. There was an emergency kit, road flares, a shotgun, a camera, and other necessities. Michael stood there for a moment staring. He had never seen the trunk of a police car and had never thought about what kinds of things might be stored in the trunk. Despite his exhaustion, he was fascinated. He thumbed through the items in his mind, wondering which ones, if any, he could use. He was going to be meeting April tomorrow where they had their first picnic. Would the camera help keep him from standing out? Possibly. But if he took it, wouldn't they be on the lookout for a guy with a camera? Probably. Michael shook his head. There was nothing there he could use. He tossed in the officer's guns and debit cards and closed the trunk. He pulled out Gary's cell phone and dialed 911.

"This is 911. What is your emergency?" an older male voice came across the phone.

"Yes my name is Michael Bander. I was taken to a house and tortured by two police officers tonight...

Chapter 15

Detective James was on the way back to the station. He needed to find out what information that the CSI's had found so far, if any, that might point him in any meaningful direction. He was going to crash at the office and begin early. He'd be lucky to see four hours of sleep tonight. *It's going to be a long night...* the sheriff's words echoed in his head. The detective was nearly to town when his phone rang. He had a CB, but for most of his business, he was being fed information that he preferred to keep out of earshot of the residents of Angel Falls. It could only hinder an investigation. Not to mention small towns like these, gossip travels faster than the speed of light and one question about a person of interest over the radio would be a guilty verdict without the trial. So, Detective James wasn't too surprised to hear his phone ringing.

"Speak." The detective answered his phone in his typical 'skip the formalities and get right to the fucking point' tone.

"Detective, we've got a problem." It was Officer Garrison. He sounded a bit frantic. He had been given a position answering the phone and 911 calls after crippling arthritis forced him from working the streets.

"What is it Garrison?"

"Well, the chief wanted me to give you a call. We had a 911 call come in."

"And…?"

"Well, sir…it..it's Frank and Gary." The officer was stumbling. He sounded nervous which was out of character for him.

"What about Frank and Gary? They aren't questioning the perp are they?" Detective James' voice began to get agitated. If they tried something like that, they could blow the whole investigation. Often times, officers would get power hungry and try and shortcut their way to detective. It almost always ended badly.

"No sir. The call came in from Michael Bander."

"Bander? Isn't he in custody?"

"No sir, er, not anymore."

"What the hell does that mean, not anymore?" Detective James yelled as he jerked the car over to the side of the road and stopped.

"Well sir, Michael Bander made a 911 call from Gary's cell phone. He said he had been taken to a house and tortured. He said he no longer felt safe in police custody and that he left the squad car at Angel Fall's National Bank and their weapons in the trunk." There was a pause. "Sir, he said they waterboarded him."

"Where are they now?" The detective asked

"Michael...er uh the perp, said that he left them tied up at the house they had taken him to."

"Did he give an address?"

"514 Lincoln Street."

"Who's picking them up?" The detective asked impatiently.

"That's why the chief wanted me to call you. Frank and Gary were supposed to be on patrol tonight. He's just sent everyone else home. He wants me to call in an ambulance, but he asked me to call you first. He wants you to go assess the situation, take some pictures and try to figure out what happened."

"Jesus Christ, I don't have time for this shit Garrison. I'm in a murder investigation."

"With all due respect sir, if this guy was tortured by our guys, you may not have an investigation. He'll walk and you know it." There was a pause.

"Of course, you're right." Detective James conceded. "I'm on my way. Send one CSI to meet me there would you?"

"I'll call it in right away sir."

"Why the ambulance? How bad is it?"

"Well sir, this Bander guy said he broke Frank's knee and that Gary took a shot at him and was hit by his own ricochet."

"Jesus Christ! Did he have his vest on?"

"No sir. But he was apparently hit in the arm."

"Tell the ambulance to hold up outside the house until I give them the ok to enter. Got it?"

"Yes sir, I'll call it in right away."

"Alright. Did this Bander guy give any clue as to where he was going next?" Detective James asked.

"No, he just said he had a murder to solve."

Chapter 16

Detective James pulled up in front of the house on Lincoln Street. The house was clearly vacant and was overgrown with weeds. There was nothing to indicate that anyone was at the home or that there had been a disturbance there. Aside from the tire tracks, it didn't look as if anyone had occupied the place for a long time.

The detective got out of his vehicle and stood for a moment taking in his surroundings. He had many rules to which he lived by, and one of them was to never make assumptions. For instance, taking the story Officer Garrison had told him at face value meant that the officers had done something terrible, the perp was long gone, and the scene was secure. But that would be an assumption. Suppose the Bander guy got a jump on the officers and forced them to this location. Suppose he made the call to lure another unsuspecting officer into a false sense of security. Hell, he was a murder suspect. If he killed once, isn't it logical that he could continue doing so in attempt to cover up his crime? Couldn't he be simply attempting to destroy evidence? *He's sent everyone else home...* Garrison's words echoed in the detective's mind. He drew his weapon and kept it pointed toward the ground. He reached back in his vehicle and snatched up his Maglite. The ambulance turned onto Lincoln Street. They had the lights flashing but the siren was off. *No need to wake up the neighborhood*. Detective James thought. He approached the driver's side of the ambulance. The window was already down. A guy with curly brown hair stuck his head out of the window. He looked to be in his mid twenties.

"We were told to stay outside until the house was secure." He said in a too chipper voice for nearly four in the morning.

"If I'm not out in ten minutes, call for backup." The detective said.

The curly haired EMT was chewing gum. He looked at the handgun and back at the detective and nodded. "Good luck." He said.

The detective turned and headed back toward the door. He stopped at the door, put his flashlight under his arm and pulled out his cell phone and dialed the station. Officer Garrison answered.

"Garrison?" The detective asked.

"Yes Detective."

"What's the ETA on the CSI?"

"Should be there any moment sir."

"Have him stand by outside the door with his collection kit and camera. Did the perp say where in the house the officers are to be found?"

"He said they were in the basement tied up. That's all he said."

"K. I'm going to secure the upper floor. Tell him not to enter until I've cleared it."

"I will let him know. Watch your six."

The detective flipped his phone shut and entered the house. It was old and smelled of mildew and cat pee. There was a broken window to his right. He figured all kinds of animals were likely to be living in here. The detective went room to room securing each one. He checked closets and behind doors. Nothing. There were pieces of dry wall, ceiling, and other debris scattered about. In one room, there was an old mattress, a tattered playboy, and drug paraphernalia. Nothing important. Nothing valuable. The place probably served as a hideout for young boys or the occasional homeless person. No noise could be heard even from the basement.

The detective stuck his head out of the front door five minutes later and found a CSI tech standing nearby. It was the Martinez kid from Syracuse. He had been working as a tech in Angel Falls for the last three years. He was good. He was smart. He was late twenties and balding. He had glasses which he reached out now and pushed up on his nose. "Long night Detective?" He asked.

"You and me both Martinez. You and me both" The detective replied shaking his head. Technically, it had been a long night for both of them. CSI's didn't typically work nights in Angel Falls. There wasn't enough crime to mandate it. But they were on call 24/7 to handle anything that arises. Because they might go a month with nothing major, they were usually anxious to put their skills to the test when duty called. They loved a challenge. *They're about to get one now.* The detective thought. "You have your kit? Camera?" The detective asked.

"Ready when you are." The CSI said holding up his kit.

"Ok, I've cleared the upstairs but not the basement. You stay up at the top of the stairs and wait for my signal to come down. Then you work the house like you would any other crime scene." The CSI nodded. "Also, you keep your eyes peeled in all directions as if the upper floor hadn't been secured. Got it?"

"Yes sir." The CSI said.

The detective nodded back and the CSI tech followed him inside and to the left. The detective pointed toward a door with graffiti on it. "That's the stairs to the basement, but like I said. I haven't been down it yet so stay on your guard." The detective pulled the door out a little and pointed his Maglite down the stairs. "Angel Falls Police! Anybody down there?" The detective yelled.

Two voices came yelling back up the stairs confirming they were police officers.

"Anybody else down there with you?"

One voice echoed up "No."

"Get us the fuck out of here." Came another.

Detective James descended the staircase slowly sweeping his light and weapon from side to side. Assume nothing. When he reached the bottom of the stairs he paused at the sight. He was so stunned by the scene before him, he forgot all about securing the rest of the room. Right in front of him, on an old wooden table, both police officers were naked and strapped to one another. The detective shook his head as if trying to clear up what must surely be a false image but the scene remained the same. The detective's mouth opened slightly as if to say something and then closed again.

"Don't just fucking stand there. Get us out of these Godamn straps!" Frank yelled from the bottom of the pile. The detective snapped out of it and moved his light around the room taking it all in. There were two lamps with broken bulbs that appeared to be connected to a battery. There was vomit on the floor next to the table. The floor was wet everywhere. Since it hadn't rained in a couple of weeks and this place didn't likely have water turned on, it gave some credibility to the waterboarding story.

The detective turned around and hollered up the stairs. "Martinez!" The CSI tech began to head down the stairs. "Grab a couple 100 watt bulbs from your car. Tell the EMT's to stand by at the top of the stairs. The tech went back up and out of the house. Long night...*doesn't even begin to describe it*. He thought. "Which one of you is shot?"

"I am." Came Gary's voice. The one on top. The detective wanted to shine his light in his direction to assess the situation, but the sight of Gary's ass crack in the air was appalling, gross, and...well gross.

"Where are you shot at?" The detective asked trying to focus his light in another direction.

"I'm shot in the arm." The officer said. The detective spotted the opening into the next room and stepped into the doorway and peered around. There was nothing of interest. He turned back and searched the floor. He spotted three pairs of underwear, one pair of pants, a shirt, and a vest. Three pairs of underwear... The detective flipped open his phone. He was about to call in that the suspect may be wearing police clothing, but remembered there wasn't anyone on the street to look for him. He clicked his phone shut and put it away. But why three pairs of underwear? The detective shook his head again.

Footsteps came from the stairs and the detective focused his light in the direction to verify it was Martinez. The CSI tech had his kit over one shoulder, his camera around his neck, and a pack of bulbs in the other hand. He made his way down the stairs and set his kit to the side. The detective flashed the light in the direction of the lamps. Martinez went to the first lamp and carefully unscrewed the broken piece from the lamp and pulled a new bulb out of the box. Martinez screwed in the bulb and the light of the lamp filled the basement and illuminated the two police officers lying one on top of the other, naked on the table. Martinez' mouth went ajar as he stared in disbelief. He didn't know whether to cringe or laugh. His expressions seemed to go through all the emotions that were flowing through him. Bewilderment seemed to dominate them.

The men on the table were beginning to groan and get restless. "Will somebody please get us off this fucking table?" Frank yelled.

"Martinez!" The detective pulled the CSI tech out of his trance. Martinez looked toward the detective who pointed at the other lamp with his Maglite. Martinez went over to the light and replaced the bulb.

"We'll have you guys out in a moment. Hang tight. Martinez, snap pictures of everything before we disturb the crime scene." Martinez nodded and began taking pictures.

"Crime scene?" Gary responded. "We didn't do anything."

“Who said you did anything?” The detective responded. “Gary, while he’s working, why don’t you tell me what happened?”

“I’ll tell you what happened,” Intervened Frank, “That murderer got the jump on us and escaped custody.”

“I tell you what Frank, let Gary fill me in, then you’ll get your chance to add to it.” The detective noted that Gary seemed to be the weak link and the most likely to botch a fake story. Frank didn’t say anything. He just made a huffing sound. “What happened Gary?”

Gary paused for a moment. He tried to move, but he was bound so tight he did little more than wiggle his lower legs. The detective cringed at the sight. *You’ve got to hand it to the Bander guy, he’s got a sense of humor.* He thought.

“We were taking the perp back to the station.” Gary began. “When he started acting like he was having a seizure in the back, we pulled over and got out to check on him. When I opened the door, he jumped me, grabbed my gun, and brought us here.”

“He jumped you and grabbed your gun with his hands cuffed behind his back?” The detective asked skeptically.

“Well...he...er...had gotten out of his cuffs.” Gary said.

"I see. Any idea how he could have done that?" The detective asked.

"Well, we didn't exactly pat him down seeing he was in his underwear and all. We could see he didn't have a weapon, but I guess he must have had something that could pick a lock because he didn't have his cuffs on." Gary stated confidently.

"How can you be sure he didn't slip his hands out?" Asked the detective. Flashes were going off around the room as the CSI tech made his way around snapping pictures.

"I checked them myself." Gary said. "They were tight. No way he pulled his hands out."

"Gary's right, I checked them as well." Added Frank. The detective had pulled out a notebook and was making notes as they went along. The CSI had photographed most of the room and had made his way around the table to where Frank and Gary were facing. The CSI held the camera up in their direction.

"I don't fucking think so!" Yelled Frank. The CSI tech lowered his camera a moment and looked at the detective. "You fucking snap our picture and I'll shove that camera so far up your ass, you will be shitting black and white for a week!" Frank yelled again.

The detective nodded at the CSI to continue. The tech looked back at Frank, shrugged, and focused the camera. "Sorry boys," the detective said, "evidence. You understand. Can't charge him with kidnapping if we can't show the jury proof can we?" The detective stated with a hint of humor in his voice.

"Show the...you better not show anybody that fucking picture! I'm going to smash that thing as soon as I get out...of...here!" Frank was wiggling as hard as he could. He wasn't making any leeway, but the more he wiggled, the more humorous it made it look as Gary wiggled with him on top. The CSI lowered his camera but was laughing quietly. He looked over at the detective who was also trying very hard not to bust out laughing.

"Alright, alright, let's get you boys out of here. Before I do, whose puke is on the floor?" There was a silence. Apparently the officers hadn't thought of including that into their story. "It's going to be DNA tested, so we are going to find out anyway. Whose is it?" The detective asked sternly.

"It's the perps." Said Frank. "He vomited after he started torturing us. Guess he couldn't handle it."

The detective nodded. "Martinez..." Martinez looked up. The detective had moved out of sight of the officers. "I need to take a couple pieces of evidence with me, so I need you to quickly bag, tag, and sign a transfer of evidence form." The detective held his finger up in front of his lips in a shushing gesture. He had spotted the cell phone, open and under the straps, and had guessed what Bander may have been up to. The detective held up his cell phone and pointed to it and then down and then made a gesture as if he was dropping it into an evidence bag and sealing it. The CSI looked down and then back and nodded understanding. “I need you to bag some of that vomit for me so I can get the lab started on DNA.” The detective finished.

“I’m on it.” The CSI tech said as he nonchalantly grabbed the open cell phone as he passed by. He came around the table and opened his kit. He pulled out an evidence bag. He held the phone out so the detective could look. The screen was dark. The CSI tech had white latex gloves on his hands. He pushed a button to activate the screen. The screen lit up and showed that a call had been in progress for one hour and twenty minutes. The CSI Tech looked up at the detective who had a sly grin on his face. The detective motioned for him to close the phone and bag it. The tech filled out a chain of evidence transfer voucher and set it aside. He then used a plastic putty knife to scoop most of the vomit into another evidence bag. He filled out a chain of custody form on it as well and stood up.

“Take those up and wait in your car. And send the EMT’s down. After everyone is gone, go ahead and finish working the scene.” Martinez nodded and headed up the stairs.

The EMT’s came down and helped unstrap the officers and get them up the stairs. Gary walked up on his own but Frank had to be moved out on a stretcher.

Before the ambulance took off, the detective stuck his head in the door and addressed the two officers. "Detective Hammond will be up at the hospital in a couple hours to take your statements. Give him your full cooperation. As typical in these kinds of situations, you will probably be put on paid leave while they sort things out." The detective shut the door and shook his head as he walked away. The day pigs fly. He thought. That's when those two will return to active duty. The detective walked over to the CSI tech's vehicle and signed the chain of custody forms for the cell phone and the vomit. He sent Martinez back in to finish and he took off for the CSI office.

The detective was feeling exhausted as he entered and knew he had another long day ahead of him. He spoke to the supervising CSI and asked for DNA to be placed on rush. First, he wanted the girl's DNA tested to confirm identity and second, he needed proof of identity that the man who had escaped custody was indeed Michael Bander. If they couldn't prove that, they may not get a search warrant. It could have been anybody in the woods. There needed to be definitive proof that it was Michael Bander. If they couldn't produce it; no warrant, and no DA would touch the case. Michael Bander would walk. The detective told the lead CSI where the vehicle was reported abandoned and asked for a full workup on the car after they had finished running the other tests. The detective made his way to the waiting room, took off his jacket and tucked it under his head. He began running through the details of the crime scene in his head trying to put the pieces together. Something about this one wasn't making sense. It's as if all the evidence was pointing right at Bander for the murder, but his instincts were crying foul. Something wasn't right and he couldn't put his finger on it. *'...And their weapons in the trunk...'Why would a murderer on the run from the law, leave behind two guns?* The question floated its way up to his consciousness as he drifted off to sleep.

Chapter 17

Michael quietly worked his way along a neighboring street. It hadn't taken him long to find an unlocked garage. There were vehicles in the driveway which gave him some hope that there might not be any in the garage. His concern was that someone would come in and his snoring would give him away. Michael opened the door quietly and stepped in. He put his left hand over the front of the Maglite to block most of the light. He turned it on and looked around using only the smallest beam necessary. He exhaled relief. No car. He looked up and found a loft with a pull down ladder. *Even better*. He thought. Michael was happy to have at least one thing go right in this long night where everything else has gone so wrong. He reached up and pulled the rope to extend the ladder. He climbed to the top of the ladder and looked around before climbing all the way in. There were boxes stacked everywhere. One was marked Christmas tree, another was marked pictures, and others were marked books. There were a few older bicycles, some wooden chairs, and a couple of trunks. There was plenty of floor space to sleep on. Michael climbed the rest of the way into the loft and reached back through to pull the ladder back up. Michael searched through some of the boxes and found a couple of quilts that he laid out and a small blanket that he bunched up and used as a pillow.

Michael lie down and let his body rest. The hard wood floor offered no comfort and the quilts weren't very thick. If only he could rest his head on a fluffy pillow on a warm bed in a cozy room. He imagined April next to him, curled up under his arm. The thought made him smile and sleep carried him away to a better place. A place where love and laughter filled the air and dirty cops didn't exist. A place where April was waiting for him, smiling with her hand stretched out toward him. He smiled at her and grasped her hand. She looked at him and smiled. She said something to him but no sound could be heard. Michael smiled as if he could hear her and she led him away.

Morning came. Car doors in the driveway opened and closed. Engines started and drove away. Michael remained asleep, lost in his own world. He mumbled occasionally and his head would move from one side to the other. Michael was oblivious to the world around him. Dreams came and went. Darkness would take him. Then, out of the darkness April would appear and the world would open itself to him. She kept saying something, but no sound reached his ears. She led him to the same place over and over. He followed her, wanting to be led. She was trying to tell him something but he couldn't understand. What did she want him to see? He would walk with her to the same place. There were people everywhere. Children ran by with cotton candy. A Ferris wheel turned slowly up ahead. There was a tilt-a-whirl somewhere to the left. Everywhere he looked, there were vendors beckoning them to play some game. She always led him to a place by the water where people stood around feeding the fish. She stopped there and looked around as if she was looking for something. A concerned look would cross her face and she would say something to him and then look around. Michael looked around with her but didn't know what she was looking for. She looked back at him and her look went from concern to panic. Michael watched her lips. What was she telling him? What was she trying to say? Michael could feel his own heart beginning to beat faster as he began to feel April's panic. She was saying two words over and over. Michael looked around. Everyone seemed to stop what they were doing and was staring at them. The game vendors had stopped beckoning. People walking by stopped dead still and turned their heads. Children lowered their cotton candy and stared wide eyed. Michael's heart was beating fast. He turned his head back toward April. A man in a dark suit and sunglasses was standing about twenty yards away holding a gun pointed in their direction. April was kneeling and in her arms was a young girl with brown curly hair. Her arms hung down to the sides and an ice cream cone had fallen to the ground. There was blood coming from the girl's stomach and head. She looked beautiful like an angel. Michael's heart sank at the sight of her. April looked up with tears streaming down her face. She spoke to him again. All sound had faded away but her words shot through him loud and clear. *"Find her!"*

Michael bolted upright out of his dream. Sweat was pouring down his face. He wiped it off with his hands. For a moment he had forgotten where he was at. On some level he expected to wake up back in his own bed next to April. That none of this had happened and that it had all been just a dream.

Then everything that had happened sunk back in and he stood up with the weight of the world on his shoulders once again. Michael folded up the blankets and stowed them away. The loft had grown hot and he was ready for some fresh air. He was going to meet April at 2:00. He was dirty and hungry and not sure what he was going to do. *Find her*. The words seemed to find their way to his consciousness. Find who? Hadn't he already done that? Isn't that what got him in this mess to begin with? Michael shook his head and cleared the thoughts away. He lowered the ladder and was about to leave. He took one last look around and his eyes stopped dead center on a box on the left side of the room. Michael nodded and knew exactly what he needed to do.

Chapter 18

It seemed like seconds rather than hours. At least that was the thought going through Detective James' head when a CSI tech woke him up to inform him of the information that he inquired about was ready. The waiting area also served as a break room and there was coffee brewing on a small counter and the television overhead was on with the morning news quietly streaming. The detective pushed himself across the floor to the coffee and poured himself a steaming cup and then made his way inside the building and to the far end where the CSI supervisor, Thomas Crane was sitting at his desk going through paperwork. Crane was short, with grey hair and spectacles. He was another example of a CSI that was far too brilliant to be stuck in little old Angel Falls. He was called 'Doc' by everyone who knew him. His parents were so sure he would be a doctor, that they nicknamed him when he was eight years old. Somehow it just seemed to follow him.

"Sit down Detective." Crane motioned with his hand without looking up. He flipped through some more papers making little grunting sounds like 'hmf' and 'mm hm'. He had a high pitched voice but not so high that it was annoying. It was quite soothing actually and really allowed anyone speaking to him to be able to hear his passion for his work clearly in his voice. He finally put the papers down and looked up at the detective while pushing his spectacles up on his nose. "So what do you make of all this Detective?"

The detective rubbed his eyes and pulled at his face both indicating exhaustion and trying to wake up at the same time. "You tell me Doc. You're the expert."

"Well, I have intellect and evidence, but as you know, many of innocent people have been wrongly imprisoned based on intellect and evidence. Experience with people and pure gut instinct have found truth where science has failed. I would never suggest one without the other, but I am curious what is experience and instinct telling us about the case?"

The detective exhaled and took a long draw on his coffee. "Well doc, logic tells me that this guy has to be guilty. He was found in the dead of night digging up this girl's body. How could he possibly do that if he didn't know she was there? And how would he know she was there unless he helped put her there? But why buy a house close to where you buried the body? And he left the officer's guns in the vehicle. I still have to press forward with the idea this guy's our perp, it's just there are more inconsistencies than I like to see. I don't feel right about it if you know what I mean."

Crane put his elbows on the desk and removed his spectacles and rubbed at his eyes. "Well, I'm afraid this isn't going to get any easier for you. We don't have a ballistics match yet but we haven't finished searching the database. We just now got the squad car back here and we've compared Bander's fingerprints with the database and nothing has come up. No record. He's a Biology teacher at the school you know. He has an impeccable record. The call made from the cell phone you recovered was to Bander's cell phone. It was likely sent to his voicemail which recorded for quite some time. That will be an interesting conversation."

"What about the DNA? Any hits on that?" The detective asked.

"This is where the puzzle gets really interesting." Crane turned a file folder around facing the detective. "We have DNA results back on the girl. You can see her allele's right here." Crane pointed with his finger to a series of black bars scattered over a graft. Alleles are an alternative form of a gene and found at a specific spot on a chromosome. The coding determines specific traits that can be passed on from one generation to the next.

"I don't see anything odd about it. Did she come up in the database or something?" The detective asked.

"Well, no, that's not what's going to bother you." Crane said.

"Bother me? What are you talking about doc?" The detective asked, getting agitated.

Crane held up a clear plastic sheet with writing on it. "We also had finished the DNA on the vomit you gave us."

"Let me guess, you got a hit in the database for an unsolved?" The detective asked. It was rare around here, but sometimes they would get DNA from a perp and it would solve a whole series of cases in which DNA was found at the scene but there was no person to match it to in the database. It was always a relief because of how many cases you were able to close all in one shot.

"No, that's not it I'm afraid. This is Bander's alleles." Crane held up the clear sheet and then slid it over the top of the girl's. The detective's eyes locked onto the sheet and froze there. He was so shocked, he about spilled his coffee.

The detective looked up at Crane and then back at the DNA records. "It's his kid?"

"99.9 percent match. I told you it wasn't going to make your job any easier." Crane said.

"A jury would have convicted Bander on what we already have. This is icing on the cake. He's got to be our guy. We get a search warrant yet?"

Crane nodded. "Ready to go. The morning shift is in, so whenever you are ready..."

"What about the DA? Does she know about Frank and Gary?" The detective asked.

"You think I'm going to break the news to her?" Crane put his glasses back on and shook his head. "That'd be like taking food from a bear. We scooped the vomit, you play with the bear." Crane said smiling.

The detective stood up and smiled. "Just throw me on the grenade why don't ya?"

"I said experience and instinct were important Detective. Just not *as* important as science and intellect. A fellow can sacrifice a pawn and still take down the king. But you very rarely throw your queen under the bus."

"Are you suggesting that I'm a pawn?"

"Of course not, that would be silly. I'm suggesting that I'm the queen. You're more of a..." Crane looked up for a second. "A knight. Still valuable, but not as likely to get the job done without the queen."

"I think when this is over, I might have to challenge you and prove you different."

"I look forward to it. If you survive the bear that is..." Crane said. The detective laughed and headed out the door.

Chapter 19

April only slept a few hours. Her sister had called and was adamant about meeting for lunch. They agreed to meet at the diner at noon. April had gotten showered and dressed. She looked in the mirror only to find that her eyes were still puffy from crying all night. It was her first night away from Michael. She couldn't bear it. She was tossing and turning and she kept having the same weird dream over and over. *You're my mommy silly*. What the hell was that supposed to mean? She didn't mind it so much because she was always there with Michael. *Michael.* She let the sound of his name echo through her mind. *What have you gotten yourself into? What have you done?* She had known Michael since grade school. Michael was respected. People looked up to him. Kids looked up to him. She couldn't imagine him hurting anybody. *He must have known she was there...* It just didn't make sense. There was a knock at the door. April dabbed at her face with a cloth, threw it in the hamper and went to the door. Her sister was supposed to meet her at the diner, not here. April opened the door. There was a lady holding a microphone, a man with a news camera, and two other people taking pictures.

"Mrs. Bander, how do you feel about your husband Michael being charged with murder?" The girl held the microphone out to her.

"Wha..."

"Has he ever done anything like this before? Has he ever struck you?"

"No...I..."

"Do you think he killed one of his students or was he having an affair?"

"I...he.." April was shaking her head. A tear came trickling down her cheek. She shut the door and leaned up against it. She wiped away the tears and went from window to window drawing the curtains closed. *How was she going to get out of here? How was she going to leave? Michael wouldn't have an affair...would he?* "Oh God." She sat on the couch and put her head on the sleeve of her robe and cried. "Why is this happening to me?" Another knock came at the door.

"Angel Falls Police, we've got a search warrant. Open the door." A harsh voice echoed into her home. April looked out the window and could see a man and woman wearing black jackets that said CSI on them, one officer in uniform, and a tall man with a mustache wearing a brown suit. The news people had moved back toward the road. April went to the door and opened it. The officer and CSI techs pushed in past her. The man in the brown suit stepped up to the door.

"Mrs. Bander?" He asked. He had a polite look about him. She nodded. "My name is Detective James. I'm sorry to inconvenience you." He held out a folded paper for her. She took it and opened it. "It's a warrant to search your residence. I'm sorry for that. I know you are under enough stress right now."

April looked up, tears welled up in her eyes. "Why? Why are you doing this to us?" She began hitting him in the chest with her hand that still clasped the paper. She was crying full force. He didn't move to stop her. He just let her get it out. April finally stopped and put her head down, teardrops falling onto the paper. She was tired, confused, and ashamed. She was crying so violently she was struggling to catch her breath in between sobs. The detective put his hand on her shoulder and patted her gently.

"I'm sorry Mrs. Bander. I really am. We'll get this all sorted out. I promise." He grabbed her shoulders gently and pulled her back. "You want to help your husband?" He asked. She looked up at him with tears and makeup running down her face. She nodded. "Then help us get this sorted out. Let's get you cleaned up." The detective stepped in and closed the door behind him. There were sounds of drawers opening and closing from the other rooms as the CSI's went room to room looking for anything they could connect to the crime scene. "Where is your kitchen at Mrs. Bander?" April pointed straight ahead and walked with him around the corner. "Do you have any wash cloths in here?" April was trying to wipe off her face with the back of her hands. She pointed to the second drawer. The detective opened the drawer and took out a wash cloth and a hand towel. He went over to the sink and wetted the cloth with cold water. "Please…let me help." He told Mrs. Bander. He dabbed away her makeup and tears that had streaked down her face. Detective James believed you always get more bees with honey. Meaning, you treat people nice and they will work with you more often than when you treat them like criminals. Even some of the worst criminals still had the same basic needs as the rest of us: the need for acceptance, for love, the desire to be understood, and to be forgiven. And of course the other basic needs of shelter, food, and water. Sometimes it was just a series of bad decisions that separated the good from the bad. And sometimes the people with the biggest hearts went behind bars while some of the coldest criminals enjoyed the life of luxury and freedom. Mrs. Bander was someone's daughter and if she had been his, he would want someone treating her with a little respect and allow her to keep some of her dignity. The detective put the cold rag in her hands and let her finish washing her face. After a couple of minutes she began to feel herself returning to normal. The detective handed her the hand towel to dry her face with.

"Thank you." She said as she took the towel in her hand and dabbed herself dry. "This has all happened so fast." She said.

The detective nodded. "Can we sit down and talk?" He pointed to the kitchen table.

She nodded. “Sure. I don’t know what more I can tell you though. I told the other officer everything I knew last night.” April pulled out a chair and sat in it.

“Would you like me to get you a water or anything?” The detective asked before he sat down.

April was about to say that she was fine when she noticed that her nervousness had given her cotton mouth. “I can get...”

“You rest. You’ve had a long night. I’ll get it. Where are your glasses?” The detective asked. April pointed toward a cabinet on his left. He opened it and took out a glass. He filled it with cold water and sat it in front of her.

“There is coffee made and cups on the bottom shelf.” She pointed to the same cabinet. “Please, get yourself some.”

The detective nodded hoping she would offer him some. On days like this, it was the only fuel he had. He took a cup out and filled it up. “Thank you.” He said. He lifted the cup to his nose and smelled it. “Mmm...smells good.” He pulled out a chair next to her and sat facing her.

The female CSI approached them. “They are finishing up in the bedroom. I’m going to get started on the garage. Is it unlocked?” The girl said directing the question toward April.

April nodded. “It should be. He doesn’t usually keep it locked.”

"K. Thanks." The CSI had a long q-tip and a glass tube. "I need to do a swab for DNA real quick first." She figured she would ask while the wife was not combatitive. April looked aghast and looked at the detective.

"It's to rule you out as a suspect." He said. April nodded but still looked concerned.

"I just need you to open your mouth for a moment. I'm going to swab your cheek. It won't hurt." The CSI tech said in her nicest voice. April did as she was asked and let the girl swab her cheek. She rubbed it around a couple of times and stuck it in the glass tube and capped it. "Thank you. We'll try and be out of your way as quick as possible." She said. April nodded and took a drink of water. The CSI tech disappeared out the door.

The detective pulled out his notebook and a pen. "I hope you don't mind." He said to April. "My memory isn't what it used to be."

"It's fine." She said. "I know you guys are just doing your job. It's just...none of this makes any sense. If you knew Michael at all, you would know that. He's just not the murdering type. He couldn't have done this."

The detective ran his fingers over his mustache while contemplating. "Mrs. Bander, can I ask a favor of you?"

April nodded. "I suppose. What is it?"

“Just for about ten minutes, I want you to step outside of this situation. Step outside of your marriage and see Michael Bander as just a man like any other. Can you do that?”

“I can try.” April said. But Michael wasn’t like any other man. That is why she had fallen in love with him. He was sweet, compassionate, and humble. Those qualities alone made him one in a thousand. He always put her up on a pedestal and treated her like she was the last star in the sky. How could she see him as just a man?

“How long have you known Michael?” The detective asked.

“Since Grade school.”

“Were you close then?”

“Not close, but we were aware of each other. We didn’t become friends until our freshman year.” April said.

“Is that when you started dating?”

“We didn’t date each other until our sophomore year.”

“Have you guys been together since then?”

“No, we broke up after our senior year. We both went to two different colleges. We tried a long distance relationship but…it didn’t work out. We stopped after about six months. Then Michael moved back into town a few years ago and we just found each other again. We’re like magnets I guess.”

"Did you guys have any children?" The detective asked as he was writing in his notepad.

April was about to answer but paused. *You're my mommy silly*. "No, we haven't had any children yet. We've talked about it, but we just kind of got settled in."

"Did he mention having any children prior to you guys finding each other?" The detective asked.

"No, he said he dated a little in college but it was nothing serious. He wanted to focus on his work."

"And he is a school teacher, is that correct?" The detective asked.

"Yes. He teaches Biology."

"Does he ever leave on trips or disappear for any time at all?"

April hesitated. She looked slightly shocked at the question. "N..no. He always comes home after work. He doesn't really go anywhere."

"Does he own a gun?" The detective asked. He knew the questions were getting more difficult for her as he began to press for clues that her husband pulled the trigger.

"Well, yes but only for hunting." April said.

"Does he have any handguns?" The detective asked.

"No, nothing like that. Just a couple of shotguns." She took a sip of water and set the glass on the table. The detective wrote some more in his notepad. He asked her questions for about fifteen more minutes. The CSI techs and officer were done with their search. They left with only a couple small bags of things. They had collected some clothes, a cell phone, and a shovel. The detective sent them on their way and got up from the table. He stowed away his notepad and pen into his inner jacket pocket.

"Mrs. Bander, has your husband contacted you at all?" The detective asked after placing his pen into his jacket?

April paused. She wasn't sure how to answer. They were going to check her phone records and know that he had called. "Yes. He called last night."

"Did he happen to say where he is or where he's going?"

"No, he only said that he didn't kill that girl."

"Is he supposed to meet you somewhere or contact you again?"

April's heart began speeding up like a freight train. She felt like it was going to explode. Did they know about the meeting? Had the sheriff overheard them? "No." She said. "I'm meeting my sister for lunch but that's all."

The detective nodded. He pulled out his card and handed it to her. “You think of anything else you need to tell me…”

She nodded. “I’ll call.” She finished the sentence. She walked the detective to the door and held it open for him.

The detective stepped outside and turned back around. “Oh…I almost forgot.” He had saved the crucial information for last. Her reaction would tell him whether or not she had any involvement. He doubted that she did, but just the same, it needed to be the last thing she heard because if she didn’t know, she was going to lose it. “The girl that they found in the woods?” April nodded. “DNA tests show that she’s Michael’s daughter.”

April’s eyes went big and her hand went to her mouth. She began shaking her head. “That’s…that’s not possible. Michael doesn’t have any children.”

That was about the reaction that he had expected. The poor girl had no idea. Michael had kept it a secret from her. “The tests are 99.9 percent positive. There is no question Mrs. Bander. The girl was Michael’s daughter. And if he did kill her, then there is another young girl whose life may be in danger.”

April was still in shock. “Wh..what do you mean? Why?”

“Because Michael had at least two daughters. Twins. Whoever killed this girl, was going to kill both of them. And the man who did it matched Michael’s description. If you hear from him again, you *must* contact me or you could be responsible for her death if he gets to her. You understand?" The detective asked.

April stood there with a vacant look. She was running back every memory she ever had of the two of them together looking for any signs, any clues that Michael had ever had a child. She couldn't find any. She nodded her head vacantly at the detective and turned around and disappeared into her house.

The detective climbed into his car and made a phone call. "You guys in position? Ok, she'll be going to town in one of two ways. I want both directions covered. Stay back far enough that she doesn't know she's being followed. I had a GPS placed under her car in case we lose her. She claims to be meeting her sister for lunch but it will more likely be him. Keep your eyes peeled for anything suspicious."

Chapter 20

April had lost it. She cried. She paced the floor. She cried some more. She even smashed the picture of her and Michael together screaming "liar!"April went outside and jumped in her car. Her hands were trembling as she tried several times to get the key into the ignition. She banged her head on the wheel and sobbed. "Why...why...Michael? How could you do this to me? How could you do this to *us*?" April sat there for a moment with her head on the wheel. When she had finally begun to calm down and her heaving subsided, she placed the key into the ignition and started the car. She had promised her sister to meet for lunch at the diner and she had promised Michael to meet him at two. How could she do it? How was she supposed to look him in the face knowing that he had had children and not told her? Would she see the kind wonderful man that she married or would she see a murderer and a liar? She couldn't do it. She just couldn't. All she wanted to do was run away. She didn't even want to meet with her sister. She was embarrassed, humiliated, and violated. On some level she wanted to keep on driving right out of Angel Falls and never look back. She gave the thought some consideration. She used her sleeve to wipe her cheeks dry. April turned on the radio and tried to lose herself in the music. Every song seemed to bring her back. She listened to Adele belt out "Rolling in the Deep" as she headed into town. *"There's a fire burning in my heart, reaching a fever pitch and it's bringing me out the dark...The scars of your love remind me of us, they keep me thinking that we almost had it all...Rolling in the deep." I'm rolling in the deep alright.* April thought as she drove into town.

April's sister Becca was sitting at a far table on the right. She smiled and waved. Becca was about 5'6, nearly the same height as April. She normally had brown hair as well but had dyed it blonde. Her hair was long and slightly curly and hung down to her shoulders on each side. She was gorgeous no matter what her hair color was. She was wearing a green shirt and skinny tight jeans. She looked good. April plopped down on the other side of the table. She felt horrible. Her eyes were all puffy again. She had wiped all her makeup off. She sat for a moment looking at her sister. She was sitting there looking so pretty. So happy. Not a care in the world. The thought made tears well up in April's eyes and they began to fall down her cheeks.

"Oh...honey, don't do that." Becca said as she got up and came around and sat next to her sister. She put her arm around her and pulled her close. April put her head on her sister's chest and sobbed. Becca just patted her shoulder and pulled her close. "I know. I know honey. It'll be ok." Angel Falls was a small town and the news that Michael Bander had escaped police custody and was wanted for murder had spread fast. The diner was mostly empty but the few people scattered about all seemed to be staring in April's direction. A waitress approached the table, but spoke quietly.

"Can I get you something to drink?"

"Two iced teas please." Becca said. The waitress nodded and disappeared. Becca pulled her sister back a little. She grabbed a napkin and dotted her face. "How did you get away from the news reporters?" She asked.

"I...I didn't. They followed me for a while but then some car cut them off and they stopped."

"Oh, you poor thing. This is terrible. How could this possibly happen? Michael just doesn't seem like the killing type." Becca said.

"He's not...er...I didn't think he was. But...but...oh I don't know what to believe. Nothing makes sense anymore."

Becca brushed back a strand of hair behind her sister's ear. "Has he contacted you?" She asked.

April nodded. "Ya, I'm supposed to meet him at two."

"What? You can't do that. He's a fugitive. They'll arrest you. They're probably following you anyway."

"I don't know what to do. I don't want to believe he did it, but...but...Becca, they said it was his daughter!"

Becca's eyes got huge. "The girl they found?"

"Yes." April was crying again. "They did a DNA test. They said it was 99.9% positive that it was *his* daughter. And *he* is the one found digging her up. What am I suppose to believe? What would you do?"

"Wha...has he ever mentioned a daughter before?" The waitress came and dropped off two teas. She opened her mouth to ask about food and Becca shook her head. "Just give us a few minutes please." The waitress nodded and moved on.

"No, he's never mentioned anyone before."

"Well, you *can't* meet with him. What if he kills you?" Becca said wild eyed.

April shook her head. "He wouldn't do that. He wouldn't." Becca sat back in deep thought. April took a sip of her tea. "They said there was another."

Becca looked at her. "Another? Another what?"

"The detective said he had another kid. That the girl in the woods was a twin and that Michael matched the description the other girl had given of her killer."

Becca's expression turned to shock. "That does it. You are staying with me. No ifs ands or buts. Got it?" April nodded and wiped at her face with a napkin.

"I just don't think I can meet with him. I wouldn't know what to say. The detective thinks he may be after the other girl. What should I do?"

"You need to turn him in." Becca said. "If he kills someone else and you don't, then you're as responsible as he is."

April took another sip of tea and set the glass down and looked at her sister. "I know, but what if he's innocent? What if he didn't do it? I'll be betraying my husband."

Becca flipped her hair back over her shoulder. "Listen sis, I know you don't want to do that, but if he's innocent then he can sort it out in court. Let's look at the facts: one, he dug up the girl." Becca stuck out her finger as she listed it off. "Two, the dead body was *his* daughter that he never told you about." She stuck out another finger. "And three, he escaped from police custody. Now why would he run if he was innocent?"April nodded. It was a good point. "Look, after we're done eating, I'll call this detective you've been talking to and tell him what's going on. You head out to my place and I'll handle this so you won't have any involvement."

April didn't know what to do. She nodded her head solemnly and looked down at her lap lost in thought.

Chapter 21

Michael had gone to the back of the loft to change. He had found a box marked Halloween costumes and that got him to thinking about what he was wearing. He would stand out like a sore thumb. There were several boxes that were marked clothes. After going through three boxes, Michael had settled on a pair of overalls, a hat, and a long sleeve shirt. It would be the least inconspicuous. He'd look like a farmer.

Michael was hungry but he didn't want to risk any public places where police officers may cross paths with him by coincidence. He had seen them at fast food places, diners, and gas stations. In the end, he settled for Walgreens drug store. He kept his head down through the store and even at the checkout. He purchased a pack of doughnuts, a small chocolate milk, a small notebook, and a pen. He headed down to the park and walked a path along the river to a small grassy clearing. He sat down and pulled out a white powdered doughnut.

Michael looked out across the river and imagined the times he and April had met here with a picnic lunch. It seemed like so long ago. It was as if the last day had propelled him two years away from her. He felt different. He felt older somehow. He pulled out his notebook and pen and began to make notes. He wrote the word 'Maria'. He remembered the name in the back of his mind. He felt like it might have been the name of the girl buried out in the woods. He wrote 'female' next to her name and underneath it, he wrote ‘orange nails’.

Was that all he knew? Maria, female, orange nails? It didn’t seem like very much to go on. How had he found her? He couldn’t have known she was there. Had she called out to him somehow from some other world? Michael didn’t believe in ghosts or an afterlife for that matter. It just didn’t make sense. Michael stared out across the river. A turtle was near shore and poked its head out of the water. It stared at Michael for a few seconds and then disappeared under the dark water. *How am I going to sort this out?* He wondered. He couldn’t go back. He knew that much. Not unless he found out what happened to this girl and cleared his name. Michael wasn’t sure that that was going to be possible. Sometimes, not even detectives can figure those things out even with a team of CSI and all the equipment in the world. Michael didn’t have any equipment and he was on the run. How could he prove he didn’t kill the girl when all he had to go on was Maria, female, and orange nails? Michael lay down in the grass and looked up at the sky. *What is the next step?* He wondered. He tried and tried, but the answer just wouldn’t come. *April will be here soon. Maybe she’ll know what to do.* Michael let himself drift off to sleep.

Chapter 22

Detective James got the call from his guys. They had followed April to the diner down town. The news van was in pursuit so they had to cut them off to let her get away. She had met with another girl presumably a friend or a relative perhaps. The detective gave the order for them to split up so each unit could follow one of the girls. April had left in her car but apparently the other girl had remained in the diner. The detective was on his way there but still five minutes out. He had a feeling that April would try and contact her husband somehow. He had expected her to do so directly, but going through another person made sense as well. It sounded like Michael might show up at the diner any minute and he wanted to make sure that he was there when he did. The car suddenly filled with the sounds of Sonny and Cher singing *"I got you babe"*. The detective reached down and grabbed his cell phone and flipped it open. "Detective James speaking."

"Detective James?" A female voice came through on the other end.

"This is he. What can I do for you?" He answered. Usually the calls coming in were from officers, CSI, or the D.A. He didn't recognize the voice.

"My name is Becca. I'm April Bander's sister." The girl said

The detective pulled off to the side of the road. He grabbed a pen and pulled his notebook from his inner jacket pocket. “Yes Becca, what can I do for you?”

“My sister wanted me to call you. Michael wanted her to meet him by the park in just a little bit but she doesn’t want to go. I don’t want my sister in any danger. Can you pick him up?” Becca’s concern and love for her sister radiated through the phone.

The detective hesitated for a moment. This could be a diversion to get them off her trail so that she could have the meeting. He decided it was best to keep his men following April. “Do you know where and when they are supposed to meet?” The detective asked. He decided he might be able to keep both girls within sight and if Becca was telling the truth, collar Michael in the process.

“They have a special place by the river near the park. She was supposed to meet him there at two.”

“And where is she now?”

“I sent her back to my place. I told her I would meet with him and I still want to do that before you arrest him.”

“Mrs...”

“Becca.” She interrupted

"Becca. Michael Bander is wanted on murder charges. I'm sure you know that."

"Mmmhhm." She agreed. "What's your point Detective?"

"My point is that I don't think it would be a good idea to put you in harm's way. You point out the spot and we can pick him up." The detective didn't want it to end in a hostage situation.

"No deal. I promised my sister I would see him. I want to look in his eyes. I want to tell him to leave her alone. You want Michael; I'll lead you to him."

There was another silence while the detective ran through the possibilities. On one hand, having her lead them to him increased the odds of catching him. But on the other hand, it increased the odds that something would go wrong. "Alright. Fine. You wear a vest and get no closer than fifteen feet. Deal?"

"Deal." She said.

They agreed to meet at the diner in five minutes. The detective wrote down her information and shut the phone and put the car in drive.

Chapter 23

Michael lay in the grass drifting in and out of sleep. The previous day had taken a toll on him both physically and emotionally and his body remained exhausted. When Michael would wake up, his mind would begin pouring over all the events that had unfolded. When he would drift off to sleep he would dream of April. The dreams would all begin different, but they always ended up at the same place. The amusement park. Michael recognized the place of course. He and April had gone there once as teenagers. It was an amusement park called "Great Rides By The Bay" and was nestled in next to Alexandria Bay some forty five minutes away. When they were sixteen, April's church had put together a trip for the youth group. Michael remembered sitting next to April on the church bus all the way there and back. They had split off from the others and had went on nearly every ride, side by side. They screamed together going down "The Giant Dragon" roller coaster. They squished each other spinning around on the "Twister". They had bumped each other on the bumper cars. And right there, down by the water, on a beautiful summer night, perhaps the most beautiful night Michael could remember, as the sun began to set over the bay, right there where they had been feeding the fish only moments earlier, Michael put his arm around April's waist and pulled her to him and right there they each melted away into the night as they shared with one another their first kiss.

Michael was lying in the grass, eyes open, remembering the moment. A large smile had crossed his face as he experienced it again in his mind. Church bells rang off in the distance signaling the time as two o'clock. Michael sat up and looked around. No April. He didn't figure she would be late. Not today. Not with all that was on the line. He needed her to be here. He needed her comfort. And he needed to explain. How could he explain? What would he say? He just figured it would come to him in the moment. But the moment was here and she was not. Michael scanned along the river bank to where it met the trees. Nothing. The clearing was surrounded by trees. Michael heard the sounds of branches cracking behind him. He stood up and turned in that direction. There were sounds of more branches cracking and a young woman stepped through into the clearing. Michael recognized her right away. "Becca, what are you doing here? Where's April?"

Becca stared at him for a moment with an angry look in her eyes. "She doesn't want to see you Michael." She said. She had taken a strong stance with her hands on her hips.

Michael hesitated with his mouth slightly ajar. He hadn't expected this. He loved April. He trusted her. Why wouldn't she show up? Why wouldn't she believe him? Michael looked down toward the ground and then back up at Becca. "I didn't do this Becca." Michael struggled for the words. He thought he heard more branches cracking in the woods. "I don't understand what's happening, but you gotta believe me. I didn't kill that girl."

"You know what you are Michael Bander? You are a liar!" Becca was shouting and pointing her finger at him. "They got the DNA test back on that girl. They know she was your daughter. You married my sister and didn't tell her you had a daughter? Then you conveniently dig up her body in the woods and you expect to convince me that you are innocent?" Becca turned her head sideways at the sound of more noise coming from the woods.

Michael stood there motionless. He was oblivious to the noises in the woods. His mouth was ajar and his eyes went blank as he tried to process what Becca had said about the DNA test. He looked away in thought and then back at Becca. "Becca, I don't have a daughter. I don't know what you are talking about." Michael pleaded.

"DNA tests don't lie Michael. Stay away from my sister. You go near her again or try to contact her, I'll kill you." Becca stared him down for a moment and then turned and headed into the woods.

Michael remained speechless. He stood there frozen staring after her. DNA test? Daughter? Becca was right about one thing. And as a Biology teacher he knew it all too well. DNA tests don't lie. As Michael filtered through what had just taken place, more sounds came through the woods and when Michael looked up, there were five men in a semi circle formation standing in front of him with guns drawn. Three of them were police officers in uniform. One was a young man wearing all black with a badge hanging from a necklace. And the fifth one was directly in front of him. He was wearing a brown suit. There was a badge clipped to his belt. He had brown curly hair and a brown mustache. Michael looked from one to the other and then for any escape route. He found none. He was caught.

"Michael Bander?" The man in the brown jacket called out to him. Michael looked at him. "Michael, my name is Detective James. I need you to come with me. I need to ask you a few questions."

"I didn't do this. You've got the wrong guy." Michael said.

"I'm sure you're right. There is probably a reasonable explanation for all of this. But I need you to come with me right now so we can get this all sorted out."

"Last time I went with you I was tortured and nearly raped." Michael said angrily.

The detective paused. Images of the underwear on the floor came back to him and he put the pieces together. "The officers who took you have been relieved of duty pending an investigation."

The other officers were getting fidgety. They creeped forward a step and Michael matched theirs by stepping backward toward the river. “She said that DNA tests show it was my kid.” Michael nodded toward Becca who had stopped just inside the woods and was watching the situation unfold from behind a sycamore. “Is that true?” Michael asked.

“Yes. What she said is true.” The detective responded. He knew his only chance was to talk this guy in. If they rushed him, he was likely to take a dive.

“That’s impossible.” Michael said.

“99.9 percent accurate. Odds say it’s your kid Michael.” The detective said matter of factly.

The other officers creeped forward a little more. Michael took another step back. “I don’t have a kid, I didn’t put that girl there, and I sure as hell am not trusting you torturing, rapist cops to figure out what really happened.” Michael turned and leaped toward the river. One of the cops fired twice as Michael leaped.

“Michael don’t!” The detective hollered as Michael had jumped. “Hold your fire! Hold your fire!” He yelled at the officer that had shot at him. The officers moved forward toward the river. “Jeff, call in a boat!” The detective yelled at the officer in black. “The rest of you, follow the river and find him. You see him you drag his ass out!” The detective looked at the officer who shot at Michael. “Do not shoot unless you see that he is armed!”

The officer pointed at the river and spoke angrily. “We can’t let that murderer escape custody and end up back on the streets!”

“Did you see him commit murder?” The detective asked.

“Well no, but...”

“Then he’s a suspect at this point, not a murderer. Got it?” The officer nodded. The detective looked down where Bander had dove toward the water. Two large rocks were glistening with red. The detective ran his finger over it and held up a finger with Michael’s blood on it. “You say he’s a murderer and that might be. But if you just killed him and we find out he was innocent, what will that make you?” The officer had a look of shock cross his face. He hadn’t considered that. “Go find him.” The detective said. The officer turned toward the river and started off down the bank. “And Paul...?” The detective shouted after him. The officer turned around. “If you see a weapon, you don’t hesitate to shoot, guilty or not!” The officer stared for a second, then nodded and headed back into the woods. The detective turned back and spotted Becca standing with her hand cupped over her mouth with a look of shock and horror. She turned and headed into the woods.

Chapter 24

Michael hit the water and the cold rushed straight into him nearly sending him into shock. The water was so cold that Michael hadn't felt the bullet that had grazed him on the leg. He had heard the gunshots though. And for that reason Michael had kept his head down as long as possible. He let the current drag his body quickly downstream. When he felt like he could no longer hold his breath, Michael came back up for air. He looked around him. Police officers were scrambling to keep up along the bank. They must have noticed him because they were pointing in his direction. Michael knew they would probably bring in dogs and boats. If he was going to remain free, he was going to have to stay in the water and wait it out. That was his only chance. Michael looked downriver as he floated. There was a cove on the side of the river the officers were moving toward. From where he was, Michael thought it looked like steep cliffs and lots of overhanging trees and brush. Michael was sure they would expect him to continue downstream. He felt his shirt pocket and when he found what he was looking for, he pulled out the pen he had used to write with earlier. A boulder hit his legs as he was pushed quickly downstream. Michael winced at the pain. He had to keep his arms treading the water to keep his head up. Michael put the pen between his teeth and swam toward the cove. His shoes were filled with water and threatened to take him down. Michael wanted to kick them off as they were draining his energy, but he knew finding another pair would be most difficult. He couldn't kick fast enough to get anywhere so he let his hands do the work. Slowly, he made his way over to the cove. The police officers were still in pursuit but they were a ways back. Michael's feet finally reached bottom and he breathed in deeply as he was able to catch his breath. Michael was just around the corner and out of sight of the officers. He pulled the pen from his mouth and bit down on the end of it with his teeth. He wiggled the pen back and forth in his mouth until the cap came off and he spit it out into the water. He then grabbed the writing part between his teeth and did the same. After he had pulled it out, he was left with a hollow tube. Michael looked toward the bluff to make sure the officers hadn't rounded it yet. There were no sounds and nobody had yet emerged. Michael waded into the cove and found a deep area under some branches that hung out over the water. Noises were coming from above. The officers had rounded the bluff. Michael lowered himself into the water and used the tube as a breathing device. The water was dark and concealed him well. The officers pushed on past, not noticing the small pen tube that was protruding from the water. Underneath the water, Michael could hear all the sounds of rocks tumbling and sand being pushed from one area to another. After about fifteen minutes the sounds of boat motors filled his ears as well. Breathing out of a tube was difficult. Michael struggled to remain calm. He wanted to leave. He wanted out of the water. He wanted April. Even if she had betrayed him. How could he blame her? With DNA evidence against him, she probably thought he had lied to her. Michael's thoughts were getting him worked up and he began to need more air than he could get from the tube. He risked coming out of the water despite the sounds of the boat motors. Michael popped his head up for a moment and breathed the air. He could see two boats. One was heading into the cove and the other was heading upstream. Michael took three deep breaths and then lowered himself back into the water. He tried not to think about April. He tried not to think about the boats or the officers searching for him. He tried not to think about the girl he had dug up in the woods. In fact, he let his mind clear and didn't think about anything at all. He just lay still and breathed slowly through the tube.

Chapter 25

Becca arrived back at her home about forty five minutes after watching Michael get shot. She was struggling to keep it together. Twice she had broken out in tears and had to pull over. How was she going to explain to her sister that her husband had been shot? How was she going to explain to her that he had been tortured? And how was she going to explain that she had read his eyes and found no trace of guilt in them? Becca shook her head. She pulled into her gravel driveway and put the car in park. She sat there for a moment thinking. Her sister was going to need her. This was such a mess and Becca felt helpless to untangle it. Becca sighed and stepped out of the car and headed inside to bare the bad news. April was waiting for her at the door. She was trying to read her expression. Becca tried not to give her one. April held the screen door open for her sister. Becca flew past her and into the kitchen. She opened the fridge and pretended to be looking for something. Finally she grasped a diet coke, stood up and shut the fridge. April was standing on the other side, arms folded, apparently not fooled by her sisters attempts at avoidance. Their eyes locked on each other.

"Are you going to tell me what happened?" April asked.

Becca tried to maintain a calm look but her eyes gave her away in the end. They were filling up with tears despite her internal protest that they remain unemotional and unreadable. Too late. A tear fell and ran down her cheek.

April's look went from one of anger to one of concern for her sister. She thought maybe something had happened to her. The thought that something had happened to Michael had not occurred to her. April threw her arms around her sister and pulled her close. "Oh honey, I'm sorry. I shouldn't have had you do that. This shouldn't have been your problem." She pulled back to look into Becca's eyes. "Are you ok? What happened?" April asked softly.

Becca opened her mouth and then closed it. She opened it again and then closed it again. She didn't have any idea where to begin. "Let's sit down." She said and motioned toward the couch in the living room. April followed her lead and sat right next to her. For a moment they both stared into each other's eyes trying to read one another. Each finding only pain and confusion. *And it's about to get a whole lot worse*. Becca thought. "I uh..." Becca glanced around and then back at April. "I did what I had said I would. I contacted the detective."

"Was Michael there? Did they bring him in?" April's voice was low but panicked for information. She wanted to get to the bottom of this whole situation.

"Um, ya he was there." Becca began. "But they didn't exactly bring him in."

April gave a shocked look. Her mouth was slightly ajar. "What happened?" She asked.

"Well, I approached him first. You know, where you told me he would be?" April nodded. "And I told him about the DNA test and him having a kid..." April nodded again.

"And...?"

"Well, he kind of looked shocked. He didn't know what I was talking about. He was still claiming that he didn't do anything."

"Well, what did you say?" April asked.

"I didn't say anything really. I stepped back and let the detective and officers move in to arrest him."

"And they didn't?" April asked.

"Well, they tried to...but he dove into the river. They're out looking for him now."

April's face looked bewildered. She couldn't picture Michael escaping from the police once much less twice. She shook her head. "I don't understand. This just doesn't make sense. He doesn't seem like the type to run from police...or anything really." April said.

"Well...about that..." Becca began and looked around not sure how to break it to her that her husband had been tortured by police officers. Finally, not finding anything of importance for her to focus her attention on, she turned back to her sister and looked her in the eyes. "Apparently the police who took him from the crime scene...?"

"Ya?" April nodded.

"Well, apparently they took him somewhere and tortured Michael." There, she said it. "And that is why he escaped and probably why he didn't let them take him into custody again."

April cupped her hand over her mouth and stifled a gasp. Her eyes had went wide. "Wha..what did they do to him?" She asked.

"I don't know. He didn't say. But he did say they attempted to rape him. He referred to them as torturing rapist cops."

April turned and vomited. It was too much. She was too weak. She couldn't handle anymore. Her face had gone pale. She was leaning over now, crying, and another wave of nausea hit her but there was nothing left to throw up. "How.."she began with spit hanging from her mouth. She spit it out. Becca had leaned forward and was rubbing her back and trying to pull April's hair back so it didn't get in her vomit or spit. "How could this happen? How could this happen to him? To me?" She was sobbing. "I don't understand..." April stood up. "I'm sorry about your floor. I'll get some paper towels."

Becca stood up and grabbed April's hand and turned her around. She pulled her close and hugged her. "I'm sorry this is happening to you. I really am." She stood there for a moment hugging her. After a couple of minutes she pulled back and looked at April whose eyes had gone all puffy again. "I'll clean this up. I want you to go lie down and get some sleep." April nodded and Becca led her to the bedroom. Becca was about to get her sister into the bed but she was running the scenario through her mind. Tell her now and be done with the bad or tell her later and drag it out? She wasn't sure what the right thing to do was. She knew that if she didn't tell her, it could come back and bite her later and her sister might not forgive her for it. She decided to get it over with now. April began to head for the bed when Becca grasped her hand. "Hold up a moment hun." She said. "Let's go get your face cleaned up a bit first." She led her around the corner to the bathroom. Becca opened a cabinet and took out a wash cloth and ran it under some cold water. She dabbed at her sister's cheeks. "There's more..." Becca said quietly while looking down. She didn't want her sister to see the worry in her eyes.

Becca looked up but vacantly and began dabbing April's face again. April's hand came up and gently stopped Becca's. "What is it?" April asked looking for an answer in Becca's face and finding none.

"Sis, they uh..." Becca began but turned her head. She was crying now. "They..." She sniffled and was holding back an all out emotional breakdown.

"They what?" April asked as she reached out and turned Becca's head so she was facing her. She could read it now. Something *had* happened. Something had happened to Michael. "Becca...what happened?" April asked with a little sternness in her voice. "What happened to Michael?"

Becca had tears running down her cheeks. She clasped her sister's hands that rested on her face. Her sister with such a gentle, soft, kind heart. Her sister that she loved. Her sister that was a broken mess. "They shot Michael." She blurted out and collapsed into her sister's arms bawling in total emotional chaos. "They shot him. I'm so sorry. I didn't know they'd hurt him. I'm so sorry." Becca was crying in her sister's arms. April's face had gone pale and expressionless. Her hands had grasped her sister's shirt and had formed fists full of cloth. Becca pulled back and looked at April. Her face had gone from pale to red. She wasn't breathing and her face was vacant. Her knees began to shake and she suddenly collapsed to the floor unconscious.

Becca scooped her up into her arms and took her to the bedroom and slid her into the bed. She pulled the covers up and over her and tucked her in, drying her own eyes with her sleeve in between bouts of sniffles. She had to take care of her sister now. That's all that mattered. She would feel better when she woke up. She hoped. Becca collapsed in a chair that was in the corner of the room. She was running all the events through her mind. He just didn't look guilty. *He didn't look like a man who had just killed someone*. The thoughts haunted her and carried her off to sleep.

Chapter 26

Detective James looked down at his watch. He was standing on Jerick Stanton Bridge downstream from where Michael had jumped into the water. He had been watching it closely for any signs Michael may have floated downstream. He was standing just over the rail on a small gravel patch. He glanced at his watch again. Damn. It had been about three hours and there was no sign of him. The detective glanced upstream again. Nothing. He turned and stepped over the guardrail and went to the other side to look downstream. The sun was beginning to set and he put his hand up above his eyes to block out the light. He was hoping to catch a glimpse of a bobbing head, a person swimming, or even Bander floating...but he could see nothing. Damn. He looked at his watch again. Time was running out. He needed to have a net thrown across the river to catch his body in the event Paul had more than wounded him. He could be dead floating on down to Pennsylvania by now. There wasn't enough money or manpower for a net. So if Bander was dead, they weren't likely to find him. They would drag the river tomorrow but he didn't expect to turn up anything. The water was too shallow and moved too fast. The best odds were that he would get hung up on some rocks or branches and a fisherman would find him. That wouldn't help his case though. Dead men don't talk. Dead men don't confess. Still, something was nagging him about this Bander guy. All the evidence was pointing one way but his gut and instincts were telling him something different. He had seen his face when that girl had told him about the DNA and him having a kid. It was a genuinely shocked and surprised expression. He had no idea that he had a kid. It wasn't uncommon of course for a guy to have a kid and not know about it. It happens all the time. But for a guy to be found with a dead kid that he didn't know he had...that was a different thing altogether.

The detective lowered his hand and went back over to the other side of the bridge and continued looking upstream. He had a walkie talkie clipped to his belt and listened in to the boat and land chatter as the men continued their search. He looked at his watch again. It was getting late and they didn't have enough manpower to continue the search into the night. With each passing minute, the odds of finding him diminished. He wondered if he had made the right decision allowing the girl to approach him. The detective shook his head. No, that wouldn't have changed anything. Bander would have hit the water no matter what. And who could blame him after what had happened to him? What guy would want to risk being tortured again guilty or not? This was going to be a mess for the DA and difficult to prosecute. Detective James' cell phone rang. "Detective James." He spoke as he flipped the phone open and put it to his ear.

"Are you sitting down?" The voice was from Dr. Crane, the supervising CSI.

"Oh, hey Doc. No, I can't say that I am. Bander escaped again and I'm up here on Jerick Stanton trying to find him."

"He jumped in the river?"

"Yep. We've been searching for damn near three hours. No sign of him. Hell, he may be dead for all I know. Paul took a shot at him when he leaped. He hit him but I don't know how bad."

"Did you put a net up to catch him?" Crane asked.

"Nope. Not enough men, not enough money. You know the speech. Just couldn't do it. Hell, I don't have enough guys to continue the search. And they're talking about making more cuts next month. You believe that doc?"

"Oh I've been paying attention. I sent the board a letter but I believe it was likely used to line the bottom of a bird cage somewhere. This will come back to bite them in the gluteus maximus."

"The gluteus maximus doc?"

"Yes, the buttocks in layman's terms."

"Oh it'll bite them in the butt doc. Let me ask you doc; you keep a spare tire in your trunk?"

"Of course. One never knows when a flat or blowout may occur and leave one stranded."

"Well did you have a flat today?"

"No."

"Yesterday?"

"Nope. Can't say I did."

"Well, one could argue that the spare isn't necessary since you've gone so long without a flat."

"Yes, I see your point. The city is arguing that the extra manpower isn't necessary because of the low crime."

"Exactly. And you don't get rid of your spare because you know the day will come when you will need it. Well, this week it might be a murderer gets away. Next time it might be a terrorist. Either way doc you are right. This will bite them in the gluteus maximus."

"Agreed."

"So what news have you got for me doc?"

"I'm afraid this isn't going to make your day any better. Or perhaps it will, depending on how you look at it."

"Well, what is it doc? Don't keep me in suspense." Detective James was craning his neck to look at something. "Hey, hold on a minute doc." The detective opened a pouch he had attached to his belt and took out a small pair of binoculars.

He put them to his eyes and stared out onto the river. He set his phone down on a guardrail post and pulled out his walkie talkie and pushed a button. "Water teams one and two come in. Over." There was a pause and then a click and both water teams on the boats checked in. "I've got some movement under some branches on the northeast corner of the cove on the eastside of the river. Can one of you check that out please? Over."

"Water team one. We're right near there, we'll check it out. Over."

The detective put away his walkie talkie and picked his cell phone back up and watched through the binoculars as the boat approached the cove. "Sorry Doc, go ahead with what you were saying."

"We ran the DNA test from the swab you had taken from the girl."

The detective was busy watching as the boat inched in closer. He could just make out something white moving under the branches. "Ya, you already told me that doc. The test matched alleles with the Bander guy."

"I'm not talking about the DNA from the vic detective. I'm talking about the DNA swab you had taken on the wife. Bander's wife."

"Ya, go on..." The boat was having a hard time penetrating the bushes and trees.

"The wife's alleles are also a match." There was a pause. "What I'm trying to tell you Detective, is that Bander's wife is the mother of the girl you found."

"Wha.." The detective dropped his phone. He reached down and picked it up out of the dirt and brushed it off. "What?"

"You heard me correctly. The Bander's *are* the girl's parents."

The detective was stunned. *Who would have seen that one coming? I must be losing my touch.* He thought as he remembered comforting the grieving wife. He felt cold chills run up his spine. "Alright doc, thanks." The detective hung up the phone and placed it back in its pouch at his waist. He held the binoculars back up and saw an officer in the boat lift up a milk jug into the air. The walkie talkie crackled and a voice from water team one came through.

"Sorry Detective. Someone set out a trot line and attached it to the jug. There was a few fish pulling it around. Nothing more. Over." The officer threw the jug back under the bushes and the boat pulled out away from the cove.

The detective ran his hand through his curly hair and sighed. This was getting complicated. He pulled out his phone and speed dialed the officer who was tailing the wife. "Where is she?" The detective asked. The officer ran through the details with the detective. Nothing much to report. The wife had gone straight to the sister's house and hadn't left. The sister arrived home about an hour and a half later. "Alright. Go ahead and bring her in for questioning." The detective turned and headed toward the car. "And one more thing...consider her and the sister armed and dangerous. Check her for weapons before you put her into the car and don't turn your back on either one of them is that understood?" There was an agreement on the other end. "Ok. Be careful." The detective sounded worried as he hung up the phone and got into the car. He got behind the wheel and sighed outloud shaking his head. "It's going to be another long night." He said to nobody inparticular. "I'm getting too old for this shit." He started the car and headed for the station.

Chapter 27

Officer Harris hung up the phone with the detective. He and his partner were going to have to bring April Bander in for questioning. This was not something he had expected, or hoped for. He wasn't sure what to expect from the girls. What he knew for certain is that when it came to arrests, he would rather bring in a guy anytime over a girl. Girls fight harder, they are more clever, and no guy ever likes having to fight with a girl. Guys on the other hand, usually went calmly, and those who didn't got the rough treatment and usually they didn't put up a fight for too long. Officer Harris looked over at his partner. "You ready?"

"Are we arresting her?" Officer Fitch asked. Both officers were new to the force. Officer Harris was only twenty-four years old and had a good complexion with a short, high and tight haircut. Officer Fitch was twenty-five and had dark curly hair. Both were strong, young, and energetic. Neither of them were too keen on having to collar a female.

"Nope. Just bringing her in for questioning." Officer Harris said.

"She gonna go easy?"

"Do they ever? We're to consider them armed and dangerous."

“Jesus” Officer Fitch said with the unexpected news. “This shit just keeps getting stranger by the minute.”

Officer Harris put the car in drive and headed from the road down the long gravel driveway to the sister’s house. He pulled in behind Becca’s car, put it in park, and turned off the engine. Both officers shared an expression before getting out of the car.

The house was a beautiful log cabin ranch with a huge bay window overlooking the front yard. The front porch was made to look like something out of an old western. It was rustic looking but clean with potted plants scattered about. There was a glass storm door and a doorbell beside it. Officer Harris reached out and pushed the button. A chime could be heard from inside. After about ten seconds footfalls could be heard coming toward the door. Becca opened the big wooded door and pushed open the glass storm door. Her expression was not pleasant.

“Yes. What can I do for you Officers?” She asked gruffly.

“Ma'am, we need to speak to Mrs. Bander please.” Officer Harris said using as polite of a voice as he could muster.

“Well, she’s sleeping. You’ll have to come back later.” Becca said and began closing the door.

Officer Fitch was on the right and caught his hand between the glass and pulled it back. “I’m afraid it can’t wait, it is important that we speak to her now ma'am." Officer Fitch said politely but sternly.

Becca looked back over her shoulder and stepped out of the storm door forcing the officers to take a step back. She shut the storm door behind her. She had on baggy pajama looking pants and a white cotton shirt. Her blonde hair hung down past her shoulders. She lowered her voice to a near whisper. "Is her husband dead? Did you find him?" She asked.

The officers looked at one another and then back at her. Officer Fitch shook his head. "No ma'am, we haven't been able to locate him."

Becca's mouth was slightly ajar. She had assumed they would have found him by now dead or alive. She looked distant picturing him on the run, maybe coming here. She shook the thought away and eyeballed the police officers angrily. "Well, then why are you here? What do you want with my sister?"

"I'm afraid we can't discuss that with you ma'am. We've been asked to pick her up and take her down town. They just want to ask her some questions." Officer Harris said trying to maintain a level of politeness. Becca's confrontational demeanor was begging to poke at him like little daggers.

"Do you have any idea what this poor girl has been through the last two days?" Becca looked from one officer to the other. "She just passed out from stress not two hours ago. I'll be damned if you're going to march her down to your little station and inflict more trauma on her than has already been done." Becca was shaking her finger at the officers.

Officer Harris was about to respond when he looked past Becca as the storm door opened and April, hair in a tuffled mess, looking like she just got out of bed, stuck her head out of the door. "Is everything ok Becca? What is it?" April had overheard her sister raising her voice at the officers and saw her jabbing her finger at them.

"They want you to go down town with them to answer some questions." Becca said. "I told them now was not a good time."

"I don't understand." She looked from one officer to the other. "I've already spoken to Detective James and the sheriff. I've told them all I know."

"I'm sorry ma'am. We were asked to bring you in. They didn't say why. I'm sure they wouldn't have asked if it wasn't important." Officer Fitch said.

"Fine. I'm going to go get changed and cleaned up. I'll be right out." April said.

"Actually ma'am, your fine the way you are. You need to step out please. You won't be gone that long." Officer Fitch said as he held the door open and kept it from closing.

April's face went pale. Her heart started beating rapidly. She suddenly felt like she was on the wrong end of the investigation.

"What's this all about?" Becca asked. "Get your hands off my door. I haven't invited you into my house. All we have done is cooperate. You have no business coming to my home and treating us like we are criminals!" Becca shouted.

"Calm down ma'am." Officer Harris said to Becca. "I need you to step away from the door please." He motioned his hand backward a bit from the door.

"I need you to step outside please." Officer Fitch said. April began stepping outside the door.

Becca hadn't budged. She looked bewildered at what was happening at *her* home. Officer Fitch had put his hand behind April and was guiding her down the porch and toward the car. "You get your fucking hands off of her!" She said. "She said she'd go with you, she has the right to get cleaned up!"

She moved toward her sister but Officer Harris stepped in front of her. "Calm down ma'am. We don't want any problems. I'm sure she'll be back in no time."

"Don't you tell me to calm down! This is my house and you are on my porch! Get out! Get out now!" Becca was pointing toward the driveway.

Officer Fitch had April next to the car. “I need you to put your hands on the car please.” He told her.

April looked at him with wide eyes. “What?”

“I’m sorry ma'am, but I need to frisk you before you can get into the car.”

“Wha...what for? I haven’t done anything. I thought you weren’t arresting me.”

“We aren’t ma'am. It’s just precaution to make sure you aren’t bringing any weapons into the station.” *Consider them armed and dangerous*. The words echoed in his mind. He didn’t want to take a chance that they’d get shot in the back on the way to the station.

They attempted to rape him...Her sister’s words rang through her head and she had a look of horror cross her face. The officer read her expression. “I’ll be using the backs of my hands. No groping. I promise.” April looked at his face and seen he was sincere and turned and put her hands on the car. Officer Fitch began to pat her down using the backs of his hands.

“What are you doing? Don’t you fucking touch her! You get your hands off of her!” Becca yelled as she tried to push her way past Officer Harris.

Officer Harris spun her around and pushed her up against the house and held her hands behind her back. “Ma'am, if you don't calm down, I'm going to have to arrest you for interfering with a police investigation." He said to her.

Becca had tears coming down her cheeks. "Why are you doing this to us?" She sobbed. "She hasn't done anything."

"Then let her go and get questioned and be there for her when she's done. You can't help her by getting yourself arrested." Officer Harris said calmly. He looked over at his partner. He had finished the pat down and had just gotten April into the back seat and shut the door. He nodded to indicate he was ready. "I'm going to let you go now, but if you try anything, I'm taking you in. Do you understand?" Becca nodded and he released her.

Becca turned and stared Officer Harris in the eyes. "If you harm one hair on her head..." She said angrily.

"Be careful how you finish that sentence ma'am. Your sister won't be harmed." He said and then turned and headed toward the car.

"Is that what you told Michael Bander before you tortured and raped him?" She shouted.

Officer Harris stopped, paused, shook his head, and then kept walking. Becca slid down the side of the house to the ground crying. The car turned around and headed out of the driveway.

Chapter 28

Detective James arrived at the CSI headquarters before the officers. There were interrogation rooms at the police station, but he preferred the ones in the CSI office. For one, there was better coffee. There were also better couches to crash on when he got tired, his evidence was right at hand, and the interviewer's interrogation chair was much more comfortable. All in all, it was the right place to interrogate when it was going to take some time. And he had a feeling this was going to take a while.

The detective poured himself a cup of coffee, met up with Dr. Crane, and went over the evidence. The DNA from Mrs. Bander had matched that of the girl almost perfectly. It had to be her daughter; there was no doubt about it. And if she hid the fact that it was her daughter they had found in the woods, then it goes to reason that she helped put her there. It didn't look like Mrs. Bander was going back home tonight. She may not go back home for another thirty years from the look of it.

The two officers found Detective James and notified him that Mrs. Bander had been left in the interrogation room. The detective nodded and went for a refill on his coffee. He grabbed a glass and filled it with water and took it into the interrogation room.

Mrs. Bander looked up at him as he entered the room. She looked like they had dragged her out of bed. Her brown hair was all tousled and her eyes were baggy. She didn't look happy. *She was about to be a whole lot less happy*. He thought.

The detective placed the glass of water in front of her. It's an old interrogation trick. It gave an extra opportunity to read body language. Many suspects would take a sip of water directly after telling a lie or when an uncomfortable subject was touched upon. Usually that would indicate a point of focus for the interrogator. In most cases they were also able to legally obtain fingerprints that way as well. The glass was always collected with a cloth and handled as evidence. The detective slid the glass toward her. "I'll be right back in a moment. Is there anything I can get you?"

April Bander looked directly at him. "You can get me my husband, Detective."

The detective smiled and exited the room. When he came back he had a legal pad and a pen. He set his coffee and pad on the table and pulled up his cushioned chair. The chair they sat the suspects in was very uncomfortable. The longer they sat in that chair, the more likely they were to start talking. Most people were able to be broken within twenty hours. Once the butt is sore, the stomach is hungry, the mind is tired, all the nerves just become unglued. The emotions flow and the words just start coming out. Lying becomes difficult because the suspects begin making mistakes as their mental ability to remember their own deceit becomes more and more difficult the more weak and irritable they become.

She was already fatigued, weak, and irritable. The detective looked at her and decided that this probably wasn't going to take all night. He looked at the clock on the wall. Quarter after seven. He sure hoped not, because he was likely to be the one messing up if he didn't get some sleep soon. He looked across the table at April. "I'm sorry to ask you to come down so late in the evening and on such short notice. Please understand that we are trying to do the best we can to help you and your husband out and solve a crime at the same time."

"And shooting my husband helps him out how?" April asked sarcastically. She reached out and grabbed the glass for a drink of water. Not because she was nervous, but because she hadn't had a drink in hours and her lips and mouth were dry. The detective took note that they had her fingerprints but decided there was nothing more to read into.

"I'm sorry. That was not my intention to shoot at him. I called for the officers to cease fire immediately."

"And was it your intention for him to be tortured and almost raped?"

The girl sitting across from him seemed to be a whole different girl than the one who was crying in his presence earlier that day. *A lot has happened since then*. He thought. "Look, Mrs. Bander, he is a suspect in a murder investigation and tried to escape. The officer that took a shot had no idea what had happened to him and the other officers will be investigated and tried. We don't condone that kind of behavior by anyone on our team. Now, if there is a logical explanation for all of this, by all means, let's get to the bottom of it so we can get the two of you back home and you can return to your normal lives.

"Have you found him? Is he ok?" April asked, her tone changing from sarcastic to concern.

"No ma'am, I'm afraid we haven't. I'm inclined to think that is a good sign. If he were fatally injured he would have surfaced by now. We've checked the rapids and the shores and there has been no sign of him. He hasn't checked in at the hospital. No news, means he's probably still on the run." April didn't comment. She didn't seem too convinced. The detective took a sip of his coffee and picked up his pen. "I'm going to ask you some questions that might help us get to the bottom of whatever is going on. Understand that you are not under arrest, but if you would prefer to have an attorney present during the questioning, we will be more than glad to let you use our phone to call one and we can wait until they arrive to begin. Do you understand your right to have an attorney present?"

April's angry look returned. "Why would I need an attorney? I haven't done anything. I have nothing to hide. Ask me anything you need to."

The detective scootched his chair up. That was what he wanted to hear. With an attorney present, his odds of obtaining a confession diminished more than seventy-five percent.

Suspects were often afraid to ask for an attorney for fear it might make them look guilty. The detective groomed his mustache with his left hand. “Let’s start from the beginning, tell me where and when you first met Michael Bander.”

April stared at the detective for a moment and let out a long sigh. “Detective, we’ve already gone through this. I met Michael Bander in grade school. I didn’t really get to know him until high school.”

“And what year was that?” The detective asked.

“Um..I don’t know. I graduated in 1994. We started to date our sophomore year so I guess in 92’ sometime.”

“And how long did you date each other?” The detective asked.

“Until our senior year. We both left for separate colleges.”

“At what point were the two of you romantically involved?” The detective took a sip of coffee. Perhaps at his own embarrassment having to ask the difficult question.

April looked a little shocked. “You mean when did we start sleeping together?” The detective nodded. “I don’t know...I guess it was sometime in our junior year. Summertime if I recall. I don’t know how this is relevant.” April was trying to be mad but she was just too exhausted. She wished her sister was here to help her.

"I understand Mrs. Bander. Some of these questions will seem difficult. I apologize for that. "So you two became sexually active sometime in 1993 is that correct?" April nodded. "Please answer with yes or no so I don't misunderstand your body language." The detective said. Often times transcripts or tapes were played for a jury and not video footage so a jury would be unable to decipher a nod. The room was both videotaped and recorded.

"Yes, we became sexually active in 1993. Can we move on please?" April took a sip of water. The detective took note.

The detective cleared his throat and scratched notes onto the legal pad. "Did you practice safe sex?"

April looked aghast. "Did I ...Oh I see where this is going. You think because that girl was Michael's kid, that maybe she was *our* kid..." April looked perturbed. "I don't think so. You're barking up the wrong tree Detective. Michael and I have never had a kid."

"Have you ever given birth?"

"No!" April said angrily.

"So back to my question; did you practice safe sex?" The detective asked.

April looked bewildered. She cupped her head into her hands and slumped to the table with her head in her arms. “Yes we practiced safe sex.” She said with her face toward the table.

“Mrs. Bander, I can’t hear you when your face is toward the table. Can you please repeat that for me?”

April looked up from the table. “Yes, we practiced safe sex. He always wore a condom unless I was blowing him. Is that enough information for you?” April was getting tired. When she got tired, she was grouchy. He was about to find out that this was a bad time to be questioning her.

The detective scribbled some more. He slid out a manila file folder from under the legal pad. He opened it and produced a picture and slid it in front of her. The picture was of a young girl in her twenties maybe. The girl had brown curly hair and brown eyes. She had a great complexion. She was very beautiful. April stared at it for a moment. It almost looked like a picture of her when she was that age. Almost, but not exactly. The girl in the picture seemed to be a little more stylish and wore makeup. April didn’t wear makeup in her early twenties. “Do you recognize the girl in the photo?” The detective was watching her expressions closely. This is where he expected to find his answers. She looked at the picture a little too long. Perhaps she was reliving the past in her mind.

April shook her head and slid the picture back to the detective. “No. I’ve never seen her before.”

The detective nodded and slid the picture back into the file folder. He pulled out another one and laid it in front of her. “Do you recognize her now?”

April’s hand went up to her mouth and stifled a scream. She pushed the photo back to the detective right away. She was shaking her head. “Why are you showing that to me? Is that her? Is that the girl that died? You think I’ve seen her? Are you out of your fucking mind? I want to go home! I want out of here! You don’t put that in front of me! I don’t want to know.” April was crying and had her arms across her chest rocking herself back and forth. “I don’t want to know.” She said again.

The detective put his pen in his jacket and left the room for a moment and came back with a box of tissue and sat it in front of April. He had shown her a picture of Maria on the morgue table with the bullet wounds visible. Her reaction didn’t tell him much. He would have expected the same either way. If she had killed her, the memory and sight of the girl on a morgue table could easily be traumatizing. And if she didn’t, the idea that her husband may have put her there would be equally as traumatizing. April took a couple of tissues and dabbed at her cheeks.

“Mrs. Bander, I had to show you those pictures because…” Her reaction here was going to tell the whole story. He thought. “Because that girl was *your* daughter.”

April stopped her hand mid wipe and stared at the detective. Her mouth opened to speak and then closed again. She turned her head to the side and then back. Her face slowly formed a grin and she began to laugh uncontrollably. The detective's face went blank. That wasn't the reaction he was expecting. He picked up his coffee and took a long swig.

Chapter 29

Six hours is a long time. That's what Michael was thinking having stood in the water for that long. That's how long it took the police to call off their search. That's how long it took for Michael's body to look like a swollen prune. He didn't have to stay under water for the whole six hours. He only went under when boats would get in visual range of the area he was hiding in. In the six hours, he had been bitten by flies, nibbled on by fish, and had the pleasant experience of seeing a water snake and two turtles close up. Very close up. All those things couple with the fact he was being hunted like he was number one on the FBI's most wanted list, kept his heart beating like a rabbit on a six hour energy drink. In six hours he had a lot of time to think. He thought about April, about the dead girl, and about drowning himself in the river. He decided there was something about standing neck deep in a river while police searched the whole city for you that really placed a bleak perspective on life. Drowning in the river suddenly didn't seem like such a bad idea. He pushed the thoughts away. He wouldn't go out that way. He wanted, no he needed April and his family to know that he didn't do this. That was all that mattered to him now. He didn't even care if the rest of the town saw him as guilty, he just wanted them to know that he wasn't...then he could drown himself in the river. But now, darkness had fallen, the sound of boat motors had all but drifted off into the distance, and search lights were no longer bouncing along the shores. Michael decided that it was time. He lowered himself into the water and out from under the branches that concealed him.

Michael was happy to be out of the water. Well, happy wasn't exactly a good word to describe a man who was on the run from the law and wanted for murder. But he was highly uncomfortable in the water and now he was less uncomfortable now that he was out. Well, that might not be exactly correct either he thought as he leaned over in the grass and flipped his hair violently back and forth getting all the excess water out. Because now he was wet and his clothes were going to chafe his skin.

Michael took off his shirt and rung it out. At least he wasn't in need of a bath, he thought, as he put his shirt back on. There's always a silver lining...Michael had come out of the water at the exact place he had gone in. He decided it was the least likely place they would be looking for him and he knew the area enough to make his way around in the dark.

Michael took a step toward the trail in the woods that would lead him back out and into the park. His shoes made squishing sounds with each step that he took. His wet overalls were already starting to chafe at his skin. Still having no underwear on, he had no way to keep himself protected. But he did have a plan. He was wide awake and had lots of energy. He was sure the cops wouldn't be feeling the same way after the long day in the sun. They would be going home to crash so they could get up early and continue their search. If he was ever going to have a semi-safe chance at getting some clothes and food, now was going to be the best time.

Michael knew he was going to draw enough attention to himself as it was being all wet. He figured that at this time of night, there wasn't going to be many people shopping at the local Walmart. And Walmart had a self checkout lane that he might get through quickly. It was the best plan he had. Get in and get out. The biggest obstacle was that it was nearly two miles away. That's twenty minutes if he ran there. He figured a guy running in overalls might attract too much attention even in the dark, so he set off on foot, taking his time.

The night had begun to cool and a nice breeze had settled in. This would have normally felt good except for his wet clothes. It gave him a bit of a chill but his clothes began to dry as he walked. He started thinking about Becca and what she had said to him about having a kid. *DNA tests don't lie Michael...* Was this some kind of bluff by the investigators? It didn't make sense. Why would they make that assumption? And if they didn't make that assumption, how could he possibly have a kid much less have dug her up on his property? Michael shook his head as he walked. None of it made any sense.

He'd only slept with a few girls in his whole life. There was April in high school. Then he went to college. He had gone to a couple of parties. He had met a few girls. But even in his four years at college, he had only slept with maybe six girls and he wore a condom with all of them. None of them had ever said anything about being pregnant. After college he had started off as a substitute teacher and worked various odd jobs until a full time teaching position had opened up at the school. He had been in two long relationships and dated a few girls in between. The girl's arm had to belong to maybe an older teenager or a young adult. If the girl was fifteen years old, then that would have put her being born when he was about twenty. He didn't start having sex until he was sixteen. So if the child really was his, there was only a logical four year window in which that could have been possible. Michael started checking them off in his mind. He dated April until he was a senior, that accounts for two... "What the he..." A large dog ran out of a yard right toward him snapping and barking. The dog had just about reached Michael but hit the end of his chain and fell backward with a yelp. Michael darted backward a little and continued walking. The dog about gave him a heart attack. *How ironic that would be*. He thought. *Evaded police, but killed by a dog...*Michael chuckled to himself but kept on walking.

Michael was beginning to notice a stinging sensation in his leg. It was throbbing like he had been cut. He looked down and was able to see a blood stain on his overalls. Either he scratched it against a sharp rock while diving into the water, or he had been grazed by the officer's bullet. Whatever the case, he didn't want an infection and he was going to need some bandages at the store. Michael picked up his pace.

Two yards up there was a slight glimmer in the lamplight coming from the street. As Michael approached the object, he saw it was a small boy's bicycle. Michael, not wanting to break some kid's heart hesitated, but then backtracked and snatched the bike. *I hope your parents have money kid.* He thought as he set out on the bike. He could get there five times faster and evade capture much easier. The bike was a good idea. As he pedaled the bike, his thoughts drifted back to high school and then college. He decided there were only two girls he had slept with in the first two years of college. He had been kind of a book nerd and kept to himself. He hadn't really started to make friends and get involved until his junior year in college. The two girls from the first two years he had seen walking around on campus and in a couple of classes over the subsequent years. None of them appeared pregnant, nor had they said anything to him hinting at the idea. Not to mention, no broken condoms. There was only about a one percent chance... Michael began slowing the bike down. *The broken condoms...* Michael had never had one break... but he suddenly remembered one falling off and him not catching it until afterwards. It wasn't with either of the college girls. It was with April. It was the summer after graduation. Right before they went their separate ways. They had gone camping. It was dark. They'd had a couple of drinks. Michael didn't know until afterward. He never did say anything; he just hoped they had gotten lucky, or that maybe the spermacide from the condom prevented anything from happening. He hadn't seen April for two years after that. He had bumped into her when they were both back on summer break.

It was a little awkward and they didn't really spend much time reminiscing. *What if April had gotten pregnant that day? Is it possible? What if she had a child?* And if she had a child then it must have been...Michael stopped the bike dead in its tracks. His heart was beating a million times a minute as he began to put the pieces together. The condom that fell off. Their getting back together. Her wanting to buy *that* specific house, and her betrayal at the park... "Oh God!" Michael said outloud. He felt sick to his stomach. "Oh no...Oh April, what have you done?" Michael suddenly felt woozy. He leaned against the handle bars to keep from falling over. *What have I gotten myself into?* Michael thought as the full gravity of his situation came crashing down on him.

Chapter 30

Detective James stared perturbed. He was tired, agitated, and wanted to go home. And this lady was wasting his time. She had been laughing hysterically for over five minutes now. The detective looked at the clock, picked up his coffee and felt that it was empty. He looked back at April who was laughing so hard tears had begun to roll down her cheeks. She began slapping the table like she had just heard the funniest joke in her life.

Detective James pocketed his pen, grabbed his empty cup and got up and walked out of the room. He went around the corner and into the waiting area. The flat screen television that hung from the ceiling was playing an old episode of Seinfeld. George Castanza was pretending to be a Marine Biologist to impress a girl. They were on a date at the beach when they came upon a beached whale. Someone hollers into the crowd "Is anyone here a Marine Biologist?" Detective James chuckled. He didn't get to watch television all that much. Even with a low crime rate, his workload was always knee deep and months overdue. The rare times he did get to take a break, he often found himself in front of a good episode of Seinfeld.

The detective grabbed the pot of coffee. A new batch had been brewed. *Probably Doc*. He thought. Doc would have known it was going to be a late night and it's just the generous kind of thing he would remember to do. The detective sat down for a moment on the couch and sipped at his coffee. George was explaining to Seinfeld about his botched date. He held up a golf ball that had been found plugging the whale's air hole. Cramer looked around trying not to give away his guilt of having previously been hitting golf balls out into the ocean. The detective took a sip and let out a long sigh. Sometimes when things were getting complicated or fuzzy, the best thing he could do was separate himself from the confusion and clear his head. Let it all drift away. He pulled out his cell phone and checked it for messages. A text had come in that they had run out of light and had called off the search. Everyone was being sent home to rest and regroup for the long day tomorrow of dragging the river for a corpse. The detective stood up shaking his head. He took another sip of coffee and headed back into the interrogation room.

April had calmed down and was sitting quietly with her chin on her clasped hands. She had tissues bunched in-between them. She had a smirk on her face and shook her head as the detective entered.

Detective James sat down and set his coffee out in front of him. He noted that his notes and photographs had remained unscathed. It was another interrogators trick. Leave behind evidence that can easily be replaced such as a photograph. In the event a suspect loses control and destroys it by crinkling it up or shredding it, it gives the interrogator a charge to hold them on. Tampering with evidence. Never leave behind a writing instrument as the suspects were able to use them as a weapon. He had read about cases in the past where a detective or two had made that mistake and it had cost them their life. An ink pen to the throat wasn't any less dangerous than a knife. "Are you done?" He asked April. April looked up at him and nodded. Then shook her head in disgust despite the smile that remained on her face. "What is it you think is so funny? Why are you shaking your head?" The detective asked.

April looked toward the wall and back at the detective. "I'm laughing because you guys are idiots. And I'm laughing at myself for having believed your ridiculous story about Michael having a kid."

"Mrs. Bander, I don't know if you are familiar with how a DNA test works, but it doesn't lie. That girl in the photo is your child...and Michael's." The detective said calmly.

Mrs. Bander's expression melted back into a smile. For a moment the detective thought she may break out in laughter again. "See this is what's so funny Detective. I had convinced myself that you were a nice guy...and a smart guy...that you might actually be able to help us..." April looked away for a moment and tried to hold back bursting into tears. She looked back at the detective. "But here I am, a physical and emotional mess; exhausted beyond belief. And you have had me woken up and dragged down here to your little interrogation room to feed me a bunch of crap!" April was jabbing her finger downward at the table. "And now I find out that everything you've been telling me all along is a lie?" She looked away and then back at the detective who looked a little shocked. He had thought her laughing was going to be an admission to guilt and being found out. "And I..." Tears began to rage down her cheeks and voice began to get crackly "I..." She sniffled and was trying hard to hold her composure. She began jabbing at the table again. "I betrayed the man I love because I believed your lies. And now he might be dead, and it's all my fault..." April buried her head into her arms and bawled. The detective looked at the clock. He was nowhere near getting an admission of guilt. Even worse, the girl looked as if she really believed what she was saying. The detective looked at the clock again, sighed, and leaned back in his chair and sipped on his coffee. He wasn't sure how he was going to proceed from here.

Chapter 31

Michael sat up on the bike and got back in control of his thoughts and emotions. He needed to talk to her. He just didn't know how. He couldn't do it now. Not sitting on a bike in the middle of the sidewalk, still wet, and very hungry.

Michael took off on the bike pedaling fast for the store. He had to pull off into three different yards on the way there to avoid being seen by passing cars. He coasted along the edge of the parking lot and parked the bike on the side of the building.

The ride over had dried most of the clothes he was wearing. He was only slightly damp now. Unless his face was all over the news, he should remain fairly inconspicuous. He wasn't taking any chances. He kept his head down all the way into the store and disappeared into the clothing section. He knew what sizes he needed. He found two pairs of jeans on sale, a white polo shirt, and a large t-shirt with a design of a tiger on the front.

Michael found an empty cart nearby and swiped it. He put in the clothes and added a pack of boxer briefs, socks, and shoes. He did all this in less than three minutes. It was the fastest clothes shopping he had ever done. It kind of felt good. He thought. He'd always hated shopping for clothes.

Michael quickly made his way over to the deodorant section. He threw in a speed stick gel, a toothbrush and toothpaste, medical tape, bandages, rubbing alcohol, triple antibiotic ointment, a razor, and shaving cream. He wasn't going to get anywhere with anybody if he *looked* like a crook. He figured he'd been in here five minutes. He hadn't yet run into anyone, but he didn't want to linger. He looked down at his cart. It suddenly occurred to him that he didn't have a car to load all this stuff in. He quickly made his way over near the purses and luggage and found a whole aisle of backpacks. He chose the cheapest and largest black backpack he could find and threw it in the cart. Seven minutes.

Michael swung by the jewelry section and found the sunglasses rack. The more he could disguise himself tomorrow, the better. He tried on four pairs and looked in the mirror before finding a pair he could live with. Nine minutes. He darted toward the electronics. On his way there he passed the stationary aisle and added a notebook and two black pens. He passed a couple of shoppers on the way to the electronics but tried to look as inconspicuous as he could. In a small town like this it is highly likely to run into someone who knows you at the local Walmart. Nobody stopped him. Nobody hollered out his name. Twelve minutes. He kept on moving.

Now to the prepaid cell phones. One or two? Michael's funds were limited. He wasn't sure how long he would be on the run for, but he needed to make the money last. He was only going to be able to make one or two calls on a cell phone and then he would have to pitch it or they would use it to track him.

He decided one phone was all he needed for now. He threw the cheapest one into the cart and moved on to the food section. Fifteen minutes.

Michael passed some more shoppers. He was beginning to panic. Somebody is going to notice. Somebody will know...He made it to the food aisle. He made his way to the plastic cup section and picked out a small box of assorted silverware. Then after visiting the soap aisle and grabbing a bar of ivory, he trucked on over to the bread aisle and snagged two loaves of bread. Another aisle over, he found a jar of peanut butter. Eighteen minutes. He was now risking too much time. He had to get out. Michael pushed his cart quickly toward the front of the store. He passed back through the men's clothing section and stopped suddenly. He backed up a couple of steps. A hat section. Michael spotted a Yankees hat that matched the clothes he had bought and threw it in the cart. He sped on up to the self checkout. There were four of them available and they were all vacant. There was a girl with a spray bottle cleaning the equipment. She looked up as he approached and nodded. Michael didn't recognize her and she didn't give him a second look. Michael hit the start button and began feeding his things through the scanner and into the bags. Michael was just about done when the scanner wouldn't pick up the tag on the backpack. He scanned and scanned. Shit. The girl was beginning to notice that he was having trouble and was about to come over when the machine finally beeped and rang it through. Michael shoved it in the bag and scanned the last two items.

The machine gave a total of eighty three dollars and sixty four cents. Michael dug into his pocket for the cash he had taken from the police officers when suddenly it occurred to him that he hadn't gotten anything to drink. He looked to the left and spotted a cooler at the front of the registers. He darted over to it and took out four bottles of water and a Mountain Dew. He didn't want warm soda for later, but a cold Mountain Dew would hit the spot and give him enough juice to make it back home. Home. Michael shook his head at the thought. What a joke. There was no home. Michael shut the cooler door and snagged a few snickers bars on the way back to the self checkout. He fed all the items through and dipped back into his pocket for the cash. He needed Ninety-two dollars and twenty-six cents. He had folded the money up nicely but when he pulled it out it was damp. He looked at the machine. Shit again. He took a twenty and tried to feed it into the machine but it wouldn't even get started in. It just kept scrunching up. Michael turned to look for the girl but she was right there by the time he had turned around.

"Are you having trouble getting it to go in?" The girl asked. She had red hair and chubby cheeks. She seemed nice.

"Uh..ya. I guess I sweat too much. Money's all damp." Michael handed the girl five wet twenties.

She took the twenties and tried to feed them through with no success. Finally she went behind her little counter and flipped a switch that made her light flash. Michael kept his bloodstained leg strategically pointed away from her so she wouldn't see the hole or the red stain that threatened to give him away. Another employee was walking quickly toward them. She was older than the one helping him and wore glasses. She looked like a manager. The lady approached the girl and Michael. Her name tag said Kathy on it. She didn't look like the cheerful type. Michael tried to look away but was afraid he would look more suspicious looking the other direction. He looked back toward the two cashiers.

"What's up Cynthia?" Kathy said to the younger clerk.

"The machine won't take the money. It's a little damp. Can you trade them out for other twenties?" The girl asked.

The manager took the cash. She glanced up at Michael to give him a dirty look for having to go all the way back to the front register when she paused and her expression gave way to recognition. Shit a third time. Michael's heart about stopped there in his chest. The Manager's face about went pale and then she nodded and her countenance was suddenly polite. "I'll be right back with some fresh twenties." She smiled at Michael and then rushed off, looking back once over her shoulder.

Michael hadn't recognized her but she had recognized him. Quadruple shit. That meant he was all over the news. Not good news for him. He grabbed his bags and looked at the cashier. "You know, I don't really need the change. You can just keep it." Michael said as he strode past her.

"Oh sir, we can't accept tips. She'll only be a moment." The girl said.

Michael waved her off. "It's ok. Just stick it in a donation jar or something." And he headed out the doors. Michael figured he had about forty-five seconds before the manager completed her call and about five minutes before the police arrived. Unless they were already in the area in which case he was screwed.

Michael quickly took out the book bag and unzipped it. He pushed in two of the three bags of stuff he had just bought but the bread wouldn't fit. He quickly tied the bag the bread was in to a loop on the back of the backpack. Michael zipped it up and threw it on over his shoulders. He grabbed the bike and blasted off into the parking lot. It was going to take him about eight or nine minutes to get to the house he had stayed at the previous night.

Michael got to the end of the parking lot and was just about to cross the highway when flashing lights were moving his direction fast. Two cars turned into the parking lot and drove right past him no more than ten feet away and continued on to the front of the store. Michael looked back shaking his head. He bolted full force across the road. He had just been given an extra minute. Two tops. It still wasn't enough time. It will have registered with the cops when the manager tells them that he had left that it may have been him that they passed coming in. They'll know he's on a bike and wearing a backpack.

Michael stuck to the streets for the next minute and a half. It's strange how a minute and a half can seem like an hour when you are on the run. Going back seemed much easier than the trip there. The ground was slightly elevated and it sloped downward now so Michael made great time. He looked back over his shoulder and saw headlights about four or five blocks behind him. They were going slow and they had a search light. Damn that was fast. He thought.

Michael took a side street and cut down an alley in-between streets. He considered ditching the bike but decided against it. He was only about half a mile away now. Just another quarter mile, then ditch the bike. Michael was afraid if they found the bike, it may give them a reason to start snooping around. He didn't want that right where he was going to be sleeping. He needed a peaceful, stress free night of rest so he could start off the next morning with a clear head. Tomorrow, he was going to solve the case. One way or another. He was determined. And when Michael Bander was determined, he accomplishes things.

Another minute passed and Michael skidded to a stop near a dumpster and parked the bike alongside somebody's garage where they had a couple of lawnmowers, bikes, and other outdoor gadgets stored. It was a small hoarding pile and the bike fit in naturally. Michael parked it and looked back over his shoulder. No lights, no sounds. He doubted that they had given up, but they didn't know where he was headed and there were too many streets and not enough officers.

Michael walked the last half mile in peace and quiet, alone with his thoughts. He needed to confirm his suspicions. He would try and contact April tomorrow. He loved her. That much he knew. But could he forgive her if she had lied to him? What if she had committed murder? Even worse, what if she had committed murder against *their* child that he hadn't even known about? Was keeping a child a secret enough of a reason? Michael shook his head. He didn't even want to think about it. This just didn't make sense. This wasn't the April he knew. This wasn't the woman he fell in love with. No. He was pretty good at knowing good people from the bad. One thing being a teacher had taught him was looking into those eyes and into the soul and knowing where the trouble was going to come from before it even began.

Troubled souls needed the most help and the most attention. Michael had made great influences on many kids that may have otherwise chosen a different path. They knew it too. Many of them wrote him regularly to tell him how much he had helped them. So, Michael just knew there must be another logical explanation. Tomorrow. He thought. He must get to the bottom of this tomorrow. Or risk being on the run forever. Michael walked around the corner of the garage he'd stayed in the night before. He was so lost in thought that he didn't pay any attention to the light coming from within. Michael turned the doorknob and walked right in to an occupied garage.

Chapter 32

Detective James stared vacantly across the table. He was grooming his mustache with his left hand. Some people twirled pens with their fingers, others drummed their fingers across the table, Detective James groomed his mustache. It put him in think mode. But exhaustion had set in and he was beginning to space out more than he was thinking. Usually, when it came to a suspect he knew to be guilty or most likely guilty, it always became a waiting game. He would usually keep them in the room until the suspect was so exhausted, irritable, and uncomfortable, they would confess just to get out of the damn room and that painful wooden chair. Something was bothering him about this case though and he just couldn't put his finger on it. It would flow through his subconscious, nuzzle right up to the edge of his brain threatening to pop across like a light bulb revealing some new piece of the puzzle that his conscious had not picked up on just yet. But because he was so damn tired, whatever it was would get close, and then it would drift away before it had a chance to make itself known. The detective sat there shaking his head.

April had crossed her arms and put her face down sideways apparently lost in her own world. She could feel the weight of the detective's stare bearing down upon her. She ignored it anyway. She began to notice that the chair she was sitting on must be made out of some hardwood like walnut or cherry. Her butt went from falling asleep, to stinging, to the throbbing mode which it was in now. She lifted her head and eyeballed the detective. "Well...?" She said.

"Well what?" The detective stopped grooming his mustache and put his arm down.

"Are you going to charge me?"

"Charge you with what?" The detective asked.

"Murder, obstruction of justice, or something?"

"Which one do you think I should charge you with?" The detective asked.

"I could really care less at this point Detective. Do what you need to do and get me out of this damn room. If you're not charging me, then I'm going home."

"Actually Mrs. Bander, we can hold you up to twenty four hours before we charge you. So I'm afraid you're stuck here unless you have something else you would like to tell us that would clear this whole thing up." The detective said and drew the last sip remaining of his coffee. April put her head back down on her arms. "Why don't you tell me about the kid Mrs. Bander?" The detective asked. "I know you gave birth. I know you gave birth to twins. And I know where you left them. The story was in the paper. Your DNA and Michael's DNA match the girl's. So let's quit with this ridiculous charade and you can start by telling me what happened." The detective glanced up at the clock and back at April. He was going to need some more coffee. That much he was sure of.

April lifted her head up from the table. "I thought you were a detective, Detective."

"Ya, so what's your point?" The detective lifted his coffee cup, remembered it was empty and set it back down again.

"How old was the girl in the photograph?"

The detective smiled. "Twenty one years old. But you already know that don't you Mrs. Bander?"

"So I'm thirty five. That means I would have given birth when I was fourteen. That means I would have gotten pregnant when I was thirteen. But I never even had sex until I was sixteen. You see where I'm going with this Detective?"

"I see where you're trying to go with this Mrs. Bander. But you're not looking at things from my side of the table."

"Well enlighten me Detective."

"The DNA tests are 99 % conclusive that the girl belongs to you and Michael. Michael was found with the body. You both own the property she was buried on. The girl was twenty one years old. Now according to the CSI's here in this building, and I've got to tell you Mrs. Bander, they are damn good at their job and way overqualified, and according to what they are telling me about the DNA match, there is a ninety nine percent chance that you are lying to me right now. Mrs. Bander, the evidence is telling me that there is a ninety-nine percent likelihood that you gave birth to that girl twenty one years ago. So forgive me Mrs. Bander if I don't believe that you began having intercourse at age sixteen." The detective said bluntly.

"Ok, if I was pregnant, then you should be able to find some record of it. Doctor bills, parents, teachers, photos. How many people have you spoken to, to confirm your theory Detective?" April asked.

The detective looked her in the eyes. "None yet Mrs. Bander. We were hoping you would be forthcoming with the truth and that it wouldn't be necessary. But yes, speaking to your relatives, friends, and teachers is what we will be doing over the next couple of weeks."

"Well, you can't hold me for the next couple of weeks. So why not just let me go home?"

"Mrs. Bander, I don't think you quite understand the gravity of your situation. You see, we can only hold you for twenty-four hours without charging you. The DA will likely charge you tomorrow with murder, conspiracy to commit a crime, obstruction of justice, or some other charge. Either way, you're not likely to be going home anytime soon."

"How have I obstructed justice?" April asked wild eyed.

"Because you're still lying about giving birth!"

"I'M NOT LYING!" April screamed at the detective. "Isn't there any test you can do to tell if I've given birth?"

The detective was silent for a moment. "If you are willing to submit to a gynecological exam and x-rays, I'm sure that would help your case if you really are telling the truth." The detective said.

April hesitated for a moment. She looked vacantly at the wall and then back at the detective. "Fine. I'll do it."

The detective smiled. He was going to get some sleep after all.

Chapter 33

Michael's heart was about ready to blow up inside his chest it was beating so hard. He had been so focused on getting away and then so lost in thought that he had walked right into an occupied garage. There was a man sitting at a workbench in front of him. There was a long florescent light over the bench that lit up about a six foot area surrounding it.

The man had brown hair that hung down to his shoulders. He was holding up what looked to be an rc car or radio controlled car. He had it balanced carefully in his left hand and was studying carefully, trying to add something with his right. He never even glanced toward Michael. Michael's heart had started to slow a little and his adrenaline levels started to go down. He turned around and grasped the doorknob. He thought if he could make it inside unnoticed, he may be able to make it back out that way as well. Michael winced and turned the knob.

"You're not leaving on my account I hope." The man with the brown hair spoke to him.

"I..I...must have walked into the wrong place. Sorry about that." Michael said with his hand still on the door knob.

"No. No, I'm pretty sure this is the right place. It's where you slept last night is it not?" The man asked.

Michael released his grasp on the doorknob and turned around. The man still hadn't even looked in his direction. He was still staring at the object in front of him. "I'm sorry. I needed a place to stay. I'll be on my way."

"Don't be silly Michael. They are looking for you. I think you know that." The man said. "Pull up a seat. Stay a while." The man took his eyes off his work and nodded toward a stool that was near him.

Michael hesitated, then pulled the stool back a little and sat down on it. He slung his backpack to the floor. "You know who I am?" Michael asked incredulously.

"Of course. You are Michael Bander. Biology Teacher. Wanted for the murder of a young girl."

"I didn't kill any girl!" Michael rattled off a little too fast.

"I'm sure you didn't. But it's not me you need to convince now is it?"

"So you believe me?" Michael asked.

"Of course. But what I believe is irrelevant now isn't it?" The man looked at Michael and then back at the rc car.

Michael thought for a moment. "Not to me it isn't. I haven't got too many supporters out there if you know what I mean."

"You have more than you know." The man said.

"What do you mean? How do you know me?" Michael asked.

"I've had two kids in your biology class. I'm not sure that my son and daughter have ever agreed on anything before. But they've just agreed on one thing...."

"What's that?" Michael asked.

"That you are the best teacher that they've ever had in their lives and that you could not have done what they say you have." The man with the long brown hair looked back into Michael's eyes and then back at his work again. "And both of my kids are very intelligent and intuitive Mr. Bander. If they say you're innocent, I'm inclined to believe them."

Michael's eyes began to well up with tears. Not just because someone out there believed him to be innocent, but because of the sudden realization that maybe he was making a difference out there. Maybe he was touching the hearts of his young students. Michael turned his head and wiped away a tear. "Tell them thank you for me." Michael said.

"You can stay as long as you need to. My family doesn't know you are out here and I would prefer to keep it that way. I'll leave you the keys to my car. After everyone leaves tomorrow, you may take it and do what you need to do. I'll wait until the following morning to report it stolen in case you decide to keep going."

"Why are you doing this for me? Don't you even want to ask me if I did it?" Michael asked.

The man looked over at him. "Have you been able to convince the police you didn't do it?" The man asked. His light brown eyes peering deep into Michael's soul.

Michael looked ashamed. "Well...no."

"Then what would be the point in me asking if you haven't even been able to convince the police?" The man returned to his work. He sat the car down on the bench and put the cover over it. It was quite remarkable. "And I'm helping you because it's the right thing to do. If you are innocent, then I'm helping an innocent man. If you are guilty, then I would only be causing harm to my family to call in law enforcement. One, because my kids respect you, and two, because knowing a man wanted for murder was sleeping in our garage may prevent them from getting another peaceful night's sleep ever. They would always be thinking, wondering, and worrying, if there might be a murderer hiding out in the garage. So you see, if I turned you in, I could be jeopardizing any chance they have of feeling safe and secure each night as they crawled into bed. But make no mistake, if my family comes to harm, the law will be the last thing you have to worry about."

Michel nodded. He understood. "Thank you for letting me stay."

"You're welcome. The keys to the car are on the counter. Don't take it until after nine in the morning when everyone has left. I'll walk to work in the morning so nobody will know the car is gone but me." Michael nodded. "There is a plate of food for you upstairs, a blanket and pillow, and a bucket with a bag inside it in case you need to use the restroom. If you do, take the bag out with you in the morning and pitch it in the trash."

"Thank you again." Michael said. "But how did you know I was here?"

"It's a man's job to know what's going on in his household. I've got silent alarms and cameras. And there's only one man on the run in Angel Falls that I am aware of. That makes you the most likely intruder to camp out in my garage." The man got up and turned out the light. "Good luck tomorrow Mr. Bander. You're going to need it."

"Thank you." Michael said as the man headed out the door. Michael picked up his backpack and turned and found where the pull down cord was for the stairs into the loft. The light from the outside lamps flooded through the garage door windows and gave him just enough light to see. Michael climbed the stairs and into the loft and closed the ladder. He really hoped he wasn't walking into a trap. Michael expected to see police lights or hear sirens at any moment but none came. Why was this man being so nice to him? Michael just didn't understand. There was just enough light coming in the upstairs window that Michael could see a blanket and pillow laid out on the floor for him. There was a flashlight next to it that he grabbed and flipped on carefully. He found the plate of food. It was covered tightly in saran wrap. There was a large pork chop, mashed potatoes, corn, and a fork. No knife. Michael chuckled at that and opened the wrap and dug in. He suddenly felt like he was starving. His nerves had kept his hunger at bay for most of the evening. But now he was starting to calm down and his hunger had returned with a vengeance. He couldn't remember the last time food had tasted so good. It was cold, but Michael didn't care. He ate it all and sat back feeling content for the first time in days. It seemed like years.

Michael opened his backpack and took out some of his supplies. He hunted around with the flashlight until he found a shallow metal pan. Michael took off his clothes. He ripped his shirt down into a few rags. He took the water bottle and soaked the first rag and used it to clean out the metal pan that was covered in dust. Then he set the pan down and emptied the contents of his water bottle into it. Michael grabbed the soap he had purchased and another rag. He dipped the rag into the water and lathered it up lightly with the soap. He scrubbed his face, arm pits, and his wound thoroughly with the soapy rag. He then used another rag to rinse himself off and wrung it out into the pan. Dried blood had formed around the wound. Michael studied it carefully with the flashlight. There was still some wet blood, but for the most part, he had stopped bleeding. He didn't think he was going to need stitches. The bandage and tape should do fine. Michael scrubbed up the dried blood until it was gone. He treated the wound with rubbing alcohol which about made him cry out in pain. Michael bit down on his fist and waited for the burn to subside before adding triple antibiotic ointment, a bandage, and pulling it all together with the medical tape. He felt good. He felt clean. Michael tossed on his clean t-shirt and shorts and lay back on the bed. He drifted off to sleep with a smile only a good meal and clean, dry clothes could have brought him under the circumstances. Michael slept well despite his reoccurring dream that always took him to the same place where he had first kissed April by the river in the amusement park. And every time it ended with him holding a pretty little girl in his arms whom had just been shot. Michael spoke her name over and over while tossing and turning in his sleep. "Maria."

Chapter 34

Detective James had gone back to his house and managed to get a good night's sleep. He awoke feeling refreshed and awake. He had sent Mrs. Bander back to the station to be held overnight. He had left instructions that the physical exams and x-rays were to be performed first thing in the morning. The detective got dressed and headed down to the diner for some breakfast. He didn't eat out every morning, but whenever he was on a stubborn case, he found a good breakfast and coffee at the diner gave him some thinking time and an opportunity to fit the pieces together. It always began the same way. He would order two eggs over medium, two pieces of bacon, hash browns, water, and a coffee.

The detective was sitting in the same booth he always chose when it was available. Back to the wall. Eyes toward the door. He had already placed his order and was sipping on his coffee and flipping through the newspaper. Michael Bander was on the front page. They had a picture of him they had gotten from the school and a photograph of Mrs. Bander answering her door. They had only reported that a body had been found. The girl's name had not yet been disclosed as they had not yet contacted her family. Her family...the detective thought about that for a moment. According to her sister, she was all the family she had left. Except for the parents that they had never met. Obviously they were already informed of their own daughter's death. Still, with this all over the news, why hasn't the girl's sister come forward? He had tried to contact her for months but her number had been disconnected, she had quit her job, and she had moved out of her apartment. Nothing. And she was an eye witness. They were going to need her to testify that it was Michael that had abducted them. The detective sipped his coffee and wondered if the sister was even still alive. Eye witness...

The waitress approached and served his breakfast. About that time CSI Dr. Crane came through the door. Detective James had asked him to join him for some coffee and bring the morning's test results with him. The DA Cheryl Johnson stepped inside after him. They both sat themselves across the table from him. The detective nodded to each of them. "Cheryl. Doc."

"Good morning Detective." Cheryl said. "Started without us I see."

"Well if I had known you were coming Cheryl, I would have started much sooner."

The DA smiled. "Touché."

The waitress approached the table. "May I get anything for you?" She asked nicely.

"Just a coffee for me please." Dr. Crane said politely.

"I'll have a cinnamon roll and a coffee as well please." The DA said. The waitress scribbled the orders into her notebook and darted off. The DA looked up at the detective. "Did you get some sleep last night?"

Detective James smiled. "A full eight hours. You believe it?"

"Doc filled me in last night about the DNA. He said you had the wife in custody?" The DA decided to skip the banter and get right to it.

The detective shoveled a forkful of eggs into his mouth and followed it with a bite of toast. He nodded.

"Well, I guess you must have obtained a confession if you managed to get eight hours of sleep." The DA said.

The detective wiped his mouth with his napkin and took a long draw on his coffee. "I'm sorry, is that a question?" The detective asked picking up his bacon. Doc chuckled. The waitress stopped by and unloaded two cups of coffee and the DA's cinnamon roll. The DA took a bite of cinnamon roll while attempting to stare down the detective.

The detective shoved his last piece of bacon into his mouth and chased it with some coffee. "No confession." He said. "She still claims she hasn't given birth. She agreed to an exam and x-ray this morning. DNA says it's hers. She's got to be lying. What do you think Doc?" The detective asked while attempting to juggle another forkful of egg to his mouth.

"I'm afraid the girl is telling the truth." Doc said. "She has already completed the tests, and I've been informed that both doctors would testify in court that Mrs. Bander has never given birth naturally, or otherwise."

The detective's eggs unbalanced and fell back to his plate. He looked incredulously across the table at the doc as if he had just told him the sky was pink. "What about cesarean Doc. Couldn't she have delivered by c-section?" The detective asked.

"That would fall into the 'otherwise' category. No, unless she has undergone major reconstructive surgery, the girl never gave birth." Dr. Crane tore open a few packets of sugar and a couple of creamers and added them to his coffee.

"Impossible." The detective said.

The DA swallowed another piece of her cinnamon roll. "Doc, how can the evidence both say the victim is 99.9 percent her daughter and yet say that she never had a child at the same time?" She asked.

The detective's eyes lit up as if a switch had been turned on. "They had a surrogate..."

"Yes." Dr. Crane said as he pointed his finger at the detective. "That is the only explanation for the conflicting evidence..."

"I feel a but coming on here." The DA said stabbing her fork into her cinnamon roll.

"Very intuitive my dear. A big butt indeed. Mrs. Bander denies ever having a surrogate and is willing to take a lie detector test."

The detective's face went expressionless. He looked for a moment like he was going to drop his fork. After a few seconds, his color came back into his cheeks and he looked down at his plate and scooped up the remaining bits of egg that he had dropped earlier and shoveled them into his mouth followed by the last piece of toast and a long swig of coffee. He sat the cup down making a clicking sound and an "ahh" signaling satisfaction with the breakfast. He looked up at Dr. Crane. "So what do you think Doc? What the hell is going on here?"

"Well, there is only one explanation; she's lying about the surrogate. She's got to be." Dr. Crane said while pushing his glasses up on his nose.

"Give her the lie detector test. If she passes, let her go." The DA said.

The detective sat up in his seat. "Are you out of your mind? The husband's already on the run. We've got her DNA and it matches the vic. She either helped murder the girl, or helped cover it up!" The detective shot back a little too loud. Both the

DA and Doc looked around slightly embarrassed and hoping they hadn't been overheard.

"Detective, I understand your frustration," the DA began, "but I can't go to the jury with conflicting evidence. I can't put her on trial with evidence that she both had a kid and didn't have a kid. The case would be thrown out before it even began. So unless you want this girl to walk...find me something more... conclusive."

The detective sat back in his seat and turned his head focusing on something other than the DA. He was trying to swallow his frustrations and make sense of the new information.

Dr. Crane looked down at his coffee stirring it absentmindedly. Finally he looked back up at the detective. "Perhaps we'll make some progress with the husband when we get him." He said.

The detective looked at Dr. Crane and then at the DA. "You don't get it Doc. The same evidence that sets *that* girl free, exonerates *him* as well. If it wasn't *her* kid, then it reasons that it wasn't *his* kid either. And if it wasn't *his* kid, then we have no motive, no murder weapon, and no case."

"I'm afraid he's right." The DA said. "Even if you find Michael Bander, we can't charge him unless he confesses to the murder, knowing the girl, or admission of having a child. If he doesn't. He walks. Hell, he might walk anyway after this torture case comes to light. How are we coming along on that anyway?"

"Luke has the reins on this one." The detective said referring to his partner.

"Yes, we were finally able to get into Mr. Bander's messages. Your suspicions are correct Detective. Mr. Bander recorded a whole argument between the two officers about what had happened and how they were going to spin the story. I had the conversation printed out and gave Luke a copy this morning. He put out an arrest warrant right away." Dr. Crane said.

"You've got to be shitting me. Do you have any idea how bad this..." The DA turned her head sideways trying to get control before exploding in the diner. "I mean Jesus Christ! Do you realize that anybody who was arrested by those assholes are going to appeal their cases on grounds that they were tortured? I'll bet at least a couple dozen bad guys are back on the street by the end of next week!"

The detective and Dr. Crane exchanged glances. Both shook their heads solemnly. One thing was for certain, it was going to be a long week.

Chapter 35

April sat quietly in the interrogation room. She had been to the hospital where she was poked, prodded, and x-rayed. After she was done, she was ushered back to her cell where she no more than got seated and then she was ushered back to the CSI building where she submitted to a lie detector test. She expected to be taken back to lockup but had been placed back into the interrogation room instead. She was still in the same clothes and her hair was still a mess. She had finally moved on past embarrassment and humiliation and was now in the acceptance stage of her dilemma. She accepted that she was screwed. She accepted that Michael was screwed. They were both going to jail for something she doubted either one of them had anything to do with. How was she going to fight a DNA test? How could she? No, it was all over. She decided that the acceptance stage was nice. There was a lot less stress when you just let go and accept the inevitable. Even if it wasn't just. And it certainly wasn't just.

April was getting uncomfortable in the wooden chair. After a few more minutes she got up and moved to the floor and leaned back against the wall. She began to wonder about Michael. Where was he? Was he alive? Was he angry that she had betrayed him? April shook her head. Of course he would be angry. He had trusted her. The one person in the world he should have been able to depend on and what had she done? Possibly got him injured, or killed? April shook her head in disgust. She was too exhausted to do anymore crying. She had cried all night. She had small bouts of sleep but probably didn't add up to more than four hours. April reached up and rubbed at her eyes. She could feel the bags that had formed under them. She longed for a hot shower and comfy bed. The door to the room opened and Detective James walked in.

He walked in and looked at her on the floor. He plopped down on the floor adjacent to her and leaned back against the wall. "Sleep well?" He asked.

April gave him a look that said '*seriously?*' and looked away. Her arms were crossed in front of her.

"You know, I can't blame you for being mad at me. I would be mad at me too." The detective explained. April kept her gaze pointed in the opposite direction. "Look Mrs. Ba..April." April turned her head surprised he had actually called her by her first name. The detective looked sincere. Almost apologetic. "I have to look after her first. You know that don't you?" April didn't say anything. She stared blankly at him. "Suppose that girl was yours. What wouldn't you go through to find her killer? What wouldn't you do?"

April looked down into her lap. *You're my mommy silly*. In her mind's eye she was looking at the little girl with the ice cream cone.

"Now I don't know what's going on here," the detective continued, "I don't know why your DNA matches yet what you have told me is true."

April looked up at the detective. She guessed this meant that she had passed the lie detector test.

"But what I do know is that there is a young, beautiful, sweet girl who is no longer with us. She is calling out from her grave and begging for justice. And you know what worries me even more?" The detective asked April.

"What?" April said quietly. Looking up at the detective.

"That girl has a sister and her life is in danger." The detective said.

April nodded. "So what happens now?" She asked.

"Now, you go home. Your sister is waiting outside for you. She's been camped out in the parking lot all night. I think she has threatened each and every one of my CSI's that have come or gone from the building."

April smiled. She could picture Becca doing that. "What about Michael?" She asked.

"What about him?"

"Have you found him? Do you still believe he had anything to do with this?"

"I'm not going to lie to you," the detective began, "Michael isn't out of the woods yet. He was still found digging up the girl. He has a lot of explaining to do. We haven't found him yet but we know he is alive. He was spotted at Walmart last night."

April's eyes lit up at this. "He's alive?" She asked.

The detective nodded. "And still in good shape too. He managed to outrun all our officers again so he can't be hurt too bad."

April's eyes welled up with tears and she cupped her hand over her mouth. She had thought she had gotten him killed. She fought off the urge to reach over and hug the detective.

The detective stood up and held out his hand to help April up. She took his hand and he pulled her up to her feet. He walked her to the door and paused. He looked back at April. "You know you're not completely off the hook yet either until we have solved this. You know that don't you?" He asked.

April nodded. "I know."

The detective reached into his pocket and produced a business card. "In case you lost the last one." April took the card. "You call me if you find Michael or you hear anything that may help. He can't keep running. He's going to have to face this."

April nodded again and stepped through the door. She found her sister waiting in the lobby. Becca threw her arms around April. “Are you ok? They didn’t hurt you did they? Cause if they did I’ll…”

“They didn’t hurt me Becca. I’m fine.” April said. “I just want to go home and get some sleep.”

Becca nodded at her sister and put her arm around April’s waist and walked out the door.

Detective James watched them from the door as they got into Becca’s car and drove away.

“What now Detective?” Dr. Crane’s voice came from behind.

“Now we track the wife and see if she leads us to the husband…what else *can* we do?”

Chapter 36

Michael woke up with the slamming of car doors outside. For a moment he panicked thinking the police had come to get him. Then he remembered that most of the family took off in their vehicles about this time the previous day. Michael relaxed a little and untied the loaves of bread from his backpack. He pulled out two slices and a jar of peanut butter and used a plastic knife to spread it on. He folded each one in half and ate them like a taco. Not a bad breakfast under the circumstances. He knew that peanut butter and bread was the way to go. He could live off two loaves and a jar for nearly a week.

Michael reached into his pack and pulled out the Mountain Dew he had meant to drink yesterday before having to run from the police. It was going to be room temperature but he figured he could use the caffeine. He wasn't sure where he was going to go or what he was going to do. One thing was certain; he needed to speak to April.

Michael finished his breakfast and quickly changed into his jeans and white polo shirt. He wasn't sure if he'd be coming back here. He doubted it. He packed everything up into his bag. He pulled out his notebook and pen and wrote 'Thank You' on a sheet of paper and left it there for the man whom he had spoken to the night before. He stowed the paper and pen in his bag, zipped it up and threw it over his shoulder.

Michael climbed down the stairs and grabbed the keys the man had left for him on the counter. He eased the garage door open and peered outside. No police cars. No people. No sounds. There was a newer white Toyota Highlander sitting in the driveway. Michael hit the unlock button on the key fob to make sure the keys went to the Highlander. The SUV's lights flashed indicating that it had been unlocked. He closed the garage door behind him and quietly jumped into the SUV. He put the keys in the ignition and started the vehicle. Michael put the car in reverse and backed out of the driveway. He half expected a cop car to be waiting around the corner to pull him over but none came. He pulled up to a stop sign, reached over into his bag and pulled out the hat and sunglasses and put them on. He didn't want anybody recognizing him. Michael checked his look in the mirror and drove off satisfied that he would be able to get around without being recognized.

Michael wasn't sure where to go. He needed to call April. He was getting concerned that someone might recognize the vehicle he was driving and realize that the driver didn't match the owner. He couldn't afford any mistakes. Michael pulled onto highway 231 and headed out of town. Michael drove through two small towns before pulling over into a McDonald's parking lot and parked. He pulled out the prepaid cell phone. It came with a card and twenty minutes of talk time. He had to call a number to activate it. Michael read the directions thoroughly and had the phone activated in about ten minutes. He dialed April's number and waited for her to pick up...hoping that she would answer. The phone rang four times. It usually went to voicemail on the fifth ring. “Come on, come on…pick up.” Michael said to himself.

“Hello?” It wasn’t April. It was Becca. Oh great. Michael debated hanging up. He sat in silence for a moment trying to decide.

“Hello?” Becca’s voice came across the line again. She sounded tired. Michael was running through the possibilities. She was likely to report the call and he would have to abandon the phone. “Michael?” She asked. “Is that you?”

“Becca, is…is April there?” He asked quietly.

“Michael, what are you doing calling her? Are you crazy? You’re going to get her into more trouble.”

“What do you mean more trouble? Is April in trouble?” Michael sounded concerned, almost panicked at the thought of April being in some kind of trouble.

“She was. Thanks to you. They took her into custody. She spent the night in the county jail Michael.”

“Oh my God. Why? Did they charge her with something?” Michael asked.

Becca lowered her voice as if to keep from alerting someone. Probably April. “They said the girl you uncovered matched April's DNA too. They said she had to be her daughter as well!"

Michael paused. His heart began to beat faster. It was as he had expected. The condom that fell off, the purchasing of the house, the betrayal. All the pieces fit. April killed the girl. She must have dragged him out there somehow while he was sleeping. She probably drugged his drink or food. "I was afraid of that." Michael said.

"Afraid of what?" Becca snapped in a whisper.

"After we graduated, that summer," Michael began, "we went camping. April and I slept together. My condom fell off. I...I never told her. I didn't see her for over a year after that. She must have gotten pregnant."

"What? You think...!" Becca snapped a little too loud. There was a pause and Michael heard a door shut like she stepped outside the house. "You think April had a kid and didn't tell you? Are you friggn crazy?"

"Well I..."

"April has never gotten pregnant much less by you! I can't believe you would think she would do that! Oh and then what, you think she murdered that girl?" There was a pause. Michael didn't know what to say. "And they actually let you teach?"

"I thought you said the DNA matched. How else would you explain it?" Michael asked.

Becca's voice calmed down. "We don't know and neither do they. They had to let her go because she passed a physical exam, xray, and lie detector test."

Michael's mood lifted. April wasn't a killer...or a liar. His eyes welled up with tears. He shouldn't have doubted her. "I'm sorry Becca, I...I didn't know how else to explain it. Will she talk to me?"

There was a long pause while Becca considered this. "Probably. But she's sleeping right now. And I'm not waking her."

"Becca, I need to speak to her so we can get this figured out. I didn't do this."

There was another long pause. "I believe you. But if she gets caught speaking with you, they can arrest her for that. Do you understand that?" Becca asked.

"Yes, I understand. This phone can't be traced to me. Look, we have no choice but to figure this out or the police, news people, and public are going to keep coming at us until they have blood! We've *got* to figure this out."

"So what are you saying? What do you want me to tell her?"

"Tell her to meet me tonight. At the place we first kissed. If we can't figure it out, you have my word, I'll turn myself in. Agreed?"

Another long pause. "Fine. But you better not let anything happen to her Michael Bander or so help me..."

"I know. I got it. Trust me; I'm more afraid of you than the police anyway." Michael said.

Michael could almost feel Becca smile on the other end of the line. "You better be." She said, but in a nice voice.

"No more surprises?" He asked.

"No more surprises. I didn't know they would shoot at you." She said.

"I know. I don't blame you for doing what you did. But I love April. I would never hurt her or anybody else for that matter."

"What time should she meet you?"

"How about six? Would that give her enough sleep?"

"Ya, it should. But Michael...I can't promise she'll agree to meet you. But I will tell her."

"That's ok. I'll understand either way. And if I can't figure this thing out soon, I'll turn myself in no matter what."

“Good luck. I hope you figure it out. Because I sure as hell can’t.”

“Thanks. I’ll need it. Give her a hug for me.” Michael said and hung up the phone. It was all on the line now. Either he walks into a trap or her arms. Michael hoped for the latter. He didn’t think his heart would survive another betrayal. Michael backed out of McDonald's and continued his course to Alexandria Bay. He kept dreaming of the amusement park. Maybe his subconscious was trying to tell him something.

Chapter 37

It wasn't the same without her. That's what Michael was thinking as he spun around on the scrambler. He had time to kill before meeting April. He had to pay to get in so he figured he might as well enjoy some of the rides. He had to admit that nothing could force a smile on your face quite like a roller coaster. But none of it felt right without April here with him.

As he watched all the people coming and going, Michael pondered what it was that was so exciting about amusement parks. The laughing, the screaming, the smells of buffalo burgers and funnel cakes; Michael came to the conclusion that it was romantic somehow. It was all about sharing the experience with someone. Michael was spinning around on the scrambler from one side to the other. He was noticing that everybody was with someone. Except him. Which is what drew him to the conclusion; *it wasn't the same without her*. Michael was pondering this while being spun around. Out and then in. On the last rotation, Michael's eyes met up with eyes that were eerily familiar. Everything appeared slow motion as Michael locked eyes with a beautiful woman with long brown, curly hair. She was staring right at him. Time seemed to freeze for a split moment and then it sped up again and Michael was being spun to the other side of the ride. When he circled back around and came to a stop, the woman was gone. Michael's senses were on high alert. A chill ran up his spine. Had the girl recognized him from the news? Was she just waiting on someone, a child perhaps? If so, then why disappear? Michael decided it was time to lay low until evening arrived. He didn't want to blow any chances of meeting up with April.

Michael got his hand stamped so he could return to the park and he headed out to the SUV. He kept looking around half expecting to see police cars flooding the parking lot, but none arrived. Maybe she hadn't recognized him after all. Michael breathed a sigh of relief and hopped into the vehicle anyway. He started the engine, turned the air on, and jumped into the back seats which he folded down flat so he could lay down. Michael looked at the time on the Toyota's clock; three o'clock. He still had about three hours until April was supposed to meet him. Michael put the time to good use and drifted off to sleep.

Michael drifted in and out for the next two and a half hours. As five thirty drew near, Michael decided it was time to head back into the park. Michael looked over the gauges of the car. The gas was still near half a tank. He turned it off and pocketed the keys. When he stepped out of the SUV, Michael suddenly remembered that he could be walking into a trap.

For a moment, his stomach turned and he felt nauseous. He wasn't going to run anymore. He had already decided; If April sent the police instead, he would allow himself to be brought in. He figured he didn't have much of a chance proving his innocence from behind bars, but he doubted he was going to figure it out constantly on the run either. No, he couldn't put more people at risk. The man in the garage was right. If his family had found out a suspected murderer was camping out in the garage, they might never feel completely safe again and he didn't want to do that to anybody.

Michael looked around and not seeing any police, headed for the gates. He held out his hand to be checked for a stamp and once again, he was thrust into the world of sounds, smells, and sights. Michael felt like he must stand out like a fox in a henhouse. He made his way alongside the water until he came to the place he remembered from a long time ago.

There were small vending machines like the ones that vend skittles or m & m's. Instead of candy, when you place your quarter into the slot and turned the knob, you were rewarded with a handful of food pellets to feed the fish with. There were a couple of children nearby with palmfulls of pellets and were sprinkling them across the water. The surface of the water was filled with heads and bodies of large carp. Their little sucker mouths opened and closed at the surface making little popping sounds as they slurped down the food pellets. The children were giggling at the sounds they made. Michael looked around. Still no sign of April. It suddenly occurred to Michael that April might not remember where they shared their first kiss. That was all he had told Becca. Have her meet me at the place where we shared our first kiss. He had never forgotten, but it was a selfish assumption to think that she would treasure the same memory that they had shared so many years ago. And if she didn't remember? Then what? Michael shook his head. It was too soon to worry about it. It was still early. She may even be delayed. Or Becca may not have told her; or she could have called the police...Michael was going crazy running the scenarios through his mind. He looked out across the water and tried to focus on a small sailboat to take his mind off of it. After a few minutes he felt his heart and mind coming back to reality. He shoved his hand in his pocket and pulled out a quarter. Michael put the quarter in one of the machines and turned the knob. He caught a handful of pellets in his left hand. Suddenly a voice from behind paralyzed him.

"Are you going to share some of those?"

Michael turned around and found April standing there smiling at him. She looked as beautiful as she had on the night they had kissed here so many years ago. April was smiling but her eyes were tearing up. Michael's hand released the pellets and they fell to the ground as he threw his arms around her and pulled her tight. "I thought I had lost you." He said.

April pulled back and looked into his eyes. Tears were falling from each cheek. "Michael...I'm...I'm so sorry. I didn't know what to do." She said. "I thought...when they told me that your DNA matched...I thought..." April's eyes teared up some more.

"It's alright," Michael said and pulled her back in for another hug, "I'm not mad. I would have done the same thing." He pulled back a little and looked her in the eyes. Her hair was getting stuck on her wet cheeks. Michael brushed it back behind her ear and wiped away the tears with his thumb. "I'm just glad you're here."

"Me too." April said smiling. She leaned in and kissed him. "Just like before." She said as she pulled away.

"I thought you might have forgotten." Michael said.

"Michael Mcreary Bander!" She said sternly. "Do you really think I would forget where we shared our first kiss?" She punched him playfully in the shoulder. "You ought to be ashamed of yourself Mister." Michael smiled. April reached into her jeans and pulled out a quarter and handed it to him.

Michael looked at the quarter and then at April. "You want to feed them?" He asked smiling. April nodded. Michael smiled again and put the quarter in the machine and turned the knob for another handful of pellets. He stretched his hand out and poured half into April's hand. They both walked over to the water's edge and shared a smiling look before sprinkling the pellets over the water for the fish. April laughed outloud. Something she hadn't done in a long time. Michael looked over and smiled at the blissful look on her face. April was smiling as if the last few days had never happened. She looked as happy and carefree as she had when they had fed the fish nearly twenty years ago.

April brushed her hands together out over the water to get the crumbs off. Michael and April both turned toward one another. Michael took April's hands in his and they just looked into each other's eyes for what seemed like an eternity. Finally they inched together closer and closer until their foreheads were touching one another. Michael slid his hand around her waist and pulled her in tight. They shared a long passionate kiss. As they separated they both froze and turned their heads slowly away from the water. A woman was standing less than three feet away staring directly at them. She was about April's height with long brown hair that hung down past her shoulders with a slight curl. The girl had beautiful brown eyes and a fair complexion. Her mouth was slightly ajar. She wasn't staring out past Michael and April. She was staring *at* them. Michael recognized her at once as the girl who had been staring at him earlier on the ride. Her sudden presence at such a close proximity startled April and Michael.

April was about to say something. She opened her mouth and then shut it again as a couple of startling things dawned on her about the girl standing before them. One, she looked a lot like herself only much, much younger. Two, she looked a lot like the girl in the photo. The one the detective had slid across the table at her. *She had a twin*. And three, she looked a lot like the little girl in her dreams only bigger. *You're my mommy silly*. "You're her sister..." April blurted out. The girl's reaction was instant. Her eyes welled up with tears and she nodded her head.

Chapter 38

Detective James was organizing the evidence. He was laying each item out on his desk side by side. First there was the coroner's report. The coroner had indicated that the girl had died from a shot to the head. According to the coroner, she would have died anyway from the shot she had taken to the stomach. Then there was the trace analysis. Apparently there was no discernable trace found in the dirt around the body or on the body itself. There were however, shell casings from a nine millimeter semi-automatic pistol found in the woods. No prints. Then there was the ballistics report from the bullets that were removed from the victim. The computer found a match to two other unsolved homicides. Nothing that could be traced to the Banders or any other perps for that matter. There was the DNA reports from both Michael and April. There were crime scene photos taken at the scene and the house where Michael had been taken to. There were pictures of the other evidence collected; the cell phone, clothes that had been identified as belonging to Michael and some belonging to the two officers. He had typed up his notes from the interviews with Mrs. Bander and laid them aside. Dossiers of both Michael, April, and the twins had been dropped off on his desk. They included everything from pictures, to driver's license numbers, date of births, social security numbers, work history, and more. Detective James carefully organized all his evidence into separate piles.

"Have you cracked the case yet Detective?" A voice came up from behind him.

The detective turned around. "Oh hey Doc...that would be wishful thinking. It's almost like I'm in the middle of one really large hoax."

"Oh it's no hoax Detective I can assure you. But it *is* a puzzle and it's yearning to be solved. More lives hang on the balance than just the missing girl I think." Dr. Crane said.

The detective was about to reply when his cell phone rang. He flicked his cell open and put it to his ear. "Detective James." There was a pause. "Mhmm...ok...What? You gotta be shitting me! They are going to fuck this thing up. Call in the locals for backup. Have them apprehend those jerkoffs and you stick to Mr. Bander. Don't let him get away! Got it? And you don't know who the other guy is? Did you run the plates? And? Well, keep your eye on him. Bring him in if it's possible. Ok. Let me know. Thanks." The detective clicked the phone shut. "Good God Almighty. You've got to be fucking kidding me." The detective said outloud.

"This doesn't sound like a positive turn of events." Dr. Crane voiced his observation.

"My guys have been pursuing the wife's car. We put a tracking device on it." The detective was shaking his head.

"And..."

"And the wife left her sister's house and headed out of town toward Alexandria Bay."

"And you're concerned about jurisdiction?" Dr. Crane asked.

"Nope. I'm concerned about the two cars they've spotted following her."

"Two cars?"

"Both cars followed her from the sister's house to the amusement park. One of the cars had one driver; a tall thick man with dark hair. They ran the plates and it came back to some corporation in New York City."

Dr. Crane crinkled his forehead. "And the other car?"

"The other car belongs to Frank. Gary was driving."

Dr. Cranes face showed immediate concern. "Oh dear. They don't know we have the cell phone recording yet do they?"

The detective shook his head.

"They don't know about the warrant either?"

"Nope," The detective said, "They're out to get rid of the evidence. They're out to kill Michael Bander."

Chapter 39

Michael and April were staring at the girl, not sure what to say. "How...how did you find us?" April finally asked.

The girl drew a finger across her cheek to catch a stray tear. She was trying to be strong. "I don't know. I kept dreaming of this place. I would see you and him..." she wiped away another tear, "and my sister. She always got shot."

Michael looked perplexed. It sounded like the same exact dream he had been having. April couldn't stand it anymore; she reached out and hugged the girl. As she hugged her and looked out over her shoulder she noticed two men approaching who seemed a little more than curious about what was going on. Both men had angry looks on their faces. One was walking on crutches and had a cast on his right leg. The one without crutches reached behind him and produced a gun. April released the girl and pulled her back behind her. Michael stepped up beside April. A third man approached from their right. He wore a dark suit and had on sunglasses. He didn't appear to be aware of the other two men; he was focusing on the girl that was now hiding behind Michael and April. She had her arms around both of them and was watching the situation unfold from between their shoulders.

"Oh my God," she said, "That's the man who killed my sister."

"Those are cops," Michael said low enough the men couldn't hear, "they're bad cops."

"Not anymore, they've been suspended." April said barely audible. The men were getting closer. They were only about ten feet away. Frank was having trouble with the crutches and Gary was trying to conceal the gun by letting it hang by his side.

"Not those guys. The man to your right." The girl behind them whispered in their ears. April and Michael had been focused on the two cops and hadn't even noticed the other man coming in from the right. The man had his hand inside his suit jacket and was walking toward them. He stopped suddenly aware of the other two men approaching. Frank followed their gaze to the man in the dark suit. He stopped and tapped Gary to stop him. The two cops and the man in the suit had stopped and were staring at each other apparently trying to figure out who the other was and what they were doing there. Michael and April looked back and forth from the two cops to the man in the suit, not sure what was going to happen next.

April was looking past the man in the suit and had noticed two police officers in uniform staring at the other officers. One of the uniformed officers spoke into his radio attached to his shirt and both drew their weapons. Neither of them seemed to notice Michael or April. They moved in behind the other two officers.

"Turn around slowly and put your hands in the air." One of the uniformed officers shouted. Both officers turned around breaking off their stare with the man in the suit. The man in the suit quickly turned and began walking the other direction. "Put your hands in the air!" The man repeated again to Frank and Gary.

Frank and Gary slowly raised their hands and began a verbal exchange about being police officers. Michael wasted no time ushering the girls in the opposite direction the man in the suit had gone. A crowd had begun to form in a circle around the scene unfolding by the water. Michael, April, and the girl entered into the crowd and disappeared behind a building.

"What do we do?" Asked April.

Michael looked around the corner at the crowd and then back at the two girls. "We need to get out of the park. If I'm right, there will be people looking for us at the entrance and probably more on the way. We need to get to my car. They won't be looking for it."

April was about to ask 'what car?' when she decided against it and nodded her head. He could explain later. "How?" She asked instead.

"I've got an idea. I don't know if it will work, but it's worth a shot." Michael said. "There is a gift shop near the entrance right?"

"Yes, I think so. Or at least there used to be." April said.

The other girl nodded. "Ya, I was inside it earlier trying to stay cool."

Michael nodded. "Ok, you lead the way." The girl led Michael and April to the gift shop at the front of the park. They were inside for maybe two minutes and all three emerged from the building.

April opened a sack and passed out hats and sunglasses. "I don't know how this is going to help us Michael. They're still going to recognize us." April said as she pitched the empty bag in the trash.

"Ok, don't put your sunglasses on yet until I tell you. Tuck your hair under your hat." He nodded to the other girl. "You, turn your hat around backwards." The girl turned her hat around and so did Michael. Michael looked out and saw two large groups of people heading toward the gate. There was another group even further back. "I hope this works." Michael said. And led the girls out circling around the third group. "Ok, after I say the word 'gun', April you shout out 'he's got a bomb' then you..." he pointed at the other girl "you yell 'run!' got it?" They nodded. "All right, when everybody starts running, toss on your sunglasses." Michael took off running toward the group and the girls followed.

"Run! He's got a gun!" Michael yelled at the group.

"He's got a bomb!" April yelled.

"Run!" The other girl shouted. "Run Now!" The whole crowd had stopped and then their faces went from puzzled to panic and they began running toward the entrance. As they caught up to the other two groups they were all yelling about guns and bombs. Within seconds, all three groups were yelling and running toward the entrance. There were guards up front trying to stop the crowd and what looked like two officers and a couple that may have been undercover. Michael and the girls tossed on their sunglasses and blew right through security with the rest of the crowd, screaming and running. Soon they were in the parking lot and the girls followed Michael to the white SUV.

April climbed in the front passenger side and the other girl hopped in the back seat. "How'd they know to find us here?" April asked as Michael put the key in the ignition.

"I don't know. They must have been following you." Michael said. "They probably knew you would lead them to me. Do either of you have cell phones on you?" Michael asked. The girl in the back said no and April nodded and took hers out of her pocket. Michael took the phone and separated the battery from it and tossed it in his bag. He put the SUV in reverse and took off.

April took off her hat and sunglasses and stuck her head around the seat. She put out her hand. "Hi, I'm April by the way."

The girl in the back took off her glasses but left her hat on backwards. She shook April's hand. "Amber." She said.

"I have a feeling we have a lot to talk about." April said.

Amber laughed. "You have no idea."

April smiled and stared at her for a moment and then turned around in her seat. "So where to now?" She asked. "We can't go driving back into Angel Falls. They'll be looking for you there. And me too."

"And me three." Piped in Amber.

April stuck her head around the seat and looked at her. "Why would they be looking for you?"

"Because I saw who shot my sister. They will want me to point him out in a line up." She pointed at Michael.

"What? Are you saying Michael shot your sister?" April asked half panicked and half confused.

"No, *he* didn't. But they think he did. That's why they're looking for him right?"

"Yes, but..how did you know that?" April asked as Michael made a hard right hand turn onto a ramp that lead to highway 84.

"Duuuh-uuuh! It's all over the news." She said sarcastically.

"Well that's how we fix it. We go back and you tell them it wasn't him!" April said.

"Um...No! Are you crazy? They will kill me if I get anywhere near there. When I went down there to report my sister's murder, they were waiting for me when I got outside. I just barely outran them. I'm not going back there. No way. No how." Amber said matter of factly.

"Michael? Are you catching any of this?" April asked looking at him.

Michael nodded. "Mhmm." He said as if he wasn't worried.

"Mhmm? What do you mean mhmm? Michael the entire city is on a manhunt for you and will shoot you on sight. How can you sit there and say mhmm?" April asked.

Michael looked over at April and back at the road. They passed a sign that said Lamier 5 miles.

April looked at the sign and back at Michael. "Why are you going in the opposite direction? We should be going back and getting this thing straightened out."

"Because they will be looking for us that way. And we would increase our chances of bumping into any one of them."

"Oh." April said and sat back in her seat. "So what's the plan?"

"Are you hungry?" He asked her.

"Are you kidding me? How can you think about food after what we just went through?"

"It's not the food I'm thinking about. We need time and we need to figure this out. We haven't even heard Amber's side of the story. Maybe if we figure this out, we can come up with a plan."

April didn't say anything. It made sense. Besides, she really was hungry; she just couldn't believe *he* was hungry. She hadn't eaten for nearly two days.

After about another nine minutes, Michael was pulling into a little restaurant called Chung Mahoney's Diner a couple miles off the highway in Lamier. There weren't many cars there and it was late so they were hoping to get a little privacy while they ate and discussed the events that had led them to where they now found themselves. The sign inside read 'please seat yourself' and they found a cozy booth with few people in the area. A young blonde waitress greeted them and took drink orders with a promise to be right back. Michael and April sat to one side of the booth and Amber sat on the other. April was staring awkwardly at Amber. She couldn't get over how much she looked like herself at that age.

"What?" Amber said growing uncomfortable at April's stare.

"Nothing. It's just...nothing." April wasn't sure how to say it without sounding stupid.

"You look like she did fifteen years ago." Michael said.

"Oh," Amber said, "that's weird."

"Well, it gets weirder than that..." April said.

Amber crinkled her eyebrows. "What do you mean?"

"According to the police, you are our daughter."

Amber had a shocked expression. "What? *You're* our biological parents?" She asked.

"Not that I know of." April said.

Amber was confused. "What do you mean 'not that you know of?' You either gave birth to twins or you didn't."

"Then the answer to your question is no. We aren't your biological parents."

Now Amber was even more confused; her emotions were bordering on anger. "Then why do the police think you are my parents?" She asked.

"Because our DNA matches. Michael's DNA and my DNA have a ninety-nine percent match with your DNA. According to the detective working the case, you have a ninety-nine percent probability that you are our daughter."

"And you know that's not true because..."

"Because I have never given birth. I didn't even lose my virginity until I was sixteen. So you see, it's impossible. You can't be my daughter because I would have gotten pregnant at fourteen." April said.

The waitress appeared with drinks. "Are you guys ready to order?" She asked politely.

"Um..can you give us a few more minutes?" Michael said picking up a menu. The waitress nodded. April and Amber picked up their menus, silently agreeing to put the conversation on hold. For the next five minutes they all discussed the menu and what each one was going to order and what kind of food they liked. The waitress eventually made her way back over and took the food order.

After she had left, Amber took a sip of her Coke and looked at April. "So?" She said.

April looked at Amber. "So what?" She said back.

"So, how do you explain the DNA if you never gave birth? Are you suggesting that I am the 1%?"

"Well, actually it was 99.9%, so I guess that would make you the .10%." April said. "I guess that is like one in a thousand...I don't know. Michael, you're the Biology teacher. You must have a theory...How is this possible?"

Michael took a drink of his sweet tea. "I don't know," he said, "It doesn't make much sense. I think we need to hear Amber's story. Start with everything you can remember up until right now." Michael said.

Amber looked away from the table and stared out over the counter where the waitress was busy working. She had already told the story to the police; she didn't want to relive it. She didn't want to see her sister die again in her mind. *Find our parents. Tell them about me*. Amber's eyes welled up with tears a little.

Michael reached out and took her hands in his. "I'm sorry Amber. If it's too painful..."

Amber shook her head. "No, I need to. Maybe you can make sense of all of it. I've tried and I sure can't." April grabbed a tissue and handed it to Amber. She took it and dabbed her eyes. "Thanks." She said.

Amber took another drink of Coke. A courage shot. She took a deep breath and began. She told them about being adopted and about the man and woman who raised her. She told them about leaving and moving in with her roommate. She told them about going to school and working at the diner. And she told them about Maria and how she had found her there. Then she went through all that had happened since. Their food came and sat on the table getting cold while Michael and April listened intently about meeting the doctor, then getting kidnapped, and finally her sister being murdered. She told them about how she had escaped and had gone to the police only to be almost killed after coming out of the building. She had been living with a friend and hiding out since then, not wanting to be seen. She was afraid to go outside. Then there were the dreams. She kept dreaming of Michael, April, and her sister. She recognized the amusement park. She had spent three days out there walking around and looking. She felt compelled to. Like she was supposed to find something there. Or someone. She was about to give up when she had spotted Michael and recognized him from her dreams. "And you know the rest." She finished.

Michael and April were staring at her, lost in thought. Michael finally broke the trance first and picked up his fork and started in at his food. April and Amber followed suit. They all ate quietly reflecting on what Amber had just told them.

"So this doctor...," Michael said between mouthfuls, "Dr. Wimm...Wimmon..."

"Wimonowski." Amber helped him out.

"Right. Wimonowski. What did he tell you?" Michael asked.

Amber shrugged. "Nothing important. He just said that we had been dropped off on his doorstep twenty one years ago and that it was in the newspaper. He asked some questions about how we were doing. I asked if he knew anything about our birth parents and he said he didn't. We said our goodbyes and then I left. He seemed nice."

"But then you were kidnapped right outside his door?"

"Yep."

"And you think the guy who took you knew who you were?" Michael asked.

"Ya, I overheard him on his cell phone. He said 'I got'em'. Which made it sound like that was his whole purpose. Like he was supposed to grab us. It wasn't just random." April gasped and shook her head.

"Do you think he meant to kill you or was it because you tried to escape?" Michael asked.

"No, he meant to kill us. He had already stopped out in the middle of nowhere. He was going to kill us both."

"Why would somebody want you dead?" April asked.

"I don't know. We didn't really have any enemies and we weren't even in the same town as we were living. That's why I said, I just can't make sense of it."

"What had Maria been doing right before she found you?" Michael asked.

"I don't know. She said her parents had been killed in an accident. She had been trying to find our birth parents and she found out about me."

"Do you think it has something to do with her parent's accident?"April asked. "I mean, maybe she saw something she wasn't supposed to."

Amber nodded her head. "I doubt it. It was a drunk driver. She was arrested and plead guilty. Case closed as far as I know."

"No, I think this may have something to do with her poking around looking for her birth parents. I only say that because you were kidnapped outside the doctor's house. I think he may have something to do with it. Something doesn't feel right about it."

Amber looked at him puzzled. "I don't follow you."

"Well, you were dropped off on his porch twenty one years ago. Why? Why his porch?"

Amber shrugged her shoulders. "I don't know. I just assumed my birth parents must have known him."

"But you said they never figured out who your birth parents were? I would think the doctor would have known if one of his friends were pregnant. It doesn't make sense. He should have known *something.*"

"I don't know. Maybe." Amber said.

"I say we go there." Michael said.

"Tonight?" April asked.

"Why not? We're kind of running out of time. We could stay here tonight but what then? We can't use credit cards and we can't stay on the run forever. If we have even the slightest chance at figuring this thing out, I say we go for it." Michael said.

Amber looked fearful. "I...I don't know. That's where that guy kidnapped us. I don't think I can go back there."

Michael was about to offer a rebuttal but dropped it. If it was going to do more harm than good, he didn't want her going back there. "Ok," he said, "I see your point. I wouldn't want to go back there either." Michael sighed and leaned back. He took another long sip of tea.

"So what do we do then?" Asked April.

Michael shrugged his shoulders. "I have no idea. That was the only place I could think of to go. I guess we turn ourselves in and Amber can go back to her friends." Michael said. "I don't know what else we can do."

Amber shook her head. "No, that's no good either. Maria wouldn't have wanted that. I made her a promise that I would find our parents. I'm not going to let her die in vain and I don't want you in jail while her murderer walks free." Amber said. "You're right. The doctor is all we have that might lead us to some kind of an answer. I say we do it."

Michael was relieved. He didn't really want to turn himself in but he didn't want to stay on the run either. Finding the truth was all that remained. Michael wiped his mouth with a napkin and fished out his remaining money so he could pay the bill and leave a tip. "Alright," he said, "Let's do it." They all three headed back out to the SUV, somber and nervous about having to head back into Angel Falls.

Chapter 40

It took just over an hour to get back to Angel Falls and pull into the driveway. Amber had given Michael specific instructions on how to get there. Now that she was back in the driveway where her and her sister had been kidnapped, she wished she hadn't. Amber looked out each of the windows half expecting to see her sister's killer. It was dark. There was a dim light that could be seen through the window blinds. Michael put the SUV in park and shut off the ignition. They all sat in eerie silence for a moment, either contemplating or reconsidering. Or maybe both.

"Well, he must be home." April pointed out. "There's a car in the carport and a light's on."

"I'm not sure if he's going to give us the answers we need. It might be best if I go in," Michael said, "You can be the getaway driver. If there's any trouble, I'll come out and you can take off. It won't matter if they get the plates; they won't trace it back to me."

"Michael, where did you get this car?" April asked having completely forgotten to ask earlier. "You didn't...tell me you didn't steal a car Michael Bander..." April put her hand over her face and shook her head. "Oh my God, we are all going to jail." She said.

"Relax, I didn't steal the car. But if it's not returned tonight, it will be called in stolen." Michael said.

April was momentarily relieved. Then as it dawned on her that they weren't likely going to be able to do that, she began to get nauseous. "I think I'm going to puke." She said.

"I'm going in with you." Amber said from the back.

"I don't want you to get hurt." Michael said. "What if the doctor did have something to do with you getting kidnapped?"

"I met the doctor and I seriously doubt he had anything to do with it, but if this guy *is* hiding something, I want to know what. My sister is dead and if he is responsible, then I want to know how." Amber said.

"Your choice," Michael said, "I'm just saying you don't have to if you don't want to."

"I want to." She said.

Michael nodded and got out of the SUV. Amber and April climbed out at the same time.

April came up next to Michael and whispered. "Michael, I am not sitting out here and waiting in the car by myself. This place gives me the creeps." April said looking around. She could just make out the outline of the building against the night sky. A slight breeze blew and the hair on the back of her neck stood up. She had goose bumps all over her arms.

"Alright. We'll all stick together then." Michael said. Michael led the way and the girls followed him up to the front door.

All three quietly walked to the door. As they approached, it became obvious that the front door wasn't quite completely closed. It had been left slightly ajar. Light from an inside lamp was visible in the crack. April and Amber looked up at Michael who just shrugged his shoulders with a 'don't ask me' look. He reached out and knocked on the door which caused it to open further.

"Hello?" Michael hollered into the house. "Is anybody home?" There was no sound and no reply. Michael hesitated a moment and then spoke even louder. "Hello? Anybody?" Still nothing. Michael reached out and gave the door a little push so it would open the rest of the way. After a moment of not hearing any sounds Michael stepped into the house.

April grabbed him by the shirt. "What are you doing? We can't just walk into someone's house!" She whispered sternly.

"What? The door was open. I thought I heard someone say 'come in'. Didn't you?" Michael said. April gave him a very sarcastic look.

“That’s what I heard.” Amber chimed in and took a step inside.

Michael and Amber walked into the house. April decided she must have heard someone say ‘come in’ as well because she crossed the threshold and stayed close to Michael.

The light was coming from the living room to their right and that was the direction they all went. There were bookcases from floor to ceiling on the right and they circled around the far wall. Most of the shelves contained books, but the third and fourth rows from the ceiling were adorned with various trinkets, artifacts, and old family photos. As they rounded the corner, they could see a recliner chair set up near where the bookcase came to a halt. There was a small end table next to the chair that had a glass of what looked to be iced tea. The glass was sweating from the melting ice cubes. The lamp that lit up the room was slightly behind the table and arced over the top, illuminating the area and most of the room. There was a book on the table next to the glass of tea that had been laid face down and open as if someone had set it down for a moment with the intent of returning to it momentarily. Michael took another step forward and stopped dead in his tracks. His heart all but froze as he took in the scene before him. April saw Michael’s expression change and followed his gaze. Her hand flew to her mouth where she stifled a scream. Amber moved around Michael to get a better look and stood expressionless unable to believe what she was seeing.

There on the floor of the reading room was the doctor with a small hole in his forehead and blood oozing out of it and onto the floor. The doctor's glasses had fallen away from his face and his eyes were open looking out toward them. They hadn't even begun to gloss over yet. Michael realized that whoever killed the doctor had done so only moments before they had arrived.

Chapter 41

Detective James and Dr. Crane were thumbing through the evidence piece by piece. Under normal circumstances, they would have both gone home and continued putting the pieces together the next day. But this case was going to become very public with a suspected murderer on the loose and two police officers that were publically arrested in Alexandria Bay. There was no dragging their feet on this one. Michael Bander had escaped their custody once and they had failed to collar him at the river, Walmart, and the amusement park. Both Detective James and Dr. Crane knew that they would be held accountable for any more deaths that may come about from Michael Bander. They nearly had him at the amusement park, but the Alexandria police force had not been told to watch for him. They were focusing on the descriptions of the two renegade police officers instead. The other officers and detectives were supposed to watch for Michael and April at the gate until backup could arrive and sweep the entire park. But a fake bomb scare sent a large crowd of people screaming through the entrance and the officers believed to have lost Bander and his wife in the crowd. Mrs. Bander must have come to the conclusion that they were tracking her vehicle because she abandoned it there. They had tried to track her cell phone but weren't getting a signal. Detective James let out a long sigh and leaned back in his chair. He pulled at his face with his hands attempting to pull away the exhaustion. He looked up at Dr. Crane who was partially sitting on his desk looking through one of the dossiers. “We’ve got to be missing something Doc. There must be something we’re overlooking.” The detective said.

Dr. Crane looked at the detective shaking his head. “When the evidence is conflicting, and the likelihood that the current theory can’t be supported, I like to lean on the advice of the old craftsman Sir Arthur Conan Doyle.”

“Doyle?” The detective said.

“Detective, you of all people should recognize the genius behind the notorious Sherlock Holmes.”

“Can’t say I’ve read any Sherlock Holmes stories,” the detective said while grooming his mustache lost in thought, “what would this Doyle tell you in this situation Doc?”

Dr. Crane stood up and stretched his back. “Sir Doyle would tell us that ‘once you eliminate the impossible, whatever remains, no matter how improbable, must be the truth.’”

The detective thought about it for a moment. “That really doesn’t tell us much now does it doc?” The detective said.

“Are you certain about that Detective? Have you actually applied it?” Dr. Crane said with a smile.

“Doc if you’re on to something just spit it out.” The detective was growing impatient.

“You are the detective, Detective. I’m not going to tell you how to do your job. I’m merely making a suggestion on how to look at the case from a unique angle. You connect the dots.” Dr. Crane said and walked away.

The detective leaned back in his chair and closed his eyes. *God, why did Doc have to be so damn difficult?* He thought. *Eliminate the impossible…what seems impossible?* The detective wondered. *It seems impossible for the two girls not to be the children of Michael and April Bander.* The detective sorted through it in his mind. *So if I eliminate that, that means Michael and April are the biological parents. But April never gave birth nor did she have a surrogate*. Hell, it *still* didn’t make sense. The detective got up and stormed down to Dr. Crane’s office and stood in the door. Dr. Crane was behind his desk and looked up from his work with his glasses slightly below his eyes.

“The truth is that the twins, Maria and Amber are the biological offspring of Michael and April.” The detective said.

“Go on Detective.” Dr. Crane said.

“April passed two exams and a lie detector test. So it’s also true that she never gave birth. Right so far Doc?”

“I believe you are. So far anyway. Keep going.”

“That means the truth is that there has got to be a surrogate. But she passed a lie detector test. She said she never had a surrogate.” The detective turned his head sideways and put his chin on his shoulder. He closed his eyes and let his mind try and find it. It was right there, he could feel it. It just...wouldn't...connect. He felt it start to slip away. "Shit." He said looking back at Dr. Crane. "How can she have a surrogate and not have a surrogate?"

Dr. Crane took off his spectacles and laid them on the desk. He looked at the detective. "Let me ask you something Detective..."

"Alright, ask." The detective said trying to maintain some amount of patience.

"How many brothers and sisters do you have?"

"Doc, you know the answer to that as much as I do. I'm an only child."

"Are you sure of that?"

"Ya, I would think I would have known if I had grown up with an extra kid in the house Doc."

"So you would pass a lie detector test if I were to ask you while being tested?"

"I would hope so."

"How many girls did your father sleep with before he married your mother?" Dr. Crane asked.

The detective had a strange expression on his face. "How the hell should I know Doc? I don't see how that's..." Then it hit him. "You're saying I could have a brother or sister and not have known about it and passed a lie detector test."

Dr. Crane smiled and nodded. "And..."

"If Michael and April had a surrogate and didn't know about it, all the pieces fit together..." The detective rubbed his mustache. "How could you have a surrogate and not know it?" The detective asked.

Dr. Crane smiled again. "Now that is a question worth investigating don't you think?"

The detective stopped grooming his mustache and looked at Dr. Crane as if another revelation had dawned on him. "The Doctor...the one who found the twins...shit. You're a genius Doc."

"I didn't do anything." Dr. Crane said. "That was merely the collective reasoning of Sir Arthur Conan Doyle." Dr. Crane said while placing his spectacles back on.

"Well then Sir Arthur Doyle is a fucking genius. I gotta go. Thanks Doc." The detective said as he spun and headed out of the doorway. He looked down at his watch. With any luck the Doctor would still be up.

Chapter 42

"Oh my God!" Amber said as she went to the doctor's side and knelt down.

"Don't touch anything," Michael said, "we've got to get out of here."

"We can't just leave him here," said April, "we need to call the police."

"It's the police I'm worried about." Michael said. "I've already been found with one dead body. No way I'm going through that again."

"Michael!" April exclaimed and nodded her head toward Amber with a look that said 'shut up stupid'.

Michael looked down at Amber who was looking at him with a wounded expression. Michael was so caught up in reliving the being found with a dead body experience that he had forgotten that that dead body was Amber's sister. "I'm sorry," Michael said, "I didn't mean to sound insensitive. It's just, when I found Maria, they didn't exactly coddle me. They tend to treat you like you're a murderer and it's up to you to prove you aren't." Amber's look softened. "I just don't want this hanging over our heads. You don't know what it's like to try and prove you didn't do something. It won't look good. And whoever did this, did it just moments ago. Look at the drink."

Michael nodded toward the glass on the end table near the chair.

April and Amber looked toward the glass. There were still ice cubes in it and it was sweating on the outside. “Michael, we just can’t…” April began.

“No. He’s right. The guy who killed the Doctor is probably the same guy who killed Maria. He’s looking for me. If you’re with me when he finds me, he’ll kill you too!” Amber said. “I’ll go. I’ll go to the police and tell them everything.” Amber looked from Michael to April. It was obvious she was trying not to cry. “Maybe they can catch him before…” Amber turned her head away and back toward the doctor. “…before anyone else gets killed.” Amber stood up. Tears were falling down her cheeks. “This is all my fault,” she said, “If I had been brave enough to go back to the police, they might have caught this guy and the doctor would still be alive.”

Michael put his arm around Amber’s shoulder and embraced her. Amber was crying hard and laid her head on his chest. She had never had a shoulder to cry on before.

April comforted her by rubbing her back. “It’s not your fault,” she said, “you didn’t do this. It’s not your fault.”

“You know what?” Michael said. As he pulled back a little. Amber lifted her head up. Her brown hair was stuck to her wet cheeks. Michael ran his finger under the stray hairs and pulled them back. “We are going to stick together. All three of us. We’ll all go to the police and tell them what happened. I’ll have April’s sister Becca meet us there and she will make sure nothing happens to you even if we get arrested. Who knows, maybe they can make sense out of this mess.” Michael said.

Amber nodded her head and wiped her cheeks with the back of her hand. April reached around her and embraced her. “Come here you.” April said as she hugged Amber. “I forget how hard this must be on you too. Michael’s right, we need to end this for better or for worse.” She said.

“In sickness and in health.” Michael chimed in. April smiled and with her arm around Amber they all headed toward the door.

They were just about to go back through the door they had come in when a fragile voice of a female came from behind. “Please don’t go.”

Michael, April, and Amber spun around to see an older lady in a nightgown peering around the corner of the adjacent room. “Please...don’t go.” She said again. “My hu...hu...husband...he’s dead isn’t he?” She asked.

The two girls stood expressionless with their mouths half ajar in shock. Michael nodded his head. “Yes ma'am, I’m afraid he is.” He said.

The older lady nodded. She had beautiful gray hair. She looked to be in her mid sixties. Her face was smooth and didn't have many wrinkles except under her eyes. Her eyes were a dark brown color that gave away too much. Michael could see the pain in them. "It was only a matter of time." She said.

Michael looked at her. "What do you mean? You're husband was shot ma'am." Michael said.

"Yes, I know. I heard it from downstairs. I assumed that's what had happened. It's a wonder he made it this long."

"I'm afraid I don't follow you." Michael said.

"Please, take me to him will you?" The older lady asked.

"You're his wife?" Amber asked. The older lady nodded. "But he said you left him years ago. Right after you found my sister and I on your door step."

The older lady nodded. "He was protecting me. He was worried they would find me."

"They?" April asked.

The older lady nodded. "Please, take me to him. I'll tell you everything."

Michael offered his arm and she held on and followed him as he led her into the other room where her husband lay on the floor.

The older lady stifled a gasp and cupped her hand over her mouth. “Oh my poor Benjamin. What have they done to you?” The older lady spoke aloud. “Dear…” The older lady looked at Amber. “There is a closet down the hall on the right. There are sheets on the second shelf from the top. Would you…”

Amber nodded and walked around the doctor and down the hall. There was a sound of a door opening and a moment later she came back with a white sheet. She opened it up and April stepped over to help, and they both covered up the doctor.

“Thank you dear.” The older lady said. She glanced over at the tea on the end table. There was a book titled *Finding Mommy* laying open and face down. The older lady nodded. “He always liked to read about this time. Come, let’s sit down at the table and talk for a while. I haven’t spoken to anyone but Benjamin in twenty years or more.” She said and motioned toward the other room.

Michael offered his arm again and led the way into the adjacent room. It appeared to be a dining room. There was a large table and many chairs around it. There was a light attached to a ceiling fan overhead. Amber found a switch on the wall and turned the light on. “Thank you dear.” The older lady said as Michael pulled out a chair for her. “Would any of you care for something to drink?” She asked.

Michael, April, and Amber all looked from one to the other and shook their heads no. "Tell us, what happened to your husband Mrs..." April began.

"Jane dear. You can call me Jane." The older lady said.

"Ok Jane. I'm April, this is my husband Michael, and this is Amber."

The older lady froze her eyes on Amber. "My how you have grown into such a beautiful young lady." She said. "I'm so sorry about your sister. I wish none of this had happened."

"So you remember us?" Amber asked. "You remember the day we were dropped off on your porch?"

"Oh I remember you." Jane smiled at Amber. "But you weren't dropped off on our porch I'm afraid."

"We weren't?" Amber showed an expression of shock. "So you knew our parents?" She asked.

"Well, no. I mean...I didn't." She looked from Michael to April. "But I do now."

Amber felt a big lump well up in her throat as she looked at Michael and then at April. April did look an awful lot like her and her sister. "I don't understand," she said, "April has never given birth. She can't possibly be my biological mother."

"That's because she didn't give birth to you," Jane said, "but I can assure you, she is your biological mother."

"How can..." April began. "How can you know this? I don't understand. How can I be her biological mother if I never gave birth to her?"

Jane smiled at April and then at Amber. "I know this because you weren't found on our doorstep. That is just the story we made up for the newspaper to protect you."

"Then who gave birth to me?" Amber said.

Jane looked at Amber right in the eyes. "I did."

Amber stood up. Her eyes were welling up with tears. "I can't do this. I've got to go. This is creeping me out." A tear rolled down her cheek. "I don't understand." She said.

Jane's smile faded. She reached out and put her hand on Ambers. "Please. Don't go. I'll explain. You're right. The story is a strange one. Sit. Please." Jane pleaded with Amber. Amber nodded her head and wiped away a stray tear and sat down.

"I'm so sorry you have to go through this." Jane said. "Nobody deserves this. Least of all you." Jane said with a sorrowful look. "I know you're searching for answers..."Jane began. "And I'm going to give them to you. But don't get your hopes up that they will comfort you." Jane said. Amber's eyes went wide. "If you thought it was creepy before...just you wait. It gets worse."

"What happened Mrs..." Michael began.

"Jane dear. You can call me Jane."

"What happened Jane? We all need to know."

Jane took a long sigh and leaned back a little looking straight ahead but her eyes were in the past. "My husband and I had been married nearly ten years you know." She began. "He was so handsome. And kind. And gentle. He was an honest man you see. Whatever you may think about him after I tell you this, you must know that he was a good man." Jane looked around and everyone nodded their understanding. We had tried to have kids for more than five years. I don't know if he wasn't fertile or maybe it was me. I don't know. It didn't matter. But he felt responsible and powerless, that much is certain. I think in his mind, he felt like he was going to lose me." Jane looked around. All eyes were focused on her. "He wouldn't have of course. I never blamed him for it. But just the same it was a terrible burden on him." Jane took another long sigh before continuing. "I don't know why they chose him."

"Why who chose him?" April asked.

Jane looked across at April. "I don't know dear. I'm not sure he knew either. But they came to him and asked him to do things and told him that they would kill me if he refused."

"What kind of things?" Amber asked.

"They wanted him to steal things from his patients. Things that they wouldn't miss." Jane continued.

"Their sperm. Their eggs." Michael finished for her.

Jane nodded. "That is correct Michael. We never found out why. Maybe they were selling them on the black market. Maybe they sold them to surrogate centers. Or maybe it was something worse..." Jane hesitated trying to keep herself from crying.

Michael placed a hand on her shoulder. "It's ok." He said. "It wasn't your fault."

Jane patted his hand. "I know. But maybe we could have stopped them. They just seemed too powerful. They had assistants working with Benjamin. He couldn't get away and they saw everything that he did." Jane took a deep breath. "Everything but this." She said nodding at Amber. Jane looked at April. "Do you remember having surgery when you were younger?" She asked.

April nodded her head. "No not..." She thought for a moment. "I had my tonsils taken out when I was fourteen." She said. Then it dawned on her and she cupped her hand over her mouth. She began shaking her head. "You mean...you mean...he?" April was in shock.

Jane nodded her head solemnly. “That is how it happened I’m afraid. He was supposed to turn over your eggs to the people who were threatening to kill me.” A tear rolled down Jane’s cheek. “I don’t know if he thought he was protecting you, or if he thought he was helping me. Or our marriage.” Jane wiped away the tear with a shaky hand. “But he told those people that the eggs were no good. And he brought them home. Along with your semen Michael.” Jane looked at Michael whose mouth was half wide open in disbelief.

“And you agreed to steal our eggs and sperm?” Asked April in utter disbelief.

Jane shook her head no. “I didn’t find out until after.”

“After?” April asked.

Jane nodded. “Benjamin, in all his misguided intentions, drugged my after dinner drink. When I awoke the next morning, he had told me that I had too much to drink and passed out.” Jane sniffled. “About a month later, I began to notice the changes.” Jane looked at Amber. “I was pregnant.” Jane smiled. “It was the best day of my life.”

“If it was the best day of your life, then why did you give us up?” Asked Amber. “Why did you send us off to live in terrible homes?”

Jane began shaking her head. “I didn’t want to dear. I had to you see. I had to save your life.”

"I don't understand." Said Amber.

"They found out. I don't know how they did, but they found out what Benjamin had done. They threatened him and told him they were going to take you away. Benjamin had to tell me what he had done. He told me that they were going to take my babies." Jane began to cry. "I wouldn't let them. I couldn't let them. I don't know what they were going to do, but I'd be damned before I let them take you away." Jane looked at Amber who was also crying. "You may not have had my DNA, but I loved you like you were my own." Jane looked down for a moment. She wiped her tears with the cuff of her nightgown. "I gave birth when Benjamin was at work. It was the best and worst day of my life. I cleaned you both up and put on little pink outfits." She looked at Amber. "You were so cute. I got to spend the whole day with both of you." Jane looked across to Michael and Amber. "Then I made the call before Benjamin came home. I knew if the news got wind of the story that twins were left on our doorstep, that you would be safe. They wouldn't be able to take you. Benjamin knew they would kill me, so he purchased a plane ticket in my name. Then he built a secret room in the basement. He told them that I had left him and I've been living down there ever since." Jane looked at Amber again and put her hands on hers. "I'm so sorry dear. I'm so sorry this happened to you. And your poor sister..." Jane broke down into tears again. Amber scooted her chair over and put her arms around Jane and hugged her.

Michael and April looked at each other. They didn't know what to say. Or think. April smiled and put her hands on Michael. They shared a long look. And a thought...*They had a daughter...*

Chapter 43

Detective James pulled up in the driveway. It was a creepy looking place. Even in the dark. The detective noted a car in the carport and a white SUV outside. There was light coming through the blinds on both sides of the house. To the left of the door, he could make out a series of shadows against the blinds. *The doctor must have guests*. The detective thought. He was about to approach the door when he noticed something that seemed off. Two blinds on the right side of the house were lit up as well. But there was a shadow moving very slowly toward the other side of the house. It was probably nothing, but the detective wasn't taking any chances. He drew his gun and moved toward the door.

Chapter 44

It all happened fast. Amber was first to notice the thick man in the black suit cross into her line of sight. He must have been hiding out in one of the other rooms. He crossed the hallway in front of the front door and into the doorway of the dining room. Michael and April were puzzled by the sudden look of absolute horror on Amber's face. They turned around but it was too late.

"He killed my sister!" Amber blurted out pointing at the man.

The man in the black suit didn't say a word. His left eye had been replaced by a glass eye which remained stationary while the other eye moved about the room. He held a gun in his right hand that stretched out before him. After he confirmed that nobody else was in the room, a smile spread across his face at Amber's expression and he pointed the gun right at her forehead and pulled the trigger.

The detective heard Amber cry out 'He killed my sister!' and the gunshot that followed. The door to the house was slightly ajar and the detective eased his way around it and spotted a man in a suit with his arm outstretched. He was pointing the gun at Michael Bander. The detective put two rounds in his chest causing the man's gun to fire. His hand swung first and the bullet meant for Michael went wide and into the wall. The man fell to the ground dead. The detective kicked the gun away from his hand. As Detective James looked around the room and took in the scene, his expression turned to heartache as he realized he had gotten there too late. Not one body, but two were lying dead on the floor by the dining room table. April had screamed at the second shot and was clinging on to Michael shaking and crying. The detective called in the CSI and the coroner. Nobody was in the mood to talk. And he wasn't going to ask them to. Not yet. *Let them mourn.* He thought. *Sort it out later at the station.*

Chapter 45

Michael and April stood at the foot of the casket and watched as it was lowered down into the ground. April was dressed in a black dress. Her hair was down and her curls hung down just past her shoulders. She dabbed at her cheeks with a handkerchief. She looked at Michael who was wearing a black suit and tie and looking solemnly into the ground. "We never got a chance to know her." She said. "There were so many questions to ask."

Michael hugged her. "I know, she was incredibly brave. She always did the right thing, even when it cost her her own life. I wish we had met her sooner."

Amber stood next to her parents. She also had tears running down her cheeks but she made no move to remove them. "She was my birthmother. She loved me from the beginning. She gave me up to save my life. She lived twenty years in solitude as punishment, and threw herself in front of a bullet for me in the end. She doesn't deserve this. This isn't justice." Amber sobbed and Michael and April put their arms around her. There was nothing they could say to make it better. Three graves. Three funerals. They laid Maria next to the Wimonowskis. It just seemed right somehow. The funerals took up most of the day and the mourning went on well into the night. Amber did a fine job of making sure everybody knew who her sister was and the life she lived. She talked about the Wimonowskis like she had known them all her life. She would smile for a while, then cry for a while. Becca, Michael, and April all comforted her, but they were just as emotional. Maria was their daughter too and despite the fact they hadn't known about her did not make her death any easier to bear. If anything, it made it worse. Eventually, night would fall and morning would follow and begin the process of wearing down the pain and easing the heartache back into the mind and soul so the spirit would find its way back into the light.

Chapter 46

Michael stood outside the house attending the grill. It was a beautiful day outside. It had been two weeks since the funerals and emotions weren't completely back to normal. But they were close. April came out the back door with a tray full of condiments and sat them at the picnic table. Amber followed right behind with a bowl full of salad. Detective James stood next to the grill grooming his mustache and chatting with Michael. There was a cooler filled with ice and drinks and Becca was thrusting her hand into the ice for one. The smell of barbecued pork floated through the air making everybody's mouth water with anticipation. There was corn on the cob and mashed potatoes. Everybody was smiling and enjoying the day. The two crooked police officers had been officially charged with kidnapping, torture, and attempted murder. Michael was glad that the attempted rape never had to be brought up. He was content to sweep it under the rug as long as they were getting life behind bars. The day after the story hit the newspaper, the FBI had shown up at Detective James' desk. They had been investigating a company called "Fertility and More" in New York City. They had flagged the man in the suit's information. They were able to use Amber and Maria's case as the concrete evidence they needed to make the arrests. Amber agreed to testify against them in court under the condition that they use some of the seized assets to acquire the three cemetery lots to bury her sister and the Wimonowskis in. They even threw in nice marble engraved headstones.

The DA dropped all charges against Michael and the police officer who had shot him stopped by for a formal apology.

Michael was able to return the car to Jack Noble, the man who had helped him in a time of need by letting him stay in his garage. Michael had sent Jack and his family six free passes to the amusement park at Alexandria Bay.

Michael, April, and Amber had built a small memorial in the middle of the woods where Maria had been found. It was adorned with a stone, decorative rocks, and lots of flowers. An attorney had gotten in touch with Amber. The Wimonowskis had left everything to Amber and Maria. Since Michael and April were Maria's surviving parents, they inherited Maria's share which they happily turned over to Amber. Amber was looking forward to learning more about the Wimonowskis and the life they had led.

Everybody sat down at the picnic table as Michael began taking the meat off the grill and passing it around. The detective looked at Amber who was just getting seated. "So what's next for you Amber? Are you going to move into the Wimonowski place?" He asked as Michael placed some barbecued pork on his plate.

Amber pulled her hair back and put it in a ponytail. "Not yet. I don't think I'll be ready to live alone for a while. I'm going to finish college." She said. She looked at Becca. "Becca said I could come out and stay with her for a while so I can finish my degree."

"That sounds like a good plan." Said the detective. "I guess I just figured you'd stay here with Michael and April."

"I'd love to." Amber said. "But this has all happened so fast and I don't want to ruin getting to know my parents. I think jumping right into a living situation could stress our relationship. I would rather take it nice and slow. I don't plan on going anywhere so we have lots of time." Amber said.

"Spoken like a true wise man." Michael said as he passed around the rest of the pork.

"You mean spoken like a true Bander." Said April.

"That too." Michael smiled.

Michael sat down at the table. "I think a prayer is in order." He said. Everybody nodded their agreement and folded their hands and bowed their heads. "Dear Heavenly Father," Michael began, "Thank you so much for blessing this family with two wonderful and beautiful girls. Thank you for watching out for us and keeping us safe as we struggled through difficult circumstances brought upon us by terrible people. Please watch over us and bless us as we rebuild our lives and get to know one another. And watch over Maria and the Wimonoskis and give them all our love. In our Father's name. Amen."

"Amen" Everybody repeated.

Amber held up her cup "To Maria, the best sister a girl could hope for. And to Jane Wimonowski, our birth mother, who protected us with her life."

Everybody raised their glass. "To Maria and Jane." They repeated. A breeze came through and even though Amber couldn't hear it, she knew her sister's spirit was in it. Amber closed her eyes and smiled. Her sister would always be with her.

The End

Thanks for reading *Over Her Dead Body*. I hope you enjoyed reading it as much as I enjoyed writing it. Please send me an email and let me know what you think. Include the name of the book in your subject line. Include your contact information and I'll add you to the mailing list and send you a link to my facebook fan club where you can receive daily or weekly writing updates. Send to bradleylutes@yahoo.com Please visit my website for important updates at www.bradleybigato.com Don't forget to add me on facebook!

Finding Mommy

Chapter 1

The beginning is always the hardest to remember. The days in between just seem so long. It was raining. *That* she could remember. Why does it seem that whenever something tragic happens, it's always raining? Now a light sprinkle...that wouldn't have been so bad. But this was a downpour. This was God flushing his toilet. It all came down at once. And there, right in the middle of it, was one innocent mom, one seventeen year old daughter, and of course not to mention...one six year old boy, who was about to grow up very fast.

School shopping. The first day of school only five days away, and to everyone's agreement, today, Thursday August 7, had been set aside just for that. Mom, or Chevy, yup after the truck, took the day off. She even turned off her cell, which is normally non-stop during the week, just to spend some quality time with her two babies. Well, they weren't babies anymore. She was pretty sure her daughter Lauren may have launched all the way up from first ear piercing at six, first training bra at nine, first period at eleven, first dance at twelve, first kiss at twelve, first wrecked car at sixteen, first time well you know, she could only hope, seventeen. She looked over at her daughter who was flipping through the pages of *Seventeen* and popping her watermelon Bubble Yum. Her long beautiful red hair was pulled back in a ponytail. Her fierce blue eyes bounced from left to right as she discovered whom Britney Spears had been dating. Seeing her sitting there, looking so mature and innocent made her feel old. It just seemed like yesterday she herself was popping chewing gum and skipping class to run off with Roy Lanely. They would go down to the river and swim, read poetry to each other or just sit and talk while staring at the water as it trickled out over all the rocks, cleansing and purifying both the water and her spirit. No more times like that. It seems now all she could do is relive it a little at a time through her one and only daughter.

She reached out and pulled back a few stray hairs, which had escaped and threatened to block Lauren's view of her magazine. Lauren looked over at her mom.

"I love you." Chevy was holding back her eyes from watering. This always happened when looking at either of her children, she always felt like squeezing them tight to her and never letting go. Lauren smiled and reached out and turned up the radio a little bit. She thought she heard a song she recognized. Ah yes, *"You better talk to the one that made you. You better talk to the one that made that.... light...in your eyes."* Lauren was singing and nodding to the music.

"Mom, make her stop will ya?" Little Bryan in the back, only six but cocky enough to be thirteen, was making a puking gesture with his finger going down his throat.

"What's a matter Bud, you afraid your sister's gonna outsing you?"

"Oh please, Walter's violin sounds better than that." Walter was their next-door neighbor who liked to sit out on his porch and practice his newly found talent of playing the violin. What Walter and Nancy take to sound like music, comes across to their neighbors as nails across a chalkboard. But due to him dropping his old hobby, of stretching in his gym shorts (and nothing but his gym shorts), they decided the scratching sounds from the violin haunted their memory throughout the day a lot less than picturing old Walter out doing jumping jacks in the front yard with wrinkly flesh flapping everywhere.

Lauren continued to ignore the comments from her little brother as she learned to do with such sophistication last year. She just kept on bobbing her head from side to side, smiling and throwing a few smiling glances toward her mom and singing *"You better talk to the one that made you, you better talk to the one that made that...light...in your eyes."*

"Ok. Bryan." Chevy decided she would stop the war before it began. "Do you have your school list?"

"Yep" Bryan was smirking and bouncing his head back and forth on the seat. The boy never sat still.

"Ok. What's on your list?"

"Um..." Bryan unfolded his list and looked down at it. He was about to tell his mom what he needed when it occurred to him "Mom, I can't read cursive. You know that silly."

"Oh right. Lauren, grab your brother's list and read it off to me, would you please?"

Lauren who was in the middle of an incredibly big Bubble Yum bubble, slapped the *Seventeen* in her lap and while rolling her eyes turned and snapped the paper out of her brothers hands.

"Hey I was reading that!" Bryan clearly didn't appreciate having his property or what he felt was his property rather, stolen as opposed to given up. His sister however, enjoying the torture while she could, just turned and stuck out her tongue.

"Stop that Lauren, now what do we need?"

Lauren turned in her seat and began to scan the wrinkly contents of the page. "Well it says here that he needs an M-16, a rocket launcher, a couple of grenades, and a switch blade. Oh, and it says a Glock is highly recommended but not required."

"Cool!" Bryan's face lit up at the sound of a rocket launcher and switchblade.

"Um, I don't think so. Lauren quit giving him ideas. I'm sure that list is perfectly acceptable in some schools, but Landmark Grade School I'm told, frowns on M-16's and rocket launchers." Chevy looked at Lauren as if she was trying not to burst out laughing.

"Oh" Lauren mouthed as if she didn't know and turned to look at the sheet again. "Well, it says we need two pocket folders, one pair of scissors, five pencils, one box of crayons, Elmer's glue, and a book bag. Oh . . . and a partridge in a pear tree." She thought that last part was funny.

Her mother on the other hand just rolled her eyes, smiled, and said "Always a comedian."

As a senior in school, Lauren was looking forward to returning. Not because she liked school, but because it was the last year until college when she would be out on her own and free. That's right, finally free at last. Not that she was held prisoner or anything. Actually, her mom trusted her more than most moms trust their daughters. Like last Friday for instance, her mom let her go out with her friends and she didn't return until one in the morning. Some moms would have freaked out about that but not Chevy. Nope, Chevy was cool with a capital K. "Your mom is the bom." Her friends would say. But on the other hand Lauren did have a good head on her shoulders, and after all, why shouldn't she be trusted? It was Lauren after all who took a cab home three months ago when her boyfriend had been drinking at a party and was trying to give her a ride home. It was Lauren who dumped him when she found out he had driven himself home that way. Besides that, she was an honor student, president of S.A.D.D., the Environmental club, and one of the best basketball players that the Haley Eagles had seen in years. But just the same she couldn't help but dream about getting her own place, doing her own dishes and laundry, inviting her own guests over for dinner or to watch the game. It would be her place and her rules. It all sounded like fun to her. Of course she realized that she was going to have to work more hours. Right now she only worked about ten hours a week cutting roses for a flower shop. She would have to find a new job with more hours, but if that was the price of freedom, so be it. *Oh well, that's a year away.* She thought. *Why worry about that now?* One more year under Mr. Balenstine, the school principal. She was sure that there weren't many nice principals out there anyway, but she thought he was a real prick. He was always giving her that look that said 'I'm watching you Lauren. I'm waiting for you to fuck up, so I can put you in detention.' He wasn't exactly ugly, he just looked stern. He had dark eyes that could pierce you, and his glasses seemed to magnify the effect. He was thin with dark balding hair, which had been combed over to one side to make it look full. *Who was he trying to impress anyway?*

"Whatcha thinking about hon?" Chevy asked.

Lauren didn't even realize she had spaced out until now. Her mom was looking at her with concern. Lauren smiled at her and looked out the windshield to avoid her stare. "Mom, watch out!" Lauren screamed at the top of her lungs with the most horrified look on her face Chevy had ever seen.

It just seemed to happen slow motion from there. Chevy's head turned slowly back toward the front. She had about point five seconds to take in the situation: a semi truck was stopped less than twenty feet in front of her. Twenty feet is nothing when traveling fifty-five miles an hour.

An accident up ahead had caused everyone in front of her to come to a screeching halt. The two seconds that Chevy had turned to look at her daughter was all it took. Chevy knew that if she tried to swerve to the left and miss, she would run her daughter's side of the car into the semi. Even if she made it, she might go head-on into an oncoming vehicle. She quickly decided to swerve to the right and with any luck maybe, just maybe she would be the only one to get hurt. She made the turn. All in all from the time she turned her head to look at her daughter to the time she swerved to the right, three seconds was all that had passed.

Chevy swerved and felt a bang. Heard a bang as if she had hit the semi, but as far as she could tell, she had made it around. She drove off the side of the road, through the grass, down an embankment and slowed to a stop just before Sleepy Creek.

She was in shock. All she could do was continue to stare straight ahead at the creek as it flowed gently over the rocks, taking away, little by little, the shock and pain and fear. Chevy's arms were trembling. She felt frozen, like her hands were glued to the wheel.

"Breathe Mom" she heard from a distance, and in her mind she heard her daughter's voice and realized her lungs had been frozen as well. She relaxed and blew out a hard gasping breath like one does when holding one's breath under water for a long time and like a whale and its blowhole, the air is forced through the lips.

"Holy crap that was clo..." Chevy cut herself off and another wave of panic and anxiety filled her as she turned to look at her daughter and found that the seat was empty. Her eyes turned in their sockets toward the window, expecting to see some hole that her daughter must have went through. Nothing. Now she turned quickly toward the back and yelling, no screaming, the name of her one and only son. "Bryan!" And again she was in horrified shock. Her daughter whom she expected must have landed in the back seat was not there. Her son, Bryan Samuel Berry, was also not in the back seat.

Chevy's lower lip began to quiver. How could this be? They had been in the vehicle hadn't they? Wasn't this Thursday August 7th? Wasn't this the day they had agreed to go school shopping? Wasn't it her daughter's eyes she was looking into right before she swerved to hit the semi? Her head was swimming with possibilities. No broken glass. No open doors. *Was this the right day?* Maybe she was on her way to sell a house and the kids were in school... *Yes that must be it.* She thought. *The kids are in school; I was on my way to an appointment, when I swerved to avoid the semi.* She looked over at her daughter's seat and saw that the seatbelt was still buckled. *That's odd.* She unbuckled her own belt and turned all the way around in her seat and looked at Bryan's seat belt. The same. Buckled.

"If they hadn't been in the car, why would their seatbelts be fastened?" She spoke aloud and suddenly became aware that her ears were ringing. *They must have jumped out of the car. Why would they do that? Maybe they thought that we weren't going to make it... They must have reacted with more speed than I thought they could have.* With renewed hope Chevy opened the car door and jumped out. The grass was high and came up to her knees. She fell the moment her feet hit the ground. Her legs were a little wobbly it seemed. She could smell radiator fluid and looked up at her hood and saw steam and fluid spraying out underneath. *So much for driving back up.* She thought.

Chevy stood up and started back toward the road, searching the grass, certain that Lauren and Bryan must be there. "Lauren!" She meant to yell, but it came out as a weak broken up attempt. "Laaaauuurennnn. Brrrryyyyaaannn." This time it came out as an ear-piercing yell. It echoed back at her. She was now walking much quicker toward the road. Laaaaauuuuurrrreeen. Brrrryyyyyaaannn." She yelled again, and again was slapped in the face by her own echo. Now she had broken out into a run, finally approaching the road.

She stepped out onto the road and again, panic, confusion, fear, froze her. She thought at that moment, this was it. She had officially lost it. *Ladies and Gentlemen, Chevy Berry has officially gone to the nut house.* Nothing. As far as the eye could see. (And last time she checked, she was twenty twenty. No semi, no accident, no cars, no people, no motorcycle, trucks, vans, nothing but road in either direction. “What the...?”

She felt like she was going to fold up and turn inside out. Nothing. Nothing had ever happened like this before. Had she taken some medicine she was reacting to? *Am I hallucinating? Maybe I'm dreaming...* If she was, this was the most crystal clear dream she had ever felt. She could hear the wind blowing through the trees. She could smell the radiator fluid. She heard the stream. *How could this be a dream? And where is the traffic?* She stared out for a few more moments and finally decided the best course of action would be to sit and wait. *Yup. That’s what I'll do. I’ll sit here and wait. Either someone will show up and help me or I will wake up. One or the other. But still... where the hell are my babies?* Chevy sat down hard. So hard, her butt stung when hitting the pavement. Thank God she wore jeans and sneakers today. Had this been any typical day, she would be wearing a dress and dress shoes. But today was not a typical day. Chevy drew her knees up to her chest and began rocking herself back and forth. What would her friends say if they could see her now? She had always been known as Chevy, "Like a Rock." Fearless, strong, smart, and down to earth. But this...this was not her. This was different. If she had come out of the store for instance and her children were gone, yes, she would be in a state of panic. She would however, have some clue as to what might have happened. And no matter how bad she felt, she would take the next step. She would call the police of course. But this...tears now began to roll down her cheeks which were now a bright shade of red. It was all she could do to keep from full blast sobbing. *Calm down Chevy, there has got to be a rational explanation for this, just calm down. Take a deep breath.* She did. *In with the fresh air. Hold. Out with the bad. One more time. In with the fresh air. Out with the bad.* She felt for a second, that she actually did feel better. Her hands were still trembling, yes, but she no longer was on the verge of sobbing. *Good. Now then, what is the next step? Cell phone. Yes. That's it.* She could call the police. And tell them what exactly? That she swerved to avoid vehicles that aren't here? That her kids disappeared right in front of her? What would she say? She took the phone, still attached at her hip, off the clip and looked at it for a second and stared. Finally she used the sleeve of her flannel and wiped her cheeks dry. *Ok. I'll just say I was trying not to hit an animal and drove off the road. Maybe I'll get a ride into town. Yes that's it, I can call J.C.* J.C. was Chevy's best friend and co-worker. If the police wouldn't give her a lift, J.C. would take her home.

Her hand was trembling so bad she dropped the phone on the pavement trying to turn it on. She picked it up and put a death grip on it, trying to will her hand to be steady and her other hand to be good aim so she could dial the numbers. Just three, but she had never had such a hard time dialing a phone in her life. She got her thumb on the nine just fine and finally with full effort and concentration, one, one. She hit send with accuracy and quickly put the phone to her ear. Nothing. Not even a sound. She looked at the phone just to make sure she had hit send and yes, she had hit send but, she put the phone back up to her ear and sure enough, still, nothing.

This is ridiculous, she thought. She tapped the end button and pressed and held the number one, to speed dial her own home. Obviously, she didn't expect anyone to answer as she didn't figure the kids teleported back home. But she did expect to get the answering machine, which would serve two purposes: one it would prove that her cell phone was working accurately. And two, it would settle her nerves just a little even to hear her own voice along with that of her two children which were on the machine. It went something like: *beep; this is Chevy, Lauren, and Bryan, we're not home right now but leave a message and we'll call you back as soon as possible.* Everyone had said their own names and the last part they had said in unison, and if you listened long enough you could hear them all break out in giggles at the very end right before the beep. Sometimes she would call her own machine from work while the kids were in school just so she could hear their voices and that giggling at the very end. More tears began to cascade down her cheeks as she once again found herself holding in her breath and trying not to break out in sobs. She knew once *that* started, it would likely not stop for some time and she may hyperventilate on top of that. And there was no paper sack to breathe into out here.

She put the phone up to her ear smearing tears across her face as she did. She waited and...her heart sank. Nothing. Not even a sound. She looked down at the phone and shook her head. She put it back on her clip. She looked one way, then the other. She couldn't see very far in either direction, as there was a curve both ways she looked. There were trees on her side all the way down in both directions, and a cornfield directly in front of her.

"Screw this" she said quietly, but out loud. She didn't normally swear, but today was just the day to change that. She stood up and began to walk. *I'll start home and when I see someone, I will flag them down.* She thought. *When I see someone...* She thought about that. She thought about that because this was a busy road and it had been nearly fifteen minutes and not a soul had driven by.

Chevy could imagine that there may have been an accident holding up traffic. As a matter of fact, she could picture it. Not hard after all, as that was the last thing she had seen and the reason she drove off the road to begin with. The reason her children were not here now right? "Right?" She asked herself out loud. But her mind did not want to reply. *Couldn't* reply to what it couldn't explain.

How could there be an accident in both directions? That definitely did not make sense. She began to walk quickly. *Clear my mind.* She thought. *Clear my mind.* But she couldn't. She kept seeing her daughter's smile as she turned and looked at her and then as her daughter's head slowly turned back around, the expression of horror on her face as she screamed "Mom, watch out!" The sound of it echoed in her mind and she thought that last look and scream may haunt her for the rest of her life. "Where are you?" She yelled out at the top of her lungs. The echo came back to her once again. She shivered and kept on walking.

The wind picked up and was creating quite a racket with the corn brushing up against one another. It all looked dried up. She looked around and kept walking. She was beginning to approach the curve and felt sure when she rounded it the answers would reveal themselves. Her shoes were making a pat pat sound on the concrete as she went with an occasional scraping sound when she would drag her foot too close to the ground. She was still trembling, but just under the skin. Goosebumps had broken out all over. She shivered and rubbed her arms to try and warm them. *Please God let there be something. Someone. Around this corner. Please, oh please oh please.* This sounded like something Bryan would say when he wanted a particular toy or snack. He would look up at her with those big blue eyes and clasp his hands and say "please, oh please mommy, can we have McDonald's for dinner?" Or "please oh please can I stay up a little longer?" Even Lauren occasionally still did this. “Please mommy can I stay over at Tanya’s house this weekend? Please oh please? Pretty please with sugar on top.” Or her personal favorite, "please with roses and pudding on top?"

“Roses and pudding on top? Where in the world did that come from?”

Her daughter had looked slightly embarrassed but she looked at her and batted her eyes and gave her the biggest puppy dog eyes and face you can imagine a red head giving, and calmly explained, “The rose is a symbol for your incredible (and she drew out incredible so it was in…cred…i…ble) beauty. And the pudding is like the sweetness in your heart.” She said matter of factly. Really, she was just trying to recover from saying something well, dumb, but it came out sweet anyway. And it almost always worked.

The thought of Lauren and Bryan made her push on faster and she suddenly became aware that she was now jogging, something she hadn’t done in oh, twenty years. Chevy had rounded the corner and kept jogging until she came upon the light at the intersection. She was on Route 4 and heading north the way she had come and now stopped on the left hand side of the road, just left of the white line and stared. Three things were registering in her mind at once. The first was the sign of the bisecting street. Cherry Street to be exact. She knew of course that it was Cherry Street and knew that she wanted to go left toward home. Something about seeing it, made her feel at ease because it was familiar. This screwed up situation had been anything but familiar. She couldn't even compare it to her first period, because even though that was new and not familiar, she knew it for what it was and knew it would be coming. This however is "fucked up!" she spoke the words out loud. *There I go swearing again.* Lauren would have shaken her finger. Not that she hadn't been caught swearing a time or two.

Chevy looked as far as she could in all directions. The second thing her mind had registered that her eyes now confirmed, she had not heard a sound other than the wind through the trees and the never-ending song of the many birds in the woods. Not one car, truck or van. "Or semi" she said out loud. The third thing she had registered was that the traffic light was out, or not working. Not even flashing for that matter. Nothing. Dead. Her mind held on to the word dead and she thought for a second that she just might be. *If this is heaven, then it sucks!* She didn't want to admit that that was a possibility, because, no way could she handle *that* thought right now.

A bunch of birds all flew up in the woods to her left. Something had scared them. Maybe somebody in the woods? Somebody would be great right now, but somebody in the woods out here by herself didn't sound all that great either. She turned left and began to jog again. She couldn't see them yet, but she knew there were houses up ahead to the right about two hundred yards. She could see the mailboxes from where she was. She picked up her speed and crossed to the other side of the street.

When she finally got to the mailbox of the first house, she stopped and leaned down, hands on her legs and tried desperately to catch her breath. As she did so, she looked up at the house. *Finally, a vehicle.* There was a red Mustang parked in the gravel driveway. The house was brick with wooden trim. There were a few plants growing up from the gutters on the roof, but for the most part it looked well maintained. All the windows had curtains, but she didn't see any lights on. She slowly walked down the driveway and up the wooden steps to the front door. There was a doorbell. She reached her hand out, no longer trembling, but tired and weak, and pushed the button. If a doorbell went off, she did not hear it. She waited a second and then pushed it again. Finally she opened the screen door and began to knock frantically at the door. Nothing. "Please. I need help! There's been an accident. I need to call the police." She was yelling as loud as she could and pounding now on the door with her fists. "Please God, someone answer the door." More birds up and flew away making screaming sounds of panic from the woods on the other side of the road. A cold chill went up her spine. She turned around and fighting the urge to cry again, decided to try the next house over which was no more than fifteen or twenty yards away.

She cut straight through the yard and through the pine trees that divided the property. The residence had a white Ford Astro van in the driveway and a Taurus wagon right behind it. There was a swing set in the yard with several toys scattered about. The swing was moving slowly in the wind as if wanting someone to come and sit there. Not her. Not today. Goosebumps were still running wild throughout her body and the creak noise that the chains on the swing made only deepened the butterflies already going nuts in her stomach. She was sure she was going to vomit.

Two vehicles in this driveway. Someone has to be home. She thought. She ran the rest of the way up to the door. *Screw the doorbell.* She flung open the screen door, making a loud bang as it hit the railing and began pounding frantically on the door. "Hello! Is anybody there? Somebody help me!" She was now pounding so hard on the door that her hands began to hurt. "Somebody...please." She kept banging. "Answer. . . the. . ." the banging now getting softer as she was growing tired and weaker. "Fucking. . door." She stopped and put her forehead on the door a little harder than she meant and began to cry. "Please." Now sobbing and not yelling adding two more soft muffled attempts at pounding on the door.

She turned around letting the screen door slam behind her and sat down on the top step of the porch. She pulled herself down to her knees and began rocking back and forth, tears spilling down her cheeks. "Oh God. Lauren...Bryan...where are you? Where are my babies? Now she let loose. Head in her arms, the wailing and sobbing began. "Where is everyone? Why won't anyone help me?" She cried for what seemed like an eternity. She looked up from her arms and reached up with the sleeve of her flannel and wiped away the tears. She was beginning to calm down, but she still sounded like she was hyperventilating. She was breathing in and out so fast it almost sounded like hiccups.

Chevy fell down sideways on the porch and curled up in a ball, wanting to go to sleep. *Maybe, if I fall asleep, I will wake up in my own bed.* "Maybe." She whispered to herself. She was beginning to feel warm and cozy when another flock of birds took off in the woods and she heard a loud snapping sound from the distance. She wasn't sure why, but she had a bad feeling about this. She stood up and looked out. "Is something...following me?" she said in a soft voice. She looked around and didn't see anything. She didn't hear anything either. The wind blew softly at her face and her long red hair blew up against her neck, which only heightened the jittery sensation she was now feeling.

Down to the right of the house Chevy could see a bicycle tire sticking out a bit. *Just my luck.* She thought. She half expected the other tire to be flat but was relieved to find it in working order. She pulled the bicycle out and mounted it.

It was a guys ten speed with a baby seat attached. She took off quickly without looking back. She had to push hard to get through the gravel driveway, but she was out on the pavement and headed toward town in no time. Only three miles away from her home. She figured it would take about twenty minutes to get there. Although she didn't exercise regularly, she was slim and fit and would make the trip non-stop assuming, that is, that she didn't run in to anyone before that. And she was pretty sure *that* wasn't going to happen. She had a theory though; if she could get back to her bed and fall asleep, she would wake up in the morning with everything back to normal, only to realize that this is all just a dream. *It's gotta be a dream.* She thought. There just wasn't any other way to think of it. She had been riding five minutes when she came upon her next intersection. She stopped at the light. She leaned the bike sideways and rested on one leg. Again, no traffic. Again, no power to the lights. She wondered for a moment if the rest of the world knew something she didn't and had evacuated to some other city. *Maybe there had been a bomb threat. Or a nuclear power leak.* Chevy put her right hand in her pocket and pulled out a blue hair tie and pulled her hair up in a ponytail. *That ought to keep it out of my mouth for a little while at least. Now, let's keep this thing moving.*

She pushed off with her foot and made a left. A half mile down the road, she began to pass area businesses. She found herself not looking over at first. Not wanting to confirm her suspicions. But as she was now riding past Kroger grocery store, she knew, if she was going to find anybody, this would be the place. They only close on the holidays. She began to look out of the corner of her eye and then finally, turned her head all the way to see. Her heart almost jumped. The parking lot of Kroger grocery was half full of vehicles. She turned into the parking lot and headed for the store. She didn't need anything there. Home was still her destination. No, here all she needed was to see people and reaffirm herself that she was not going crazy. There was a Wendy's in the far parking lot and she could even see vehicles in the drive through. "I must not be crazy." She thought aloud.

She zig zagged through the vehicles and pulled up to the grocery store entrance. She laid the bike down, not wasting time with the kickstand. She went quickly to the door and without thinking, ran smack, face first into the glass. She took a step back rubbing her nose, eyes watering, and pushed hard on the door. They were automatic doors, obviously out of order, so she had to push very hard and the motor made a whirring sound as she forced it open. Inside she came to a second set of doors and once again, they did not open automatically. She pushed her way through and once inside, found herself standing in utter darkness. There was enough light coming through the windows that she could see the place was empty. She walked over to the nearest checkout and yelled out. “Hello, is anyone here? Hello?” Her voice came back to her as an echo and she knew of course, that there was no one here. The smell of mold and rotting food came to her. She guessed that because the freezers were not likely running, the food here was beginning to spoil. She could see down the freezer aisle just enough to make out a shiny reflection on the floor she knew was water. To her right was a miniature Coca Cola cooler. She opened the door, and was hit again with the smell of mold and water poured out at her feet. She reached inside and took out a twenty oz. bottle of Sprite. She grabbed a handful of Snickers bars and headed for the door. Never having shoplifted a day in her life, she felt strange walking out the door without paying. When she went back through the whirring doors, she squinted at the bright light that hit her outside. She looked at her watch. It had stopped and the time it stopped at had been one thirty three. She guessed it to be around three thirty now. She stood there quietly looking out over the parking lot of vehicles. Not thinking anything in particular, like why are all these vehicles here with no people? Not thinking about the fact she might be losing her mind, or that everyone in the world had been abducted by aliens except her. No, she just stood there letting the cool air blow against her face and opened a Snickers bar and began to eat. When she was finished she opened the warm Sprite and drank half the bottle. It was flat and tasted stale. With that done, she threw her trash in the trashcan, she had hesitated thinking it didn't really matter anymore but couldn't bring herself to throw it on the ground. It wasn't like anyone was around to empty the trash can anyway.

She picked up the ten-speed, mounted it, and took off for home. *Home again home again jiggity jig. Home again home again a big fat pig. Home again home again jiggity jog. Home again home again a big fat hog.* It was just yesterday she sang that very song to her six year old on the way home from school. Now she sang it to herself, trying not to think about when she would sing it to him again.

On her way back home, Chevy passed by more businesses with cars out front and all of them looked as vacant as the grocery store. She just kept going. She passed by a house she had recently sold to the Evens' only weeks ago. She longed to stop and say 'Hey, how's the new house? How do you like the neighborhood?' And so on, but she just knew, no one was there. Finally, when Chevy pulled onto her own street, Morton Street to be exact, her heart began to race and she sped up.

She pulled up to the driveway and dismounted. Her eyes had begun to water at the sight. As if she hadn't seen it in years and yet it had only been hours ago. She walked the bike to the door and laid it down gently. She opened the storm door and pulled her keys out of her pocket. She inserted the house key half expecting it not to fit. It slid in as it should and she turned and opened the door. She stepped inside. She didn't need to flip the switch to know the power was off. She knew because it was warm which meant the air conditioning was off. *Fuck it.* She flipped the switch anyway and of course. Nothing. She closed the door behind her and opened the curtains to the living room window to let in some light. She didn't call the kids' names; she knew from the silence there would be no answer. She went to the kitchen and pulled the blinds up so she could see. She stepped in a puddle when she entered and knew her freezer had defrosted all over the floor. She decided after opening the Coke cooler at the grocery store, she didn't want to smell that odor again anytime soon. The freezer and fridge would remain closed. She went room-to-room opening curtains and blinds, trying to allow maximum light while there still was some.

The last room she came to was her daughter's and after opening the window she stopped and sat on the bed. Lauren had a fluffy pink comforter and pillowcase. Chevy put her hand on the comforter and rubbed it in a circular motion as if to smooth out the wrinkles. "Where are you sweetie?" She put her face in her hands and began to cry again. She cried for a few moments and as she was wiping her tears on her sleeve, she noticed her daughter's diary sitting on the table beside her bed. Chevy reached out and picked up the diary. She rubbed her hands over this as well, feeling the cloth texture. It was pink and had a gold heart on the front with Lauren's name embossed in gold right above it. The clasp was also gold and had a little place to fit a key. She pushed the button and it clicked open. Lauren didn't need to lock it. Her mom promised to never read it. "Cross my heart and hope to die." Chevy repeated quietly now as she had four years ago when her daughter began to keep one. She had told her daughter on her birthday as she handed her her first diary. "You write whatever you want. Whatever your thoughts or feelings are. No one will read it but you."

Lauren had looked up at her mom with glistening eyes. She pulled back a strand of hair and said, "You promise you won't read it?"

"I promise"

"Ok put your right hand over your heart and say 'I cross my heart and hope to die, stick a needle in my eye.'" Chevy burst out laughing, but did as she asked and held her hand over her heart and said the lines with a big grin. “Ok” Lauren said, “Now pinky swear.”

This, Chevy was familiar with, as she had been asked many times over the years for a pinky swear. She held out her pinky and Chevy took it with hers and as they interlocked she said “I pinky swear.”

Lauren threw her arms around her mom and gave her a great big hug. “Thanks mom. I love you.”

“I love you too honey.” Chevy now found herself repeating as she had done four years ago. Except now she was talking to an empty room. “I’m sorry honey.” She began as she now broke her promise and opened her daughter’s diary with hopes of finding out where she was. “But I need to find you.” Chevy pulled the diary completely open and began to flip through to find the last page. As she flipped, she saw many pages with pictures drawn on them. Good ones too. Some were in color with markers and some were in pencil or pen. She stopped for a minute on a pen drawing of a rose and rubbed two fingers over it. “So beautiful” she whispered under her breath. It had been done with great detail. She continued on, seeing other things like photographs, stickers, and embellishments like buttons, and other scrap booking things. She finally came to the last page. Wednesday August 6th, was written on the top. Her heart all but stopped when next she read, *Dear Mom,..* Chevy froze, staring at the page and trying to understand. *Why would Lauren be writing to me? Why would she think I would look in her diary?* Then she flipped back through the pages and saw that was how she had begun each entry. Instead of 'Dear Diary', it was 'Dear Mom'. Sort of a tribute for buying her first diary is what she now concluded and turned back again to the last page. She began again. *Dear Mom, today was a great day. I went over to Lisa's house and we sat out by her pool all day talking about bo...* Chevy stopped reading. She suddenly became aware of her daughter's voice in her head. *What was she saying?* Wait...there it is again. She could barely make out Lauren's voice.

"Mom. Please don't leave me. I'm so sorry..."

Was she...crying? Yes she was sure she was. "I don't remember this memory." *It is a memory isn't it?* How else would her daughter's voice be in her head? *But she...she's sobbing. Oh baby why are you crying?*

The voice came again. *"Mom. I love you. Please don't leave me. I love you."*

Chevy could hear the pain in her voice and wanted to hold her so bad. Hold her and tell her she wasn't leaving. She wasn't leaving and everything would be fine. Chevy had her left arm outstretched as if she could see her daughter right in front of her. "I'm not going sweetie. I promise. I'm staying right here with you. I love you too. Please don't cry baby. Please."

But cry she did. Her daughter was now crying so hard saying "Moooommmmyyy." And Chevy could almost see her. See her with her arm stretched out as well while being carried away by some invisible force. Her cry was getting louder but her voice was getting fainter as if she was being carried away down some long hallway.

Chevy's arm was still outstretched and tears running like rivers down both sides of her face. "No. Baby. Baby don't go. Please. Come back Lauren. I'm right here. Come back Lauren." And Chevy came back to herself and her arm fell. She was now sobbing louder and harder than she ever had. She put her face in her daughter's pillow. The diary left her hand and fell to the ground. Chevy screamed into the pillow and was now hitting the bed with her fists and screaming, "Where are my babies? Where are my babies? Please God find my babies!" She cried all her energy out into the pillow, and without her knowledge, she began to sob herself to sleep. A noise in the background of her mind slowly worked its way into her consciousness. A noise she first had mistaken for ringing in her ears. A noise she now fell asleep to and may not remember in the morning. The slow and steady. Beep. Beep. Beep. Of what could not be mistaken as a heart monitor.